Murder's Legacy

Murder's Legacy

Anita Dickason

Mystic Circle Books

Publisher: Mystic Circle Books
Cover Design: Mystic Circle Books & Designs, LLC
Editor: Jennie Rosenblum:
https://jenniereads.com

ISBN:
978-1-958464-01-4 (paperback)
978-1-958464-02-1 (hardback)
978-1-958464-03-8 (eBook)

Library of Congress Control Number: 2023900506

Dedication

In Memory

of

Elizabeth M. Vansyckle

During the writing of this book, a very dear friend, fellow author, and the inspiration for my character, Tori Winters, passed away. For most of Beth's nursing career, she was a hospice nurse.

Beth had an exceptional talent, a way of conveying emotions within her writings. Something I truly envied. She always made it seem so easy.

I was fortunate to have the opportunity to collaborate with Beth on her books.

This Is Why: Hospice Stories of Love and Transformation
Victor the Vegetarian Vulture
The Echo Trilogy: Heart's Echo, Earth's Echo, and Word's Echo

Beth will be sorely missed. Her love of life and compassion touched the lives of all who knew her.

Love and light, my friend.

Acknowledgments

To my daughter,
Christy Kay,
for her unwavering help and love.

Pat Pratt, Author
Lou Kemp, Author
Jennie Rosenblum, Editor
for their invaluable suggestions, editing, and
critiques.

Chapter 1

An awareness, a sense something was amiss trickled through Tori Winters. The house was eerily silent.

Since daylight, a rumble of trucks and machinery, shouts, and loud reverberations had echoed. The first stage of converting the historic house she'd inherited into the Red Door Inn was finally underway.

Unable to contain her excitement, Tori had perched on the back porch, munching on a bagel. She washed it down with swigs of coffee as she watched the excavator move into place.

When the massive metal jaw struck the first blow, crushing the center of the roof of the dilapidated guest house, dust and fragments of rubble flew into the air. With the finesse of a surgeon, the operator moved the long arm, grabbing and shoving the debris to the center of the old building. Each time the huge jaw opened, and the teeth clamped onto another section of the wood and brick structure, Tori wanted to cheer.

Buoyed by a sense of accomplishment, she finally

wandered inside, refilling the cup as she passed through the kitchen. Settled in her office chair, Tori turned her attention to her to-do list.

Now, engrossed in her thoughts, she hadn't immediately realized everything had gone deadly quiet. Bothered by the uneasy feeling, she rose to find out why.

The back door slammed. Colt McLean, the construction contractor, shouted, "Tori! Tori! Where are you?" Footsteps pounded in the hallway.

Tori's heart lurched when she heard the distress in his voice. Colt wasn't the type to panic. In fact, his easy, laid-back personality never seemed to get ruffled. She scrambled around the desk. "Office. What's wrong?"

Colt came to an abrupt halt in the doorway. At the sight of her, relief flashed in his eyes. "Thank god!" Then his face tightened in fear. "Is Mia or any of the rest of your team here?"

"Not yet. Why?"

"You'd better come outside." He turned, heading to the back door.

Hot on his heels, Tori took the back steps two at a time. The momentum propelled her across the backyard as she dodged pieces of wood and broken bricks littering the ground. The excavator sat idle, its long arm with the enormous metal jaw suspended over a corner of the house.

Colt rushed toward the cluster of construction workers. At first, she couldn't imagine what had set off his panic until the men moved aside.

Stunned, Tori skidded to a stop alongside Colt and

stared at a sinkhole. Her hands fluttered in the air. "What happened?"

With a grim tone, he said, "The tunnel caved in."

"Good lord! Why?"

"Probably the excavator." Aggravated, he slapped his hand against his thigh. "This shouldn't have happened. I inspected the tunnel before we started. I didn't think there'd be a problem."

The image of a vast crater in the middle of her ten acres flashed in her mind. "Is it going to get worse?"

"I won't know until I get inside."

Horrified, Tori tilted her head to look up at him. "You can't go down there! What if it caves in even more? It's too dangerous."

Colt glanced down at her. A twinkle sparked in his grey eyes. "I'll make sure no one drives a truck across the top."

The light-hearted remark didn't stop her. "No! I still say it's too risky."

He sighed. "Tori, I don't have a choice. I've got to assess the damage. See what it's going to take to shore up the inside. We're dead in the water on the demolition until I do."

He looked toward the group of men, motioning to his foreman. "Ben, let's get inside. Find out how bad it is."

"Uh … I still don't—"

Colt interrupted. "I know what I'm doing. It's why you're paying me the big bucks."

Irritation flashed in her eyes as Tori snapped back.

"I'm not paying you to risk your neck."

Ben walked up. "Which end, boss?"

"This end first. If the tunnel's blocked, we'll use the door under the house to get to the other side. We need flashlights." Followed by Ben, he loped toward the driveway where the vehicles belonging to the construction crew were parked.

"What happened?"

Tori glanced over her shoulder.

Mia O'Brien trotted across the backyard, staring at the sinkhole with an astonished expression.

"The dang tunnel collapsed."

Mia stopped beside her. "Do you know what caused it?"

"Colt thinks it may be the construction equipment. He and Ben are headed inside." Tori crossed her arms across her chest. "I don't like it. It's dangerous."

"What can they do?" Mia asked.

"I don't know, but I'm going to get my phone." She raced back inside, grabbing it off her office desk. On the way out, Tori picked up a flashlight in the utility room.

As she headed down the back steps, Colt and Ben were already at the entrance. Colt reached down, grabbed the cover, and shoved it back. The two men disappeared down the hole. Tori picked up the pace.

Mia trotted alongside her. "What are you doing?"

"I'm going with them."

Mia said, "This is a really, really bad idea. Colt and Ben know what they're doing. You don't."

"Maybe so, but I'm responsible for what happens on my property." She shoved the phone at Mia. "If I holler, call 911."

She quickly slid down the ladder. Unbidden memories of her earlier bloody escape from the tunnel set off a nauseating sense of trepidation. Tori gulped, refusing to allow the images to deter her. She pushed the switch on the flashlight, then moved toward the voices. The men's lights illuminated the timbers and dirt that partially blocked the tunnel where a section of the wall had given way.

"How bad?" she asked as she walked up.

Colt whipped around and growled, "What are you doing down here?"

"My property, my decisions."

Though his jaw tightened, he only nodded. His light flicked across the ceiling. "It's not as bad as I feared. It's just this part of the wall. The roof didn't collapse. Those heavy wood beams are probably why."

Ben said, "It's going to be a problem clearing this out. We can't haul all this dirt and wood up the ladder."

"I know," Colt said. "Let's check the rest of the tunnel before we decide what to do." With cautious steps, he picked his way over the mound of debris to get to the other side. The beam of his flashlight cast a ghastly glow in the oppressive darkness.

Ben followed, crawling over the dirt and broken spears of timber.

As their voices faded, Tori couldn't stop the shivers

rolling down her back. Her light did little to alleviate the darkness that pressed against her. Would she ever get past knowing how close she came to dying down here? To distract her thoughts, she flashed the light over the rubble and tunnel wall. Near the top, she saw what looked like a small opening. While it seemed odd, she figured it was probably caused by the cave-in.

With a sense of relief, she saw their light beams grow larger. Tori stood back, listening as they discussed the damage. When they turned to leave, she led the way. As she stepped off the ladder, she sucked in a deep breath of fresh air. In her anxiety, Tori hadn't noticed the air in the tunnel had a slightly fetid taint.

Mia's brow wrinkled with worry. "What did you find out?"

While she explained what she'd seen, Tori watched the two men climb out.

Colt walked over. "Tori, let's go to your office. I want to look at the blueprints."

With their long-legged stride, the two men took off, their heads together as they talked.

After handing Tori her phone, Mia observed, "There's something about a man wearing a tool belt. Downright sexy."

Despite the lingering horror she felt, Tori had to laugh. Leave it to Mia to break the tension with some light humor. "Which one?"

Mia sighed. "Both."

Another chuckle erupted. Tori said, "Come on,

woman. We've got enough problems without adding hormones to the list."

Mia plopped on the couch inside the office, and Tori settled in her chair. Colt and Ben stood at the long table. On top were the blueprints for the renovations. Colt's fingers flipped the pages until he reached the one he wanted.

While she listened, Tori had to admit Mia was right about the eye candy.

Colt, six-foot-two and probably around two hundred pounds, had traded his belt and plate-sized cowboy buckle for a tool belt firmly fastened around his lean hips. A sweat-stained t-shirt, tucked into worn blue jeans, clung to his chest, outlining broad shoulders and impressive abs and biceps. Military-style boots had replaced cowboy boots.

Ben Slater wasn't far off the mark, either. Similarly attired as his boss, though shorter, five-ten or so, and stockily built, he was all muscle. Strands of dark hair curled over his forehead and down his neck. Wide brown eyes gleamed with humor.

Tori had first met him two days ago. Seeing the camaraderie between the two men, it didn't take long to realize their relationship went beyond employer and employee. They were also good friends.

Colt traced the tunnel with his fingertip. "Right about here is the cave-in. We need a backhoe to enlarge the entrance. Thank goodness for this heat wave. Still, we can't beat around the bush. A rainstorm popping up could cause the sinkhole to get bigger. Figure out what we need, and let's get it ordered."

As Ben walked out, Tori asked, "What about the demolition?"

"On hold until I know more about the stability of the tunnel. The walls may have to be reinforced before we start up again."

Concerned about the projected date to open the inn, she asked, "How much of a delay will there be?"

"I'm not sure yet."

After Colt left, Mia stood, eyeing the worried look on Tori's face. "Hopefully, Colt will know more soon. On my way here, I picked up freshly baked cinnamon rolls."

For Tori, it was a welcome distraction. "You know what a sucker I am for anything with cinnamon."

Mia laughed. "Yeah, I do."

In the kitchen, Tori's nose twitched at the warm scent of spices. She eagerly eyed the boxes spread across the counter. "This calls for a new pot of coffee."

Mia threw up a hand. "Stop. Enough with the coffee. I've decided you need a lesson in down-home cooking." She marched to the pantry, returning with a box of tea bags and a large ceramic pitcher.

"Where'd the pitcher come from?" Tori asked.

"It's been in the pantry."

"Really!"

"Yep, under your nose for over a week."

"Okay, guess I should pay more attention. So, what's this cooking lesson?"

"Texas-style iced tea. Considering the amount of tea your grandmother had in the pantry, I'd say this is one area where the two of you had nothing in common."

Mia proceeded to boil water, pouring it over the tea bags she dropped into the pitcher. "We'll let this steep for a few minutes." While she waited, she set out two plates, adding a cinnamon roll to each one.

She gazed into the pitcher. "Hmm … should be enough." Dipping into the brew with a large spoon, Mia removed the tea bags. "Okay, now for the pièce de résistance." From the canister on the counter, she scooped out a cup of sugar.

"You've *got* to be kidding!" Tori exclaimed. "You're going to dump all that sugar in the pitcher?"

"Yep, and more." She dumped, then scooped up a second cup, adding it to the mix. She stirred it. "We'll let this cool a bit, then I'll divide it into the plastic jugs I bought and add more water."

With a droll look, Tori said, "You're really going to drink that?"

"You bet I am. If you're going to live in Texas, this is how iced tea is made. I remember my grandmother making tea in a large pitcher like this one."

Overhearing the conversation as she walked in, Heidi Grant squealed, "Ooh. Iced tea! I'll have a glass."

"Not you too?" Tori groaned. "I think I'll stick to my coffee."

"Hey, you need to at least try it. You might like it," Heidi said.

Tori cast a doubtful look at the pitcher.

"Oh, my gosh! What happened?" Heidi leaned over the sink to stare at the backyard through the window.

After Tori explained, Heidi asked, "How far back is it going to set the grand opening?"

Tori shrugged. "Colt doesn't know yet."

Mia slid a plate with a cinnamon roll into the microwave. "Heidi, do you want one?"

As she eyed the box of rolls, Heidi shook her head. "I've *got* to lose some weight. I'd better pass." Then she gave Mia a disgusted look. "You could eat every piece in the dang box and never gain a pound. I look at it and feel heavier."

Tori's gaze swept the two attractive women. While both were around five-foot-seven or so, Heidi was slightly taller and heavier, though she couldn't be considered fat. Snug blue jeans and t-shirts molded their curvaceous builds.

Mia's long blond hair was pulled into her ever-present ponytail, and bangs brushed her eyebrows. As she glanced at Heidi, dark blue eyes in a round face twinkled while her mouth curved in an affectionate smile.

Heidi was a perfect foil to Mia, with her near-black hair in one long braid. Her broad face, high cheekbones and dark eyes hinted at her Native American heritage. In their late twenties, they had been close friends since grade school.

Hearing Tori's chuckle, Heidi's head whipped around. "Hey. As the munchkin in this clutch, you're as bad as Mia. No matter how much you eat, I bet you don't weigh more than a hundred or so pounds."

Still laughing, Tori's hand flew in the air. "Wait a minute. Let me make sure I've got this straight. You'll pass on the cinnamon roll because you need to lose weight, though you're going to drink a glass of iced tea that's more sugar than tea. Explain the rationale to me. I think I've missed something here."

Heidi gave her the stink eye. "Smart ass," she muttered.

Tori's laughter rippled in the air. She poured a cup of coffee and slid onto a chair at the large kitchen table.

Mia chuckled as she set the plates on the table. "I've got an announcement."

Heidi, filling a glass with ice, then tea, glanced over her shoulder. "Do tell?"

"This is a red-letter day. I handed in my two weeks' notice to the grocery store."

"Whoo-hoo!" Tori's hand shot in the air to high-five Mia.

When Tori arrived in Granbury, she discovered she'd inherited a sizeable estate, including a historic house, from a grandmother she didn't know existed. Mia, a local grocery store manager, helped Tori avoid an embarrassing moment. When Tori learned that Mia owned a home cleaning service, Tori hired her; the rest was history. Mia and the women who worked for her, Heidi Grant, Cammie Dodd, and Tina Lopez, soon became part of Tori's plans for the historic house. Tori still felt a sense of awe at how it all worked out, all because of a chance encounter at a grocery store.

Heidi's voice broke into her musings. "Okay, this calls for a celebration. I think I'll have one of those rolls after all. That is, if someone," she glanced at Tori, "doesn't have any more smart remarks."

Tori waggled her eyebrows, shooting a humorous look at Heidi while she munched on a bite of the roll.

Heidi grabbed a plate and quickly heated a roll before joining the two women.

Though Tori joined in the conversation, her eyes kept darting to the windows to see what was happening outside.

Mia hadn't missed Tori's distraction. Around a mouthful of the roll, she said, "Anything we can do to help? Once Cammie and Tina finish cleaning the Simpson house, they'll be here."

Tori swallowed the last chunk. "Not really." A note of frustration crept into her voice. "I can't even do anything."

While Mia wiped off the table, Tori stashed the plates in the dishwasher. "Dan and Parker plan to come by to-day," she told them.

Mia said, "I hope it's nothing serious."

"No. Dan has the paperwork for the new business. It's a good excuse since he's wanted to see the house. I think Parker enjoys stopping by."

"I'll make sure there's a fresh pot of coffee," Mia said. "Parker's not going to pass up a cup." She fluttered the dishcloth in the air. "I've got something else to discuss."

Tori cast a questioning look toward her.

"Cammie has a request. I think it's a good one. I know you planned to have her handle the front office, but she'd like to take over the kitchen. She's signed up for culinary night courses at a college in Fort Worth, even though she's already an amazing cook."

"Mia's right," Heidi said. "Cooking has been her passion since she was in high school."

"If you two are convinced, it's good enough for me," Tori said. "I bet she'll have some good input on new appliances for the kitchen. It's the one area Colt and I haven't finalized because I didn't know what to buy."

"She's going to be ecstatic," Mia declared. "Do you want to tell her, or should I?"

"Don't wait." Distracted by the activity in the backyard, Tori said, "I'll be back." She jumped up, heading to the back door. For some reason, she couldn't shake the uneasiness she felt.

⁂

Mia's brow furrowed as she watched Tori's determined stride across the yard. "She's really upset, though she's trying to hide it."

"Hmm … is she still having nightmares?" Heidi asked. "This business with the tunnel could bring it all back."

"I don't know. You know how tight-lipped Tori gets."

A grim tone crept into Heidi's voice. "The last time she did, it almost got her killed."

Chapter 2

While Tori didn't want to get in the way of the construction crew, she had to find out what was going on. She stood near the men clustered by the entrance. Their chatter centered around the difficulty of removing the debris.

Despite the heat from the sun beating down on her, a chill raced down her back. Maybe she should do away with the tunnel. Forget trying to use it. The house had enough appeal without the mystique of a historic secret tunnel.

Colt's head appeared in the opening. Once his feet were on the ground, he headed toward her. "It's not going to be as difficult as we first thought. The biggest issue is access. I lucked out on getting a backhoe. The owner had finished another job. He's on the way. Once I've got a trench into the tunnel, we can clean it out and haul new materials inside. It won't take long. When we finish, I'll build the stairs to replace the ladder."

"Colt, I wonder whether it would be better to forget about using the tunnel. Close it up."

"Even if you do, you still have a problem. If the wall isn't repaired, there could be another cave-in somewhere down the line. It's better to get it fixed now. The only other option is to fill the tunnel with dirt, then pack it down so there is no chance another sinkhole can form."

"How long would that take?"

"It's a major undertaking and could take weeks. To be more precise, I'd need to work out the specifications."

Unsettled by the problem, Tori felt she was floundering. She didn't know what to do. The tunnel was part of the house's history. Still, she had to make a decision.

He gazed at her with a look of concern. "Tori, I don't believe the tunnel is a problem, but it's your decision. I can stop if you need time to think about it."

Certain that time wasn't the answer, Tori squared her shoulders. "No, don't stop." Then she turned and strode back to the house.

Inside, she followed the sound of voices to the dining room that had been converted into a temporary office. The four women were grouped around the large dining room table strewn with laptops and papers.

Cammie spotted Tori in the doorway and jumped up. "Mia told me." She grabbed her, squeezing tight. "Thank you, thank you." She danced back. "I'm so excited. I can't sit still. Mia said I could help design the kitchen."

Cammie's infectious enthusiasm helped dispel some of the worry gnawing at Tori's insides. "If I had any idea becoming a chef was your ambition, it would have been decided before now."

"Chef! Oh my gosh. No, not yet. I'm not ready for the title. But I will be. I promise."

Tori glanced at the other women; each had a broad grin. Then she spotted the glasses of iced tea. "Looks like I'm in the minority here. I'm going to get a cup of coffee."

As she walked out, the doorbell rang. A quick glance at her watch told her who was at the front door. Dang, so much for her plan to change clothes. When the door swung open, Tori forgot about the worn blue jeans, t-shirt, and hiking boots. Her voice bubbled with excitement. "Dan, Parker. I'm so glad to see you."

The two men greeted her as they walked in. Dan abruptly stopped. His eyes widened in astonishment as he gazed around the foyer with mahogany wood accented by blue and cream wallpaper. Then his gaze drifted upward. "Oh, my."

Tori watched, knowing the feeling he was experiencing. She'd felt the same way the first time she walked into the house and saw the large chandelier. Then it had been dirty, now the etched glass panes sparkled.

Parker said, "Wait until you see the rest of the house."

Still gazing about with awe, Dan said, "If you have time, I'd love to take a tour."

Tori laughed. "Absolutely, though I suspect I have more time than you."

Dan Foote, an attorney in Fort Worth, had drawn up her grandmother's will when Elly bypassed the local family lawyer, Jonah Greer. Once Tori decided to move forward with the renovations, she became concerned that

Jonah's ties to the Granbury business community could create a conflict of interest. Instead, she retained Dan to handle any legal issues that might arise.

Parker Hayes was a private investigator who occasionally worked for Dan. He and David Tucker, a close friend, had been instrumental in saving her life.

Dan said, setting his briefcase on the floor, "In this case, I'll make the time."

Tori ushered him through the sliding doors on one side of the foyer into the library. Parker trailed behind them. Sunlight streamed through clean windows. A sofa and several chairs were scattered in the middle of the room, along with marble-topped tables and lamps. Floor-to-ceiling bookcases ran along one wall. Tori had slowly added to the meager number of books on the shelves, though there was still a lot of empty space. In a nook formed by the curve of the turret was a built-in bench. The old cushions, too worn to repair, had been replaced.

Dan stopped to look at the dainty writing desk and chair tucked in one corner. "This is beautiful. How old?"

"Early 1900s. A French Louis XV-style writing desk made in France. Mia could tell you more."

"Parker has mentioned her."

"She's my expert on antiques. You'll meet my team when we get to the dining room."

A puzzled look crossed his face. "Dining room?"

Tori chuckled. "It's become a temporary office. We'll head upstairs first."

As they wandered in and out of the rooms, Tori

explained the planned renovations to each one. When she reached the end of the hallway, she pointed out the stairs leading to the attic, then slid open the door hidden under the staircase. "This leads to a small room that opens into the tunnel. It's next to the wine cellar and under my bedroom. I can't show it to you as there are problems. I'll explain when we get to my office."

Back downstairs, Dan stepped to the fireplace to gaze at the oil painting hanging over the mantel in the living room. The painting depicted two people, a woman seated in a chair and a man standing near her shoulder. "So that's your great-grandfather, the infamous Frankie Leichter. He looks like someone you wouldn't want to cross."

"From what I've read about him, he ran his gambling syndicate with an iron fist. Anyone who got out of line was likely to wind up dead or missing," Tori said before sliding open the doors leading to the music room. "My favorite room and most valuable possession." She pointed to the baby grand piano.

"What a beautiful piano. I don't suppose you play?" Dan asked as he strolled across the room to take a closer look.

"As a matter of fact, I do."

"If you wouldn't mind, I'd love to hear how it sounds. My wife and I have a box seat at the Bass Performance Hall in Fort Worth."

A grimace crossed Tori's face. "I'm not anywhere close to that good, but I can give you an idea of the beautiful tone of this magnificent instrument."

Before sliding into place on the bench, Tori took off her boots. She flexed her fingers as she positioned her stocking feet on the pedals. Her mind culled through the music she'd memorized over the years. For a moment, her fingers rested on the keys before Tori struck the opening chord for one of her favorites, Gershwin's *Rhapsody in Blue.*

Lost in the glorious sounds of the music, her fingers rippled over the keys. She forgot about the two men who had quietly sat in chairs placed near the piano. When the final note rang out, Tori held her hands in position for a second before dropping them into her lap.

The silence in the room pulled her back from the thrill of the music. Six people gazed at her with amazement as she shifted on the bench. Then the sound of energetic clapping echoed around her.

Heat rose as Tori's face reddened with embarrassment. "There *were* mistakes. I'm sadly out of practice."

Mia was the first to speak. "My gosh, Tori! It was unbelievable. I knew you played, but I had no idea that you were this good."

Dan stood. "She's right. It was a superb performance. What a privilege to be able to hear you. And, if there were mistakes, I didn't hear them."

Tori motioned toward the women. With pride in her voice, she said, "Everyone, this is Dan Foote. Dan, this is Mia O'Brien. She's the General Manager for the Red Door Inn." After Dan had greeted Mia, Tori pointed to each of the other women, introducing them and explaining their role in the operation of the new inn.

"Well, it's a pleasure to meet all of you," Dan said.

"There's a fresh pot of coffee in the kitchen," Mia said, then added, "Or, if you prefer, iced tea."

"I'd like coffee," Dan said.

Parker piped up. "Same for me."

As Tori laced her boots, she gave Mia a snarky look, then laughed. "Yep, they want coffee."

Mia gave her the stink eye before heading to the kitchen.

Parker said, "Obviously, we've missed something here."

"Oh, a fun bit of nonsense over coffee versus Texas-style iced tea." Tori picked back up with the tour. "As you can see, the rooms not only interconnect but have a door opening into the hallway that runs from the front of the house to the back."

Dan quickly glanced into the dining room as they strolled to the kitchen. As they passed another open door, Tori motioned. "My office."

As she poured coffee into the cups, Mia asked, "Mr. Foote, black or would you like cream and sugar?"

"Black, please, and make it, Dan."

She graciously nodded her head, handing him the cup.

"I know you like yours black," she said to Parker.

Dan took a sip, looking out the windows at the backyard.

Parker, stepping alongside him, exclaimed, "Good lord. What happened?"

With a grim note in her voice, Tori said, "Let's go back

to my office, and I'll explain."

Dan headed to the front door to retrieve his briefcase.

Seated behind her desk, she studied the two men as she waited for them to settle. Dan had stopped to glance at the blueprints. Slim and nattily attired in a dark suit, pinstriped shirt and tie, his thin aesthetic face always had a reassuring look that exuded confidence.

On the other hand, Parker was the type of person one could easily overlook. A handy advantage for a private investigator. Short, maybe five-ten, and slightly overweight, his drooping eyes and face had a bulldog look. She had learned he was every bit as tenacious. After removing the ever-present computer bag slung over his shoulder, Parker sat in a chair in front of the desk.

Dan set the briefcase alongside his chair. Before placing the cup on the desk, he took a sip. "Let's hear the bad news."

Tori explained about the sinkhole and her options. "I'm really in a quandary here. I have to fix it or do away with it. But the tunnel is part of the history of this house."

"Here's a point for you to consider—liability. If someone in the tunnel is injured, or worse, due to a cave-in, you will face a lawsuit. Especially when it comes out, it's not the first time it has happened. I'd recommend getting a structural engineer to look at it. If the tunnel isn't safe, then there's your answer."

"David is an engineer. He and Colt both graduated from Texas A&M University. I'll ask him."

"I take it then, the two of you have gotten past what

happened over Elly's will."

"Hmm … yes." Until Tori arrived in Granbury, David Tucker, though not a relative, had been in line to inherit Elly's estate. Their relationship had gotten off to a rocky start, but now David was a good friend. Maybe more, though she didn't let herself dwell on the idea.

Dan's voice broke into her thoughts. "I need your signature." He opened his briefcase and removed a set of papers. He briefly explained the purpose of each document as he handed it to her. With the last one signed, he said, "When I get back to my office, I'll send you a copy. Once I file these with the Secretary of State's office, you are in business as the Red Door Inn. Congratulations." He slid the signed copy back into his briefcase.

As a broad smile crossed Tori's face, and a warm feeling rushed through her with another critical step in her dream for the house completed, the back door slammed. Footsteps pounded. Her fingers tightened around the pen. The sound was eerily reminiscent of Colt's earlier visit. When he appeared in the doorway with a grim look, she knew there was a reason for her growing fear.

"Tori, we found bones in the tunnel. I think they're human. I've already called the police."

Chapter 3

*T*ori jumped to her feet. "What … who …?" she stuttered.

"I don't know," Colt told her.

Parker stood. "I want to see what you found."

"I'll go with you," Dan said.

Not about to be left behind, Tori followed, grabbing a flashlight on her way out. Ahead Colt was already climbing down the ladder, followed by Dan and then Parker. She crawled down, jumping off a rung near the bottom and switched on the light.

The three men had stopped near the debris. Part of the dirt had been moved, exposing a large hole in the wall. Ben stood to one side, his light shining into it.

Colt pointed. "Until the cops get here, we don't want to dig any further."

Tori slipped past Dan and Parker to look. Inside the hole, bones protruded from the dirt while others were fully exposed. A skull, buried up to the cheekbones, stared up at them. The gaping eye sockets cast a surreal quality to the macabre tableau.

Parker said, "Tori, let me have the flashlight."

For a moment, she found herself rooted to the spot by the horrifying sight.

"Tori?" Parker said, lightly touching her shoulder.

She shuddered. "Yes, here," and shoved the flashlight at him before giving way.

Parker dropped to one knee, slowly moving the light beam over the bones as he closely scrutinized each one. "You're right, Colt. Definitely human." Then he stood, flashing the light over the wall as he examined the hole.

Her eyes darted to the dark tunnel on the other side of the debris as memories rose. Unknowingly, she'd been so close. Unnerved, Tori crossed her arms over her chest.

As if he sensed her distress, Dan's voice was soft, almost soothing. "Tori, let's wait up above for the police. There's nothing we can do down here." He took her arm, guiding her toward the ladder.

When Tori climbed out, her team had clustered near the entrance.

"We heard what Colt said. What happened?" Mia asked.

Dan answered, "They found a skeleton. It's all we know right now."

Mia eyed Tori, and from the concern on her face, she didn't like what she saw. "Tori, let's go back to the house."

Tori gathered herself together. "No. I'm okay. It's the shock of seeing it. Besides, I can't leave. The police are on the way."

While Mia's lips thinned, she didn't protest as she put

her arm around Tori's shoulders. The other three formed a barrier behind her.

Two officers came around the side of the house. Parker, followed by Colt, had climbed out of the tunnel. Colt waved to them.

When they trotted up, the officer in the lead said, "What's this about a dead body?"

Colt looked at his name tag. "In the tunnel, Officer Burch. I'm Colt McLean, the building contractor." He motioned toward Tori. "Tori Winters owns the property."

With a worried expression, the second officer stared at the sinkhole. "Is it safe to go down there?"

"Yes," Colt told him.

The three men disappeared down the hole.

Dan said, "Parker, I want you to stay on this."

Parker nodded.

Several minutes later, the two officers climbed out, followed by Colt.

Burch pulled his radio from his belt. When the dispatcher acknowledged his call, he said, "I need the crime scene unit." Then he pulled out a cell phone. After tapping a number, he said, "Sarge, the 911 call was right. There's a body in the tunnel at the Leichter place, though it's only a skeleton."

He listened, then added, "It's definitely been there a long time." He disconnected and pocketed the phone.

Burch turned to Colt. "Could we get some of the vehicles out of the driveway?"

"You bet." Colt turned to his crew, bunched together

near the entrance. "You heard the man. Move them."

Colt stepped to the tunnel entrance and shouted, "Ben. You need to move your truck."

There was a flurry of movement for several minutes as trucks were parked on the street.

Dan looked at his watch. "I need to leave. Let's go back inside." He turned to Parker. "Keep me posted."

Tori and her team followed him back to the house. Before he left, he warned them to be prepared for a media onslaught. "They monitor the police bands, and news hounds are probably on the way. Don't answer any questions. Keep it to no comment."

Tori groaned, remembering the last round with the media. On the way out, Dan retrieved his briefcase from the office.

At the front door, Tori said, "Thank you. Knowing you've got my back helps more than I can express."

He smiled. "Don't worry. We'll get this figured out."

Tori nodded, wishing she felt as confident as he sounded.

Locking the door behind him, Tori wandered to the back of the house. As she passed the doorway to the dining room, she spotted Heidi, Tina, and Cammie. Seated at the table with their heads together, they didn't notice her. Mia stood at the kitchen sink washing cups and glasses.

Tori dropped into a chair. She groaned. "What else can go wrong?"

"This is a strange turn of events. I wonder who it is."

"From what I saw, all that's left is bones."

Mia slid a cup of coffee in front of her. "Thank you." She took a sip. "Hmm … good. I do believe your coffee is better than mine." Tori stared out the window at the men gathered around the tunnel entrance. "Know what I think?"

Mia set the clean cups in the cupboard. "What?"

Her tone grim, she added, "It's murder. Which means Frankie, my not-so-illustrious great-grandfather, had his hand in whatever happened. Why else would a body be buried down there?"

Startled, Mia looked at Tori. "You're probably right."

"Frankie was murdered in 1947. That makes it eighty-some years ago. I wonder how we can find out who went missing back then?"

"If I remember my history, Granbury did have a newspaper."

Interested, Tori straightened. "If so, I wonder if it's possible to research the articles."

"That I can't tell you."

Still watching the activity, Tori saw two men carrying shovels climb into the tunnel. Parker stood nearby.

"I'm going back out." Tori gulped the rest of the coffee, grabbed the flashlight she'd laid on the table and headed out the back door. She came to an abrupt halt alongside Parker.

He glanced at her. "A crime scene tech is taking pictures. Officers are sifting through the dirt, and Colt's men are helping. This is going to take a while."

"Have the cops told you anything?"

"Not yet."

Voices sounded in the driveway.

Tori looked over her shoulder and moaned. "Well, Dan was right. The news media has arrived."

A man holding a microphone and another with a camera on his shoulder headed their way. When he got close, the one with the microphone said, "Charles Elliot, KDW4 news." He stuck the microphone toward them. "Who found the body?"

A police officer walked up. "This is a crime scene area. Move back to the driveway."

The reporter, holding his ground, said, "I don't see a reason why we can't wait here. Other people here aren't cops."

"Not up for debate. Move back."

Grumbling, the man retreated but told the cameraman to film everyone. Parker followed them to the driveway after telling Tori he'd keep an eye on them.

Tori stepped closer to the entrance. Though she could hear voices, she'd couldn't make out the words. Unable to stand still, she paced, rubbing the goosebumps on her arms that wouldn't go away. The wait was excruciating and seemed to take hours. Finally, an officer climbed out carrying several clear plastic bags of varying sizes.

Before Tori could query the officer, Parker ran up, stopping him. "What did you find?"

"Who are you?" the officer asked.

"Parker Hayes." He pulled out a leather case and flipped it open to show his private investigator's ID.

"Before I retired, I was a homicide detective with Fort Worth PD."

The officer's wariness instantly disappeared as a look of respect sparked in his eyes. "I've heard about you. You had some reputation in the department." He lifted the bags. "Remnants of clothing, a watch and a man's cufflink."

Tori stepped closer to look.

When the officer glanced at her, Parker said, "This is Tori Winters. She's the owner."

"Oh, yeah. You escaped from the tunnel. This must have been a déjà vu kind of experience for you."

Her tone dry, Tori said, "You could say so."

The officer handed a bag to Parker. "This one is the most interesting." Parker closely examined the contents before giving it to Tori.

Inside was a rusted pocket watch. On the face was printed *Railroad Timekeeper*. When she turned the bag over, she spotted two initials, DK, engraved on the back. "May I see the other bags?"

Tori closely examined filthy fragments of dark clothing that appeared to be wool. The cufflink, encrusted with dirt, looked expensive.

"What are you going to do with them?" She handed the bags back to the officer.

"I'm not sure. Depends on whether we can identify the remains."

Parker asked, "How long before you move them?"

"I don't know. It's a slow process. We're still moving

dirt, sifting through each shovelful. We're careful, so we don't miss a piece of evidence." He hesitated, looked around, then lowered his voice. "There's a bullet hole in the back of the skull. Looks like an execution hit to me."

Parker said, "I figured it was murder. Why else would a body have been dumped in the tunnel? What happens if you aren't finished before it gets dark?"

"Mr. McLean has already contacted someone to bring in lights so we can keep working. I need to put these in the van and get more bags."

Parker said, "I'll go with you. If you don't mind, I'd like to take pictures."

They trotted off toward the police van parked on the driveway, dodging the reporters who swarmed toward them.

Behind her, someone shouted. She turned. A flash of anticipation rushed over her. David, his long legs encased in tight jeans, loped toward her. Even from a distance, he had a rugged aura. The intensity in his dark eyes was set off by the scruff of beard outlining his jaw. Mia, who had gone to school with David, said he liked to walk on the wild side, always ready for a fight.

With a concerned look, he motioned toward the sinkhole. "What happened? Did someone get hurt?"

Tori rushed to reassure him. "No, everyone is okay. A wall in the tunnel collapsed."

"Then why are the police here?"

"Colt found a body in the debris."

"Good lord!"

"What are you doing here?" Tori asked.

"Colt called. I was in a meeting. He left a message asking me to stop by as soon as possible. Where is he?"

"In the tunnel helping the cops dig out the bones."

He headed toward the tunnel entrance.

"Uh … I don't think …" She stopped. He'd already started down the ladder.

"What's David doing here?" Parker asked as he stopped alongside her.

"Colt called him. I'm not sure why."

As an officer disappeared down the hole with a handful of plastic bags, Parker growled, "I'll be back." He headed toward the ladder.

"Men," she muttered to herself. They couldn't stand back and let anyone else get a piece of the action. Considering the tunnel's size, they'd probably be standing toe-to-toe.

Well, she might as well go back to the house. She wasn't solving anything hanging around out here. And she had a clue—initials on a pocket watch.

When Tori entered the kitchen, an enticing aroma of garlic, onions, and meat wafted in the room. "Oh, my gosh, is that meatloaf I smell?"

Mia stood at the sink washing dishes while Cammie stirred something in a pot.

"Yep," Mia said.

Mystified, Tori stared at the two women.

Cammie said, "Hey, this is an inn. Just because we're not open doesn't mean we can't provide a service. Since it looks like what's happening outside isn't going to end soon, we figured we'd feed everybody. Parker, Ben, and Colt need to eat. When they are ready, the Red Door Inn will serve its first meal."

Tori dropped into the chair. "Cammie, that's an absolutely brilliant idea. You can add David to the list. He's out there, down in the tunnel with the rest of them."

Mia held up her hand. "There's a correction here. Cammie said *we*. But she came up with the idea, and she's the one doing the cooking. I'm following orders."

"So, what's the menu?" Her mood lightened. Who could be down when she had this kind of team behind her.

"Meatloaf, baked potatoes, green beans with almonds, and a lemon tart for dessert. Choice of beverage is wine, courtesy of the Red Door Inn's wine cellar, beer, iced tea or coffee."

"Dang! I'm getting hungry smelling it."

Heidi and Tina walked in.

"We are too. We could smell this in the dining room." Heidi pulled out a chair and sat.

Tina wandered over to look at what was in the pot.

Cammie said, "Lemon custard."

"What's the game plan?" Tori asked.

Heidi said, "Tina and I figured we'd help serve. Get in some practice. We've cleared off the dining room table. This one isn't big enough. Besides, Cammie has fixed enough for an army."

A flush of red spread over Cammie's cheeks. "It

wasn't hard. Meatloaf is the kind of dish you can make in large quantities and is easy to keep warm. Same with the other items."

Tori's eyes narrowed as she stared at Cammie. Her fingers drummed the table as she thought.

Mia said, "You're doing it again."

"What?" Tori said.

"That look, all squinty-eyed. You do it every time you're plotting some scheme in your head. What is it this time?"

"Humph!" she grunted. "Pots and pans. Food."

"Care to enlighten us?" Mia said.

"Cammie, this is what I want you to do. Make a list of kitchen equipment you need. I'm surprised you can cook anything since everything is so outdated. Also, start on a list of appliances for Colt to order."

Cammie squealed. "Really! Oh my gosh, this is better than Christmas. I'll start on it tonight."

"As for the food, I didn't have a single pound of hamburger in the fridge. The only potatoes I've got are the flake kind in a box, and maybe, I had a can of green beans. Though it's iffy. I dang well know there weren't any ingredients for a lemon custard or almonds. Give me the receipts, and I'll write you a check."

"No. This was my idea, so I don't mind paying for it."

"I'm sure you don't, but you said it. This is an inn; therefore, the cost of food is charged to the inn. Mia, is it possible to set up an account at your store? It would make it easier for Cammie or any of us to buy whatever is needed. Since everyone is going to work here, we should think about providing lunch."

"I'm sure it can be arranged. I'll talk to the manager."

Heidi groaned. "Cripes. I'll never lose weight once Cammie starts cooking. Tori, you have no idea what you have unleashed. Low-cal isn't in her vocabulary."

Laughing, Cammie said, "Hey, I can always serve *you* smaller portions to compensate," earning a disgusted look from Heidi.

Tori's eyes sparked with mischief as she added to Heidi's torment. "I can help by running you around the property a few times each day."

"Yeah, right. When that happens, it'll be a cold day in hell, my friends," Heidi responded.

A flurry of activity outside the window caught Tori's attention. "Another confrontation between a reporter and one of the cops."

Heidi said, "It's already made the news. I heard people commenting during our mad dash through the grocery store."

Mia said, "They keep ringing the doorbell. We say no comment, but it doesn't seem to slow them down. They even want to know if it's connected to your ordeal in the tunnel."

"Great," Tori muttered. She believed she had put the nightmare behind her. Now it was getting dredged up again.

Mia said, "It was to be expected."

"I know. Well, nothing I can do about it."

"What's been happening?" Tina asked as she pulled out a chair alongside Heidi.

"They are slowly removing the remains from the pile of dirt," Tori told her. "The officers have a few pieces of evidence, bits of clothing, a pocket watch with the initials DK, and a man's cufflink. It's murder. He was shot in the head."

For a few seconds, the only sound was the clink of Cammie's spoon as she stirred the bubbling mixture. Tori wondered if everyone else had the same thought. Since discovering there was a tunnel, they'd all been down there several times.

Heidi finally asked, "Any idea how long it's been down there?"

"No, but Frankie has to be responsible. It looks like a hole was dug in the wall, then sealed off with wood."

As she thought about it, something strange suddenly struck her. The walls in the tunnel were solid dirt, except for the stretch of timbers where the hole was located. She needed her tablet. Tori straightened, looking around.

"What?" Mia asked as she filled the coffee machine.

"My tablet. I thought I left it on the table."

"I put it in your office."

Tori bolted out the door. When she returned, she carried it and her laptop. Tori set up a new page on the tablet. As details emerged, she wanted to keep track of them and her thoughts. After adding an entry about the wall, she turned to the computer and booted it.

She googled Granbury newspapers and found the

archives for the *Granbury Chronicle*. "Mia, you were right. The *Granbury Chronicle* ran from 1915 to 1948. If the mystery man was from Granbury, there might be an article about his disappearance."

"Do you know when the house was built?" Heidi asked.

"It was around 1938 or 39. I never had a reason to find out for sure."

Tori glanced out the window. A backhoe trundled across the back of the property, and two men carried a stretcher toward the tunnel's entrance.

"I'll be back. Maybe the police found something else."

Chapter 4

Outside, Tori stopped a few feet from the two medics. A chill raced over her at the sight of the folded black bag on the stretcher. She was all too aware of its purpose. It could have been her in one of them.

Stop it, she told herself. It didn't happen. Let it go. Don't think about it. But, while her thoughts were rational and logical, her emotions were a chaotic mess.

Parker climbed out of the tunnel. When he spotted her, he walked over.

"Anything new?" she asked.

"More pieces of clothing, and they found the other cufflink. It's all been bagged. Most of the dirt has been moved further back into the tunnel. Once the officers are finished, the homicide detective wants everyone out, so the medics can get down there."

He pulled out his phone and tapped a number. "Ken, I'm at the Leichter house. I need round-the-clock security set up here. I want two men watching the place during the night, one during the day. Work out a schedule." He paused to listen, then said, "No, I don't know how long."

After another pause, he said, "As soon as you can get them here," then disconnected, shoving the phone back into his pocket. At the questioning look on her face, he added, "We need to keep an eye on the entrance, make sure someone doesn't slip inside."

A commotion near the driveway caught their attention. Several of the construction crew were dragging pieces of equipment toward them.

Parker said, "Lights. Even though the police are finished, Colt and I agreed it was a good idea to keep them on all night."

Considering the horde of news personnel clustered on the driveway, Tori figured it was a wise precaution.

David climbed out, followed by Ben, then Colt.

When Ben spotted the men with the equipment, he asked, "Boss, once the lights are up and running, do you want me to release the crew?"

"Yes. But make sure they're back here in the morning."

Next out of the tunnel were the crime scene techs. One carried a camera, and the other a large bag.

Another man, sporting a badge on his belt, climbed out. He stopped to speak to the medics. After a short discussion, a medic picked up the plastic bag before crawling down the ladder. The second medic followed. The officer turned, saw Parker and walked toward him.

Parker said, "Andy, this is Tori Winters, the owner of the property. Tori, this is Homicide Detective Andy Rodriguez. He's in charge of the investigation."

When she extended her hand, Rodriguez shook his

head. With a warm smile, he said, "Not a good idea. Mine are too dirty." He wiped them on his pants. "It's nice to meet you, though I wish it had been under better circumstances. Here's where we stand. The medics will take the remains to the medical examiner in Fort Worth. We'll try to identify the victim, but we don't have much to go on, considering how long we believe the body has been down there. Until I advise otherwise, the only people allowed inside the tunnel are your contractor, his foreman and Parker."

"How long will you keep the tunnel closed?" Tori asked.

With a wry look, Rodriguez said, "I wish I could tell you. This is new territory for us. We've never dealt with a case this old. Colt told me it was urgent to get the tunnel repaired. I'll release it as soon as I can." He nodded to everyone and walked toward the driveway.

Tori frowned. "This doesn't sound good."

Parker said, "I don't think it's as bad as it seems. He's playing it safe. I expect he'll be finished by tomorrow or the next day at the latest."

She sighed. "I hope you're right. On a lighter note, we've fixed a meal once everyone has finished here. Ben, you're included. Does anyone need to leave?"

A look of surprise crossed Ben's face. "Uh … no. I don't have any plans."

David said, "I'm in. What's on the menu?"

After hearing Tori's answer, Colt said, "Even if I did have plans, they would have been canceled."

"Parker?"

"With an offer like that, I'm not going anywhere. Besides, I need to wait until my men get here."

Colt brushed at the clumps of dirt sticking to his pants. "Tori, are you sure about this? We're all dirty."

"You can wash up in the house. But don't worry about the dirt. You'd understand if you'd seen this place when I first moved in."

"Okay. As soon as the medics leave, we'll head inside."

She turned and strode to the house. Tori didn't want to see a bag of bones hoisted out of the tunnel. At least it would be one image she wouldn't have in her head.

Inside, the mouthwatering odors helped dispel the tight knots in her shoulders. Cammie was putting the tart in the refrigerator, and Mia stood at the sink with her hands in soapy water. Tina and Heidi watched the proceedings outside from their seat at the kitchen table.

"Anything new?" Mia asked.

"Not really. The medics are removing the bones. Detective Rodriguez has left. He's in charge of the case. Said he couldn't release the crime scene yet."

Mia said, "Andy! A good man."

Tori looked at her.

"What?"

"I never cease to be amazed at who you know."

Tina laughed. "We went to school with him, though he was a couple of years ahead of us. He and my brother, Tony, are buds. Tony was best man at Andy's wedding."

She hesitated, casting an uncertain look at Mia. "Tori,

I've got another idea to run by you."

Obviously, something else had been discussed while she was outside. She'd noticed that Cammie and Tina didn't feel as comfortable talking to her as Mia and Heidi did. She hoped it would change as they got more involved in the operation of the inn.

She nodded in a reassuring manner and said, "Let's hear it. I'm always open to new ideas."

"Well … uh … it seems we'll need artwork for menus, business cards, advertising, stuff like that. It's something we haven't talked about. I'd like to do the design work if you don't mind. If you don't like it, it won't be hard to find a graphics designer."

"What a great idea." Tori already knew Tina was working on a degree in computers.

Tina's face brightened.

"Draw up the designs, and it won't be my decision. This is a team effort."

The back door closed, and David walked into the kitchen.

Tori noticed much of the dust was missing, though his hands were still dirty.

"Who's doing the cooking? If the food is as good as the aroma, I hope you've got enough to feed everyone."

Tori motioned toward Cammie. "We have a new chef. She's taking over the kitchen."

David looked at Cammie. "Good lord, whoever believed you had such hidden depths. Marry me. We'll sail off into the sunset, you and me and your pots and pans."

With a giggle, Cammie slapped him on the arm. "David, don't get ridiculous. It's only a meal."

His eyes twinkled with merriment. "Ah, there is a meal, but then there is ambrosia."

While a blush stained her face, her tone was mocking as she said, "Then I'd suggest you go wash those filthy hands if you plan on eating my ambrosia."

With another laughing glance at Cammie, David said, "Yes, ma'am. On my way. The medics are getting ready to leave. As soon as they do, the others will be here. Two of Parker's men arrived." Whistling, he walked out.

Mia said, "What's this about Parker's men?"

Tori explained.

"It's reassuring to know. I wouldn't put it past a reporter to sneak into the tunnel to get a few pictures," Mia commented. "Heidi, is the dining room table ready?"

"Yep. We don't have enough everyday dishes, so I used the good ones. I've got it set for us, David, Colt, Ben, and Parker. Anyone else?"

Tori said, "No, that's it." She followed Heidi into the dining room.

Under the overhead chandelier, a smaller version of the one in the foyer, woodwork and furniture gleamed. The table, covered with a heavy damask white tablecloth, was set with Waterford glasses and hand-painted Franciscan Apple plates, first produced in 1940. Atop the wine-colored napkins were pieces of sterling silverware by Lunt Silversmiths, a company dating back to the early 1900s.

After learning their value, Tori planned to put the

dishes and silverware on display in the museum. But for the Red Door Inn's first meal, it seemed appropriate to use them.

"Oh, Heidi. This is wonderful."

With a note of anxiety, she said, "You don't think it's too much, do you? After all, these guys have been working in a tunnel most of the day."

"No, I absolutely do not. Like I told them, we can handle dirt."

David walked in. "Holy hell, what a layout." He looked at his clothes. "This should be a tuxedo event, at the very least."

Tori laughed as she headed back to the kitchen. "No big deal. The kitchen table was too small." She heard men's voices in the utility room as they washed up at the large sink.

Cammie grabbed potholders and pulled out a large pan of meatloaf.

Tori was surprised it even fit in the oven. "Heidi was right. It's enough to feed an army." Her eyes narrowed. "And … I have never seen that pan before."

With a sheepish look, Cammie said, "I bought a few extra items at the grocery store."

"Make sure I get *all* the receipts."

Cammie pulled out another tray loaded with baked potatoes. "Heidi, would you put these on the serving plate and take them into the dining room? Tina, find out what everyone wants to drink." Next was Mia, who was told to dish up the green beans.

Tori chuckled at Cammie's clipped tone as she issued orders. She was in the groove and loving it.

"What do you want me to do?" Tori asked.

Cammie looked around. "Hmm … you're in charge of the pièce de résistance."

Surprised, Tori watched Cammie walk out.

When she returned, Cammie said, "You can put this on the table."

Laughter from the women bubbled in the air.

Heidi, who had walked back in, was the first to recover. She wiped the tears from her eyes. "All the fancy dinnerware, sterling silver, Waterford glasses, and we're going to set a bottle of ketchup on the table. Oh, this is too funny."

Once Cammie stopped laughing, she said, "Look at it this way. At the Red Door Inn, we aim to please. I don't mind if someone dumps ketchup on my meatloaf. It's the way I like to eat it."

Still laughing, Tori headed to the dining room, the ketchup bottle held high.

The men slowly wandered in. Parker whistled, looking around in stunned disbelief. "Didn't expect this. Pretty dang fancy."

Then Colt arrived with a similar reaction.

Heidi said, "Have a seat wherever you like, though Tori is on this end."

Unconcerned, David pulled out a chair while Colt and Parker gingerly sat as if they were afraid any remaining dirt on their clothes would adhere to the chairs. Ben had stopped in the doorway, a look of uncertainty on his face.

David motioned to the seat next to him.

Ben sat, uneasy until he eyed the food on the table. "The meatloaf looks delicious, like what my mom makes."

Cammie, who had walked in behind him, said, "Well, I hope it tastes as good."

Seated at the head of the table, Tori said, "I'm certain this is a surprise and not what you expected. But it's the Red Door Inn's first meal, making it special."

The tension the men brought to the table eased as they dished up the food. The bottle of ketchup was handed around with a laugh.

After swallowing a chunk of meatloaf, Parker said, "Wow, this is really good. Who cooked it?"

Tori said, "Our new chef, Cammie."

She blushed. "I'm not a chef. Not yet, anyway."

Parker laughed, forking up more meat. "Couldn't prove it by me."

The conversation lagged until everyone made a serious dent in the food. Then the talk turned to the identity of the body in the tunnel.

Colt scooped up a bite of potato. "David, since you grew up in this house, any ideas on who is in the tunnel?"

"Not a clue, though I suspect the murder can be linked to Frankie. With his violent history as the head of the Dallas gambling syndicate, I can easily see him shooting someone, then burying him in the tunnel."

Parker said, "It would make it what, an eighty-some-year-old murder?"

"Probably. The house was built in 1938," David said.

Tori added, "I wasn't sure and planned to look up the date. Frankie was killed in 1947."

Finishing his coffee, Parker said, "It gives us a window of around nine years, then."

"I did a little research and found Granbury had a newspaper back in the 30s and 40s," Tori told them. "If the man lived here, there might be an article about his disappearance. Even though all the articles are online, without narrowing down a date, it will take time to do the research."

Parker said, "The newspaper is a good place to start. I took pictures of the watch and cufflink before Andy took off with them. Once I get on my computer, I'll email you a copy."

Tori nodded, then turned to David. "Dan mentioned a structural analysis," Tori said. "He's concerned about future liability. Is it something you do?"

"Yes, it is. Colt and I have already talked about it. It's why he called me. I'd also recommend hiring a second firm. You can't get around that I'm connected to this place. I wouldn't want any accusations of bias."

With a troubled look, she watched Heidi and Tina clear away the plates. Mia and Cammie had left to get the dessert.

"Colt and I talked about doing away with the tunnel. I don't want to since it's part of the history of this house. But at the same time, I can't take a chance on someone getting hurt or killed in the future. Dan made a good point. It could hinge on whether the tunnel is structurally sound."

"I'll find out. There is another firm, G&L Engineering, in Fort Worth," David said. "I've worked with them on a couple of projects. I'll call them tomorrow."

Cammie and Mia walked in and handed out small plates with slices of the tart.

From the men's expressions as they bit into a piece, Tori knew, as the old saying went, Cammie had hit another one out of the park.

After profusely thanking Tori and her crew, Parker was the first to leave. He wanted to check on his two security guards outside.

"If they need anything, let me know," Tori told him.

The other men stood. Their comments echoed Parker's.

Once they had departed, Tori high-fived everyone. "We did it, thanks to each one of you. We've set the standard for what guests can expect at the Red Door Inn."

With everyone pitching in, it didn't take long to clean up. As the women left, Tori stood on the porch and watched as they walked to their cars. Nearby, a security guard also watched.

Reassured that no one would get into the tunnel during the night, she headed to her bedroom. After a quick bath, she collapsed in bed, snuggling under the covers. Despite her exhaustion, the sense of apprehension she'd tried to ignore all day crawled through her with a vengeance. Maybe she was gun-shy from her previous experience with the tunnel. Still, Tori couldn't shake the feeling more trouble was headed her way.

Chapter 5

restless night had left her groggy and irritable. The sun wasn't even up yet, though it was hard to tell with the backyard lit up like a football stadium. Since lying in bed wasn't going to improve her mood, she might as well do something useful. After dressing, she wandered into the kitchen.

Yawning, she peered out the window at the two men seated next to the vehicle parked near the tunnel entrance. Their presence sparked an idea. She started the coffee machine, then grabbed a couple of skillets. In one, Tori cracked two eggs, in the other, she started ham slices to frying. She retrieved a package of croissants from the pantry and a small box from the utility room. Once the ham and eggs were cooked, she assembled sandwiches with a fried egg, ham, and a slice of cheese.

After wrapping them in foil, she dropped them in the box. Next, she added a thermos with hot coffee and disposable cups. Walking out the back door, the smell of fresh dew was a tonic that lightened her mood.

As she approached, the two men stood. "Hello," she

said, stopping in front of them. "I'm Tori Winters. This is my place."

"I'm Carl Degger. This is Steve Alford."

"Nice to meet both of you. Anything happen during the night?"

"No. Real quiet," Carl told her.

She reached inside the box. "I fixed a couple of sandwiches." Tori handed one to each man. "There's coffee in the thermos."

"Why, thank you. This is downright nice." Carl's face beamed with a broad smile as he set the thermos and cups on a portable table next to the truck.

"Just drop off the thermos when you leave."

"Will do," Carl said as he hurriedly unwrapped the sandwich.

Steve had already taken a bite. He mumbled, "Thank you."

On the way back to the house, she pondered whether there was another way to identify the mystery man. She could only come up with one, Jonah. His grandfather had been Frankie's attorney. He might remember something.

Inside, she tossed the box on the counter in the utility room. Before washing the skillets, she made another sandwich.

Seated at the table with the croissant and a cup of steaming brew, she tapped the screen on her tablet. She added a note to her list, call Jonah.

Eager to get to her computer, she quickly ate. She refilled her cup, then headed to her office. Settled behind her desk, Tori checked her emails. Parker had sent the pictures of the pocket watch and cufflink.

First, she enlarged the image of the watch. The hands had stopped at five minutes to twelve. Heavy tarnish stained the metal. On the backside were the initials DK. Her fingers drummed the desk as she studied the image. Who was he? Why was he murdered?

The cufflink, in the shape of a fan, proved quite interesting. Engraved on the back was a faint 18 and Cartier Paris. The mystery man had money, but it didn't answer whether he was a legitimate businessman or a gangster.

The front door opened, and footsteps echoed in the hallway. Mia stopped in the doorway. "I figured this is where you would be. I bet you're already working on the mystery of the body in the tunnel."

"Yes. Look at these pictures Parker sent me."

Mia dropped her oversized tote bag on the chair and set a thermos on the desk. "How did the security guard get your thermos?"

Still studying the pictures, Tori murmured, "I took a couple of sandwiches and coffee to them this morning."

"Hmm … may need to add a few extra items to the next grocery run if you plan on feeding the guards." Mia walked behind the desk to peer over Tori's shoulder.

"Ever come across a watch like this?"

Mia leaned closer to look. "No, I haven't."

"This is what is really interesting." Tori clicked the mouse to bring up the image of the cufflink.

"Oh, my gosh. Cartier and eighteen karat gold. Wow,

it has value. The mystery man wasn't some hour-by-hour laborer. It should make it easier to find out his name."

"You would think so."

The doorbell rang.

Mia said, "I'll get it." As she passed the chair, she picked up the thermos, then pulled a newspaper from her bag, handing it to Tori. "You made the front page."

Tori groaned, picking up the paper. A picture of the medics wheeling the stretcher with a bulging black bag on top was front and center. Atop the image, the headline read—*BODY FOUND IN LEICHTER TUNNEL*

The article stated, "*New drama at the historic Leichter mansion. Only months after Tori Winters dramatic escape from the historic tunnel, another victim has been found. Renovations underway at the mansion resulted in a collapse of the tunnel. In the debris, skeletal remains were found of an unidentified man. According to an unnamed police source, the victim was murdered. It is believed the murder occurred some eighty years ago. A pocket watch engraved with the initials DK was found with the remains. Miss Winters, the granddaughter of the late Elly Leichter, plans to turn the historic house she inherited into a bed and breakfast inn.*"

Disturbed by the publicity, Tori tossed the paper on the desk, though she couldn't fault the reporter. It was news, big news for Granbury.

Colt strolled in and greeted her. He motioned toward the newspaper. "I was going to forewarn you, but you've already seen it."

She scowled. "It's not an auspicious start."

His eyes sympathetic, Colt said, "It's a setback, but not one we can't overcome."

Mia walked in, carrying two cups of coffee. One she handed to Colt, the other to Tori. "Anything else I can get?"

Tori shot her a grateful look. "Thanks, Mia. I don't think so."

She nodded and walked out.

Colt took a deep swallow before saying, "Last night's dinner was impressive."

At the compliment, her face lit up, erasing the worry lines across her forehead. "I think so, considering it was an impromptu, unplanned meal."

"I'd say it bodes well for the success of the inn. Okay, just a quick update. Until I make sure the demolition won't cause further damage, it's shut down."

He took another swallow. "David is making the arrangements for the survey, even though I can't start until the police are finished. Once I have the word from Rodriguez, we'll be ready to go." He gulped the last of the coffee. "I'd better get outside. My crew should be arriving."

As he walked out, Tori leaned back in the chair. The feeling she'd felt before falling asleep swept over her. It was as if she was waiting for the other shoe to drop. With a shake of her shoulders, she stood, certain the anxiety was because of the tunnel. Besides, what else could happen?

The ring of the phone lying on her desk sent her spinning back. She leaned across, seeing Jonah's number on the screen.

"Good morning, Jonah. I bet you saw the news. I

planned to call you later this morning and touch base with you."

His tone stiff, he said, "I appreciate it. Even though Dan is handling any legal problems with the renovation, I'd still like to know what is happening. I might be able to help."

For many years, Jonah had been the family lawyer and a close friend of her grandmother. Jonah and his son Lincoln, also an attorney, had been part of a group pressuring her to sell the property. Their dismay over how they had been misled and that it nearly cost Tori her life affected the friendship.

"Yesterday, a section of the tunnel collapsed, and a skeleton was found amidst the rubble."

"I gathered that from the news. What caused the tunnel to collapse?"

Tori explained.

Once she finished, Jonah said, "I know Colt is friends with David, and they both graduated from Texas A&M University College of Engineering. But are you certain he is the right person to oversee the renovation? It sounds like he was responsible."

A spark of anger hit, forcing her to take a calming breath. One of the early issues with Jonah was his questioning her decisions.

"Jonah, I thoroughly investigated Colt's experience and qualifications before I hired him. This wasn't his fault. Colt had considered the possibility and examined the tunnel before he started. He didn't expect a problem."

"What about the body? What are the police doing?"

"What's left has been removed and sent to the medical examiner in Fort Worth. The police found a few items, remnants of clothing, cufflinks, and a pocket watch with DK on the back. It's the only clue to his identity."

"Obviously, this must be connected to Frankie."

"Yes. There's a bullet hole in the skull. Growing up, did you hear any talk about someone disappearing?"

There was a short silence before Jonah said, "No, can't say I did. The initials don't ring a bell. Considering how long the body has been in the tunnel, it may be difficult to find out."

"If the police can't come up with anything, I have one possibility. There was a newspaper back then, and the articles are online. The disappearance might have been newsworthy."

"Could be. From what I know about Frankie, witnesses and informants had a way of disappearing. What's being done about the tunnel?"

Leave it to Jonah to go back to the heart of the problem. "Colt plans on obtaining an engineering analysis to see if the tunnel is safe."

"That's an excellent idea."

After telling Jonah she would keep him in the loop, she disconnected.

A series of hellos echoed from the hallway as Heidi, Cammie, and Tina walked past. She picked up the newspaper and followed the women into the kitchen.

As they stashed their bags in the utility room, Heidi

asked, "Anything new this morning?"

Tori motioned toward the newspaper she'd tossed on the counter. "I made the front page." She looked out the window. "David and Parker are here. I'll be outside."

She raced down the back steps, then trotted toward the cluster of men near the entrance. As Tori neared, the two men greeted her. Colt walked over and joined them.

Parker said, "I spoke to Andy on my way here. He released the crime scene. Said he didn't have a reason why he would need to go back down there."

"That's good news. We can get started on the survey. I'll have a crew here later today," David said. "And I contacted the other engineering firm. Once I'm finished, they'll run the same tests. Then we'll compare results."

With a bemused expression, Parker shook his head. "David explained the process. Way over my head. I'd suggest you not ask."

Tori chuckled. "I won't. I trust him." She shot him an affectionate look that sparked an unexpected answering gleam in his eyes. Tori cleared her throat. "Uh … how long will this take?"

"A couple of days," David said, though his lips twitched with a wry smile as if he sensed her discomposure.

"Once we have enlarged the opening, we'll start hauling out the timber and dirt." Colt pointed toward a backhoe with an operator atop it. He twirled his hand, and the operator fired it up, moving into position.

"Parker, did the detective say anything about the

murdered man?" Tori asked.

"Only that he was doubtful they'd be able to identify him. The PD's archived records only go back to the middle 1950s."

"Let's hope I can find something in the newspapers. I'm going back to the house." As she strode away, Tori wondered where else she could search. The problem was the time period between when the house was built and Frankie was killed. It would help if the date could be narrowed down.

Then an epiphany struck—her grandmother's journals. What with getting the construction underway and making plans for the operation of the inn, she'd put off reading them.

When she walked in, the buzz of voices and a vacuum cleaner echoed overhead. She trotted up the stairs.

Mia was polishing a dresser in the master bedroom. Seeing Tori in the doorway, she asked, "Everything okay outside?"

"Rodriguez is finished with the tunnel. Colt started on enlarging the entrance."

"That's good news."

"I guess so."

Mia picked up her rags and polish. "That doesn't sound like our indomitable Tori. What's bothering you?"

With a shrug of her shoulders, Tori said, "I'm not sure. An uneasy feeling that I can't shake."

"Come on, let's go downstairs. I could use a break." In the hallway, she shouted, "Break time."

As they strode toward the stairs, Mia said, "You know what's wrong with you?"

"Okay, I'll bite. What?"

"It's the tunnel. You haven't gotten past what almost happened to you down there."

With a sigh, Tori said, "You're probably right. The same thought has occurred to me." Behind her, footsteps clattered as the rest of the crew followed.

Clustered in the kitchen, everyone grabbed glasses, filling them with iced tea. Ignoring the offer of one, Tori reached for a cup.

Heidi said, "She's being stubborn. We'll bring her around to our way of thinking."

The others chuckled as Tori sniffed, sliding onto a chair. She pulled her tablet toward her. With a flick of her finger on the screen, she brought up the latest to-do list.

"Since we're all here, let's have a team meeting." Once everyone settled in chairs, Tori said, "First, last night was a super success. I don't know about any of you, but it surprised me."

Heidi set her glass on the table. "We were talking about it earlier. All of us were taken aback by how well it came together. The credit goes to Cammie."

Cammie flushed a bright red. "What I did wasn't a big deal. We all made it happen."

Tori's lips twitched. "Yes, but some more than others, and that includes me. The four of you pulled it together. This brings me to my next topic."

She paused to take a sip of coffee, making sure she

had everyone's attention. "Even though we can't offer overnight accommodations, nothing says we couldn't host a few simple breakfasts or luncheons. Maybe for a club meeting or other type of event."

Four sets of excited exclamations sounded.

"It's an awesome idea," Mia said.

Tori looked at Cammie. "You're the chef. What do you think? Is it doable?"

A grimace crossed her face. "I wish you'd all stop calling me a chef; I'm far from that. But speaking as the inn's cook, I'd say yes, we can."

Excitement bubbled in the air as the five women tossed out ideas.

Cammie shoved back her chair. "I can't keep up with all of this," she exclaimed, heading toward the utility room. When she came back, she carried a small notepad and pen. Seeing the raised eyebrows, she said, "What! I need to make a list," and settled into her chair.

Mia groaned. "Good lord, what have we created?"

"By the time we get the inn going, we may all be making lists," Heidi observed.

Tina said, "If we can settle on what we will serve, I'll start on the menus and flyers for advertising."

"We should have a mini opening, then have the full-blown one when the inn is officially open." Tori scribbled on her tablet, making a note to purchase one for each of the team.

Heidi said, "I'd suggest contacting local clubs and organizations. One of them might want to hold their board meetings here. If we rearrange the dining room, we could easily accommodate twenty or so individuals."

Tina said, "Do you have another pad of paper, Tori?"

Rising, Tori laughed all the way to her office. She was still laughing when she handed out notepads and pens.

A ripple of snickers erupted from Heidi. "Never say one of my predictions doesn't come true. But this may set a record."

The enthusiasm was contagious. Caught up in the excitement of planning new activities for the inn, Tori forgot about her earlier misgivings.

When a knock sounded at the back door, Mia jumped up to answer it. When she walked back, Colt and another man followed her. Behind them were David and Parker.

The grim look on the men's faces was her only warning.

Chapter 6

Colt walked toward the table and handed her a paper. He turned, leaning against the counter. "Tori, this is Otto Farthing, the city inspector. He's pulled our construction permit. We're dead in the water."

Stunned, Tori's gaze flicked over a revocation notice, effective immediately and signed by Otto Farthing. Unable to hold back her distress, she cried, "What! Why?"

Farthing said, "I don't have any choice but to shut you down. Simple as that."

Anguish morphed into a surge of anger. Tori slowly rose. At five-foot-three, her diminutive, hundred-and-ten-pound frame straightened. With a thrust of her jaw, she didn't bother to hide the animosity in her voice. "No! It's not as simple as that. You'd better explain, Mr. Farthing."

Startled, he drew back. "Until I determine your property is safe, I can't allow you to continue with the construction."

"And how … did you come to your conclusion?"

"The tunnel. It collapsed."

"How did you get from there to the entire property could be unsafe? What does the tunnel have to do with the construction or renovations to this house?"

"Uh, why … uh, this property isn't safe, and the tunnel collapsing proves it."

Her hand made an angry slashing motion. "Wait a minute. You said you had to determine *if* the property was safe, and now you're saying it isn't. It wasn't an issue when you signed off on the blueprints and the construction permit."

His forehead glistened with beads of sweat. "Uh, I didn't have all the facts."

"And what facts do you now have?"

"Well, uh, the tunnel."

"Colt, did he even bother to ask what steps we are taking to ensure the tunnel's safety?"

"No, ma'am. All he did was hand me the notice." He shot a distasteful look at Farthing. "Then, tried to skedaddle off the property. He said it wasn't necessary to speak to you." He motioned to David and Parker, who flanked Farthing. "We convinced him otherwise."

"Mr. Farthing!" Her voice rose. "You didn't believe it was necessary to tell *me* … the owner of the property!"

He refused to look at her. "Your contractor had the notice. It's all I'm required to provide."

In disbelief, she stared at him.

As the silence dragged on, he shuffled his feet and cleared his throat. "Now, look here. I'm only doing my job."

Her body hummed with anger. "Mr. Farthing, if you

were doing your job, you would have investigated before deciding to pull my permit. If you were doing your job, you would have discovered there is not a single reason or justification for this asinine stunt."

Defensive, he said, "It isn't a stunt. This is serious, and there's nothing you can do. There's no reason to get all het up about it."

Tori fired back. "If you think I'm going to idly stand by and let you shut me down, you've got a surprise coming. I can and will do something about it. And you haven't begun to see me get *het up*. You can expect a call from my attorney."

"Miss Winters, I'm sure Jonah Greer will agree with the city's position once he knows the facts."

"I'm not referring to Jonah Greer. My attorney is Daniel Foote with Atkins, Smart, and Foote law firm in Fort Worth. And quite frankly, he won't hesitate to take you and the city to court over these false allegations and unwarranted actions. From now on, you are persona non-grata. If I find you on my property again, I'll have you arrested for trespassing. One of the men standing next to you is Parker Hayes, a private investigator. Parker, please escort Mr. Farthing off my property."

Parker nodded in approval. "Yes, ma'am."

Farthing nervously eyed the unfriendly faces before he turned, scurrying toward the back door.

Once the door had shut behind him and Parker, Mia let out a whoop. "It's the second time I've heard Tori let loose with both barrels. Way to go, girl."

With a grim tone, she said, "We're not out of the woods yet."

David grabbed a cup from the cupboard. "Colt, you want anything?" He filled the cup with coffee.

"Right about now, a cold bottle of beer sounds good, but I'll settle for a bottle of water."

David opened the fridge, grabbed one, and tossed it to Colt.

Tori asked, "Can he pull the permit the way he did?"

"Without checking the city ordinances, I'd hate to speculate." Colt unscrewed the cap. "But you picked up on a key point. One I find inexplicable. He didn't bother to ask what steps we're taking to fix the tunnel." He took a swig.

With the anger still coursing through her, Tori said, "Why do I have this feeling there's more here than pulling my permit? I don't think Farthing up and decided to do this. I wonder who is behind it. I've got to call Dan and let him know what happened. I'll be in my office." Her face tight with worry, she walked out.

Once Tori was out of earshot, Colt said, "She's one tough lady. I sure didn't expect her reaction. Farthing didn't either. She cut him off at the knees and left him dangling. I don't think he'll forget this for a while. What did she mean by who was behind this?"

David explained the pressure Tori had received to sell

the property. He mused, "I thought it was all over, but now I also have to wonder."

Mia spoke up, "Judd Swanson?"

"That's my thought," David said.

Colt took another deep swallow of water. "I know the name but never met the man."

Leaning against the counter, David cradled the cup in his hands. "Swanson was leading the pack. I suspect he'd still like to get his hands on this place. This is the kind of tactic he'd pull. And he's got the clout to do it."

Parker walked back in and looked around. "Where's Tori?"

"In her office calling Dan," Mia said.

Tori sank onto the desk chair. Under the anger, a new fear rose. Could they shut her down? When turning the old house into a bed and breakfast inn was just an idea, David had warned her. He said the movers and shakers could throw roadblocks in her way. Judd Swanson, a local developer, had told her the house was a liability, even dangerous, if she went ahead with her plans. Of course, he had a motive. He wanted the land to build a high-rise con-dominium.

Now, disaster had struck. Her permit was revoked. All construction stopped. None of it, though, was why she was afraid. Four women had tied their sails to her boat, and now the boat could be sinking. Tori shook her head with impatience. Sometimes metaphors were disgustingly annoying.

Nonetheless, it was true. Jeff Archer, her new CPA and wealth management advisor, recommended a profit-sharing program. All four would receive a base salary and a percentage of the profits from the inn.

Mia had made changes in the operation of her business, O'Brien's Home Cleaning. She'd even quit her job at the grocery store. While the other three worked for Mia, they also had part-time jobs they'd already quit. If the Red Door Inn went into the tank financially, she'd be all right, but not her team.

It didn't help that during the discussions regarding their employment, all four had made it abundantly clear they'd pull their own weight in the project. They would not take advantage of Tori's wealth. It's why she had to be careful about the dang electronic tablets. They wouldn't accept them as a gift. But if she told them it was for their work at the inn, it was different.

Tori scraped her hand across her face. All she could do was take this one step at a time, not get ahead of herself. She picked up the phone. Luckily, Dan was in the office.

"Tori, I only have a few minutes before I leave for court."

"Dan, a city inspector, Otto Farthing, showed up and revoked my construction permit."

In typical fashion, Dan calmly asked, "Did he cite a reason?"

"Yes, the tunnel."

"What about the steps you are taking to fix it? They should have allayed any concerns."

"It's part of the problem. The inspector didn't ask. Just shut it all down." She went on to explain the comments Farthing had made regarding the condition of the property.

"Colt's plans were all approved. I need to speak with him before I call the city attorney. Give me his number."

Tori relayed it.

Before disconnecting, Dan said, "Tell him I'll call later this afternoon. In the meantime, don't worry."

As Tori returned to the kitchen, she grumbled, "Yeah, right! Don't worry. How many times in the past have I heard that one?"

Stepping inside, she said, "Dan plans to call the city attorney. Before he does, he wants to talk to you, Colt. He was headed to court but said he would call later this afternoon. I gave him your number."

"Well, this is going to stir up the rumor mill," Mia said.

Oh great, Tori thought as she plopped into the chair. Just what she didn't need. No point in worrying about it since there was nothing she could do. There were, however, the new plans for the house. "Colt, we," motioning to her team, "are going to open the inn on a limited basis for meetings, luncheons, that kind of thing. I need a permit to serve food. Do you think what Farthing did will keep me from getting one?"

"Hmm … it could prove interesting. The existing

permit is for the new construction and structural changes in the house. So, there shouldn't be any reason you can't get one. I can file the application for you if you like and see what happens."

David said, "Good idea. If Farthing blocks the permit, we'll know some skullduggery is going on." Seeing Tori's questioning look, he said, "Swanson."

Tori nodded. "He popped into my mind. Judd has certainly been determined to get his hands on this property."

Colt said, "We'll need to make a few changes to the kitchen before someone comes out to inspect it. Where can I set up my computer? I can file the application online and need to order some materials."

"Plenty of room in the dining room," Tori told him.

Colt said, "David, nothing is stopping us from conducting the structural analysis. The sooner you can get it done, the better."

"My men should be here within the hour." He headed out the door.

Colt followed him, saying he had to get his computer from his truck. He stopped in the doorway, looking back. "I need your list of appliances." He waved a hand at the kitchen. "None of these will pass inspection. Later on, when we do the full remodel, the new appliances can be moved to the new building or into your new apartment over the garage. I'm also going to replace the flooring. I can't do much with the cabinets other than a coat of paint."

"You're sure you don't need a permit to remodel?"

"Nope. Besides, what they don't know won't be a problem." He walked out.

Mia said, "I like that man's attitude."

Parker asked, "Is there enough room for my computer?"

Tori said, "Of course. We've got more than enough room."

"I'll get my bag out of my truck." He followed Colt.

Mia said, "Has anyone else noticed Parker seems to like hanging out here?"

"After the skeleton was found, Dan did tell him to stay with the investigation. But you're right. I think he likes being here," Tori said.

With a chuckle, Mia said, "I'd better start another pot, since you aren't the only coffee addict in this house."

"I'll be in my office." As Tori walked out, the doorbell chimed. "I'll get it."

When she opened the door, Linc looked at her with a wary expression. Not surprised and wanting to put him at ease, she gushed a bit. "Linc. Good to see you. I talked to your dad earlier." She stepped back.

"He mentioned it. Both of us are concerned. I just wanted to make sure you knew we'd do whatever we could to help. Even though it's mostly a police matter and fixing the tunnel."

As they strolled to her office, Tori said, "No, not really. The tunnel and body aren't all that has happened. It's worse."

"Oh?"

Before she could explain, Colt and Parker walked into the hallway, stopping by the doorway to the dining room.

"Linc. It's been a while," Colt exclaimed.

The two men shook hands.

Then Linc looked at Parker. "I remember you. The private investigator, Parker Hayes."

Parker shook his hand. "Yes, we've met, Mr. Greer."

"Make it, Linc." He glanced into the room and the table covered with computers. After greeting the four women, he said, "What's all this?"

"We've turned the dining room into a temporary office," Tori said. "Parker and Colt are also using it."

Though a questioning look crossed Linc's face, he didn't comment.

"Would you like coffee or iced tea. We've got both."

He followed her to the office. "Iced tea? That's something new."

"Mia insisted. You know how she can get."

From the dining room, Mia shouted, "I heard that."

Linc, his attitude relaxing, laughed. "I'll pass, but thanks."

Tori settled behind her desk while Linc sat in a chair. "I thought you were in the middle of your renovation. Why isn't anyone working?"

"Until the tunnel is fixed, we stopped the demolition. But it doesn't matter since the city revoked my construction permit."

"What! Why?"

"According to the city inspector, Otto Farthing, it's

because the tunnel collapsed, but it seems to be an arbitrary decision. He never inquired about the steps I planned to take to fix it."

"That's odd. It doesn't sound like Farthing. I've known him for years. Always seemed to be a straight-up kind of guy. Are you completely shut down?"

"Yep."

"What do you plan to do?"

Tori wasn't certain why, but she felt edgy about confiding in Linc. "I don't know yet. This all happened about an hour ago."

"If Dad or I can help, let me know. So, what about the tunnel?"

"Colt's going to repair it. Did your dad tell you about the body?"

"Yes. He said you were trying to identify the person. He's checking the archived files but hasn't come up with anything. What about the police?"

"Nothing. The homicide detective is doubtful they can identify him."

He glanced at his watch. "I'd better get back to the office. I've got a meeting with a client. Call if you need help."

"Thanks, I will."

As Linc passed the dining room, he stopped to say goodbye, then headed to the front door. As he drove away, Tori stood on the front porch for a moment, wondering whether she could ever fully trust him again.

Mia opened the door and stepped out. She put her

arm around Tori's shoulders. "It's tough when trust is broken. You can't always get it back."

Tori gave her a skeptical look. "Sometimes, Mia, you are downright spooky. Are you reading my mind now?"

"Under the circumstances, it'd be hard not to." She squeezed Tori's shoulders. "Come on. We've got decisions to make for our new project."

Inside, Colt and Parker were busy on their computers.

As she walked in, Colt looked up. "I filed the application," he said.

Heidi and Tina stood behind Cammie, looking over her shoulder at her computer screen.

Heidi beckoned. "Come take a look at these," moving aside so Tori could squeeze in.

"Bright, bold colors," Tori observed, looking at a set of dishes.

Cammie said, "Fiestaware has been around for a long time, since the late 1930s. It all depends on what look you want in the dining room. I'd recommend staying with a known brand for ease of reordering. It will get broken." She clicked through other selections.

"Okay, I've got a problem here. I like all of them. How are we going to decide?" Tori said, feeling overwhelmed.

Tina said, "Here's my take. White goes with any color scheme. We can change the look of the table with accessories. And you don't have to worry about a contrast to the wallpaper, which you haven't yet selected."

"Cammie, go back to the white set."

She clicked the mouse.

"I like this one. The lace pattern is distinctive and elegant. What do all of you think?"

Everyone had a resounding yes.

"Okay, put it on your list, Cammie."

"Do you want to look at cookware or the silverware?" Cammie asked.

Tori shuddered. "No! Absolutely not. I trust your judgment. Order whatever you need. Where are you on the list of appliances?"

Colt's head twisted toward Cammie at the question.

With a nervous hesitation, she said, "Uh … still working on it."

David walked in, breaking up the discussion. "Colt, I'm headed into the tunnel. We could use some help with the lights."

Colt and Parker both closed their computer.

As they filed out, Tori's worried look returned. "I'm going with them."

Outside, she hurried to catch up. Two men stood near the entrance with an assortment of equipment on the ground beside them, none of which she could identify.

She stayed back, not wanting to be in the way while she watched. After a short conversation, David headed down the ladder. Each piece of equipment was handed down to him before the rest of his men followed.

Turning, she scanned the back of the house. The excavator sat silent, its huge jaw resting on the ground. Anger shot through her at the latest machinations to stop her.

That's what this permit business was all about. Well, it wasn't going to happen. She'd get her ducks in a row, starting with ensuring the tunnel wasn't a liability.

Wandering over to the entrance, she could hear the rumble of voices. She wanted to be down there, hearing what was said. Instead, she had to wait. Tori clasped her arms across her chest. The sun had disappeared behind the clouds. A slight haze clung to the ground.

Easy for her imagination to run wild as a shudder rolled over her. Who was the man in the tunnel? Why had he been killed? Standing around out here wasn't finding the answers.

Still, it seemed she couldn't escape the past. It kept clawing its way into her life.

Chapter 7

Seated at her desk, Tori studied her to-do list. Many of the entries were on hold until the problem with the permit was fixed. She had no idea how long it could take. At somewhat of a loss as to what to do next, she decided to search the newspaper archives.

After accessing the *Granbury Chronicle's* website, she discovered it was a near-impossible task. While the daily papers were archived, she didn't have a way to refine the search parameters. Just the thought of the day-to-day hunt made her groan.

Since David said the house was built in 1938, she started on January 1, 1939, and slowly scanned the headlines for each day's paper. By the time she decided to take a break, she'd read the first three months. Only eight years and nine months to go.

Giving up, she headed to the kitchen. With a bottle of water from the fridge, she sat at the table, guzzling the cold liquid while watching the activity in the backyard. David and one of his assistants stood on top of the tunnel. The man slowly rolled a piece of equipment across the ground. David was watching a device he held in his hand.

Her phone chimed. It was Dan.

When she answered, he said, "Tori, I spoke with the city attorney, Will Marshal. He's aware of the issue and will call back when he has more information. I tried to call Colt, but his phone went right to voice mail."

"He's down in the tunnel. He and David are going ahead with the structural survey. Colt said he didn't need a permit."

"Smart thinking. We might end up in a hearing before the city council. If so, it would be helpful if you had documentation proving the tunnel was structurally sound. In the meantime, not much else you can do. Is there anything new on the investigation? I haven't been able to reach Parker."

With a wry chuckle, she said, "He's also in the tunnel. I suspect he's looking over the crime scene. The homicide detective is finished."

Dan laughed. "That sounds like Parker. He's got a nose like a bloodhound. Can't stay away from a mystery, and this is a good one. Keep me posted, and ask Colt to call when he gets a chance. I'll be in my office the rest of the day."

"Will do. And thanks, Dan."

She tapped the disconnect button, laying the phone aside. As always, after speaking with Dan, she felt somewhat reassured.

Mia and Heidi strolled in, plopping into the chairs.

"Hey, you look deep in thought," Mia said.

"Got a call from Dan."

"And?"

"He spoke with the city attorney."

"Will Marshal."

Tori wasn't surprised Mia immediately came up with his name. It wasn't often Mia didn't know someone.

"What do you know about him?"

"He's fairly new to the area. I think he worked for some law firm in north Dallas before the city hired him. I haven't heard any complaints."

"I hope Marshal gets it fixed soon, though Dan mentioned the possibility of a hearing before the city council. The delay is infuriating because there isn't a reason for it."

Mia nodded. "Here's a small bit of news. The account is set up at the grocery store. I added all our names as authorized buyers."

"Any problem in getting it?"

"Are you kidding? When I brought up the idea to the manager, he practically foamed at the mouth. Tori, you can't get around the fact your money opens doors."

Tori ignored the fear digging into her gut and plastered an encouraging smile. "Well, let's hope you're right and the city sees it the same way. The Red Door Inn is good business for the city and tourism."

Heidi said, "If there's a hearing, you should tell them."

"You're right. I should," Tori exclaimed. "You know what? We need a website. Come on, let's get Cammie and Tina in on this." Tori grabbed her tablet and stood.

As they tromped into the dining room, Cammie

looked up from her computer. "What's up?"

"Team meeting," Tori said as they settled around the large table. "Tina, can you do a website?"

"Sure, it's easy. I can design it and hold off on publishing until we're ready. I already have a logo." She tapped the laptop in front of her, then turned it for everyone to see.

Tori breathed a sigh of satisfaction. Tina had cleverly incorporated the three RD poker chips Tori had inherited into the design. The poker chips from her grandfather's Red Door Casino were the inspiration for the inn's name. "I absolutely love it. It's perfect."

Tina said, "We can also use it in all our advertising. I'll need pictures of us, so I can post them on the website. I could do them, but they need a professional touch. I know a photographer. His shop is just off the square."

Heidi mumbled, "I hate having my picture taken. I always look fat."

Mia chuckled. "Suck it up. Besides, look at it this way. It gives us a reason to get gussied up. Heaven knows none of us has had a date lately. What's next?"

With the advertising decisions out of the way, Tori moved to the next item. "What do we do about this room? How can we increase the number of guests?"

They debated the pros and cons for several minutes, finally deciding to replace the large table with smaller ones. Of course, it meant they had to find replacements to fit the style of the room.

Mia slid her hand over the gleaming wood and

sighed. "This table is beautiful. I hate that we can't use it or the chairs. They won't fit into the museum. What are you going to do with it?"

Tori thought, then said, "I'm not selling it, that's for sure. If I take out the leaves, I bet it will fit into my new apartment over the garage."

Parker strolled in, a cup of coffee in one hand.

Mia exclaimed, "How can you drink that stuff? It's hours old."

He grinned as he pulled out a chair. "It's okay. Reminds me of my days as a homicide detective."

Tori asked, "How is it going out there?"

"David is still working on the survey, though I must admit I wasn't paying much attention."

Tori eyed him. Instead of his laid-back demeanor, he had an air of suppressed excitement. "Dan has been trying to call you. I told him you were in the tunnel. What were you doing?"

"Examining the area where the bones were found. The location itself is different and quite interesting. The two rooms your infamous ancestor built were framed with wood. Even the ceiling of the tunnel is reinforced with heavy timbers. It's what, in my opinion, kept the damage from the cave-in to a minimum." He took a swig of coffee.

"What is different?" Heidi asked.

"A hole was dug into the side of the tunnel. After the body was stuffed inside, dirt was packed around it, then the opening was covered with wood slats. That's the only section on the tunnel wall with wood." He reached into his pocket. "I found these." He laid two poker chips on the table.

Stunned, Tori stared at them. "Good lord! Not more poker chips. What a peculiar place to find them. Why would he have poker chips in his possession?"

Mia spoke up. "Back in those days, gambling was a form of entertainment at parties for the men. Maybe he was here for a poker game when he was killed."

Tori reached across the table and picked one up. A dark gold color, the surface was dirty and eroded. Despite the degradation, three lightning bolts were visible. She flipped it over. A dollar sign and 25 were printed on the other side.

"How odd. The chips Elly left me had RD, which stood for Frankie's main casino, Red Door, printed on one side. The back side only had handwritten numbers."

Parker said, "I don't know much about poker chips, though the ones I've seen all had a value on one side, a dollar, five dollars. Back then, twenty-five dollars would have been a high-dollar bet."

Tori flipped the chip from side to side. "What's really strange are the lightning bolts. What do they mean?"

He shrugged as he slid the other chip toward her. "If you think that one is strange, look at this."

Picking it up, she turned it over. "Wow, this is weird. The lightning bolts are on both sides and no value. Why?" She passed them to Mia.

Parker said, "Another mystery."

"I need to learn more about the history of poker chips." Tori added an entry to research them to her list on her tablet. "Are you going to tell Detective Rodriguez about them?"

"Yes. Since these were found at the crime scene, he needs to know."

"Dang, I was hoping to keep them," Tori said.

"I doubt he'll want them."

Then Tori told him what she had found out about the cufflinks.

"It certainly adds to the mystery," Parker said. "Evidently, the man had money. Any luck with the newspaper?"

"Not yet."

Parker looked at his watch. "I need to leave." Retrieving the chips that had been passed around, he laid both in front of him, then pulled out his phone. After taking pictures, he handed them back to Tori. "I'll stop by the PD on my way out of town and show Andy the pictures. If he wants the chips, I'll let you know."

Tori walked with him to the door.

"I'll check back with you tomorrow," he said before leaving.

As she passed the dining room, it was empty. She followed the voices into the kitchen. Cammie was on her knees, a ruler in her hand, measuring the baseboard behind the refrigerator.

"What *are* you doing?"

"I may have a problem with the refrigerator. If Colt

removes the baseboard, I think it will fit."

Mia laughed. "She's been like a nervous hen, checking and rechecking her measurements on her list of appliances."

"I need to make sure I don't make any mistakes," Cammie mumbled as she pushed to stand up.

Tori said, "There is nothing any of us, including me, can do that can't be undone or fixed by Colt. Stop worrying. Besides, this is all temporary anyway. Once Colt starts to remodel, it's all going to get changed again."

Heidi said, "I'm out of here unless you need something."

"No, I'm good. You all might as well go home. We've done enough for today."

Mia said, "Are you sure? I don't mind staying."

"No reason to, but thanks. I'll see you tomorrow."

Leaving the women to gather up their belongings, Tori headed outside. Colt, David and his two men stood near the tunnel entrance. Parker's security guard was close by. It seemed a heated argument was underway.

As Tori walked up, she heard David say, "I'm telling you, it's not a problem."

In an emphatic tone, Colt responded, "Well, *I* think it's necessary."

"What's wrong?" Tori asked.

With a glare at his friend, Colt said, "A slight disagreement on the reinforcements."

"Didn't sound like a slight one to me," Tori said. "Who's going to explain?"

Chapter 8

avid's lips twitched with a grin of appreciation. Tori was the spitting image of her grandmother. Russet hair framed a face with dark eyes under black eyebrows. Even her stance, fisted hands on her hips, eyes flashing, and her jaw thrust forward, was just like Elly.

"Colt wants to add posts sunk in concrete along the tunnel. I'm telling him it's not necessary. Even though I'm not finished with the survey, I've seen enough to know the tunnel is structurally sound."

With a glance at David's two assistants, who unabashedly listened, Colt said, "Since you're done for the day, let's talk about this in Tori's office."

David nodded as he turned to his men. "Let's get this gear loaded up." Then he looked at Tori. "I'll be inside in a few minutes."

"What happened to the lights?" she asked, suddenly realizing what looked different.

"Since there won't be any activity after dark, Parker said he only needed one," Colt told her.

They moved toward the house, leaving David and his men to finish up. Inside, Tori asked if he'd like something to drink.

"A bottle of cold water will do."

She snagged one from the refrigerator on the way to her office.

Uncapping it, Colt swigged half the bottle. Easing into a chair, he said, "A busy day. Tomorrow I'll start repairing the tunnel."

"I thought we couldn't do anything."

"The construction permit is only for the new building, adding your apartment to the garage and the structural changes to the house. I don't need a construction permit to fix the tunnel."

David walked in. He had also grabbed a bottle of water.

Colt said, "I was telling Tori about going ahead with the repairs."

David grunted as he settled into a chair. "Farthing won't be able to do a thing about it."

"At least it's some good news," Tori said.

"I talked to Dan. He had questions about the city's procedures for issuing a permit and the progress of the survey." Colt took another long swallow.

David said, "As soon as I finish the report, I'll get it to you. The second survey team will start tomorrow."

Colt said, "Tori, we are on solid ground here, no pun intended. A hole was dug in the wall. It wasn't reinforced with wood like the other two rooms since it probably happened after the tunnel had been built. I figure the only reason was to bury the body. Then wood was used to cover up the opening."

"Parker said much the same thing before he left," Tori told them.

"He was down there most of the day, sifting through all the dirt." Colt finished off the water. "The hole created a weak point, and it's why that section of the wall collapsed. Once we get it fixed, there shouldn't be a problem."

"It's what I keep telling him," David said. "He doesn't need to add additional posts."

"I know I don't, but I think it's necessary. Dan is talking about a hearing. The additional posts, even though they aren't necessary, will add weight to our arguments."

David leaned back with a thoughtful look on his face. After a few seconds, he said, "On that basis, I can concede the point."

"Unless you object, Tori, I am going ahead with the posts."

"No, I don't. How long will it take?"

"Once I get the entrance enlarged, a couple of days. Where do you stand on the changes to the kitchen?"

"Cammie has the list of appliances." An idea struck. Tori said, "What about some of the other renovations in the house? What can you do without needing a permit?"

"Anything that doesn't involve a structural change."

"Then I could go ahead with the new wallpaper and flooring on the bottom floor?"

"Yeah. Good use of the downtime for my crew."

"It would make the house even more attractive to clubs and organizations who might want to hold an event here," Tori said.

David motioned with the bottle. "A great idea. This house has a huge appeal."

"Yes, it does. I want to play up the appeal if this goes to a hearing. This house is good business for Granbury, and I plan to make sure the city officials know it."

With a smug smile, David said, "They won't know what hit them."

Colt said, "I like it. Good thinking. But if we're talking wallpaper and flooring, I need your selections pronto. I can start stripping the old wallpaper tomorrow. Once we finish the downstairs, we might as well replace what we can upstairs."

"Mia is going to love this. She's been chomping at the bit to get the wallpaper replaced." Tori pulled the chips from her pocket, sliding one across the desk. "Parker found something today."

David groaned as he picked it up. "Not more poker chips."

"Yep."

"What's wrong with poker chips?" Colt asked.

David handed it to Colt. "Already had one mystery with the poker chips her grandmother left Tori. Now, these pop up."

Colt fingered the chip. "Lightning bolts, how odd." He handed the chip to Tori. "Looks like you have another mystery to solve." He stood, picking up the empty bottle. "Time for me to leave. I'll see you in the morning." He turned and walked out.

As Colt's footsteps faded, David said, "Farthing didn't slow you down one iota."

Her lips twitched upward with a satisfied smile. "No, he didn't."

"Any plans for supper?"

Anticipation surged through her, though all she said was, "No. Got any ideas?"

"We could order a pizza. Or would you rather get out of the house?"

Tori eyed his filthy clothing. "I'm not sure you'd be allowed through the front door of any restaurant. Pizza sounds good."

"If you'll order, I'll try to get rid of some of this dirt."

With a chuckle, she picked up her phone. The pizza place was already on her speed dial. Once she'd ordered, Tori headed to her bedroom. When she moved into the house, the upstairs was in such disarray that she opted to live in the servants' quarters off the kitchen.

After hastily washing up, Tori put on a dash of makeup and lipstick, then changed out of the boots she'd worn all day. Feeling somewhat presentable, she wandered into the kitchen.

David was already seated at the table with his laptop open in front of him. "A lot of articles and images about poker chips."

"Anything on the ones Parker found?"

"Not finding one that's even close."

Knowing David and his friends played poker, rotating houses for the game, she asked, "Do you use poker chips in your games?"

"Nah. Too much trouble. Easier to toss the money on the table." He closed the lid, shoving the computer to one side. "How long on the pizza?"

She glanced at her watch. "Twenty minutes or so. Wine or beer?"

"A beer sounds good. I noticed a pitcher of tea in the fridge. Whose idea?"

"Mia. Said I had to learn how to make iced tea the Texas way. The only problem is that it's laden with sugar. Too sweet for my taste."

"It's the way it's served down here. Any fast-food place usually has a couple of sweet tea dispensers as opposed to one for the unsweetened version."

"I had no idea it was so popular."

"Hey, it's a Texas staple, right up there with barbeque."

Tori grabbed a can of diet soda and a can of beer. She set them on the table before easing onto a chair.

With a flick of his finger, David popped the top and took a swig. "So, tell me more about these plans that are about to tick off whoever is behind this latest stunt to derail you."

Even though his question was slightly convoluted, it caused Tori to chuckle. "The dinner last night sparked the idea. We can't open for overnight guests, but there's no reason we can't use the house for daily events. Today, we got a lot of the details worked out. Cammie is taking on the cooking, and Tina is now officially in charge of advertising. Between the two of them, they've already come up with some great ideas. How did I get so dang lucky?"

"I must admit, it's hard to beat having those four in your corner."

"Don't I know it." Her lips twisted in a wry smile as she picked up the can of soda. "Even though this business with the building permit has turned everything topsy-turvy, we can still get some of the renovations done."

The doorbell rang.

"That was fast. My treat. I'll get it." He walked out.

Tori rose to get the plates, setting them on the table. David's voice rising in anger sent her rushing toward the front door.

A woman holding a microphone and a man with a camera stood in the foyer.

David said, "I'm telling you, no comment. Leave before I call the police."

When the woman spotted Tori, she pointed. "There's the owner, Tori Winters. Get a shot of her."

Behind them, one of Parker's men stepped inside, grabbed the man by the arm, pulling him out the door.

The man shouted, "Get your hands off me, or I'll be the one calling the cops."

The security guard said, "You were told to leave. You're trespassing."

The woman, ignoring the ruckus, rushed toward Tori.

"Miss Winters, how did you feel when you found a skeleton in your tunnel?"

"No comment," Tori said.

The guard reached for the reporter, but she nimbly scampered aside, avoiding his arm. David and the guard stepped in front of her, forcing her to back up until she was outside, though she still hollered questions. The guard followed.

David slammed the door shut, snapping the lock in place behind them. "I wasn't paying enough attention when I opened the door. They were inside before I could stop them."

"I wonder which paper they work for. I think the man managed to get a picture before his abrupt exit."

"We'll find out tomorrow. You need a peephole."

"I know, but I hate the idea of cutting into the wood."

As they started back to the kitchen, the doorbell chimed again. More cautious, David cracked the door open and peered around the edge before he threw it open. The smell of onions and pepperoni wafted ahead of the teenager walking in.

Tori waited until David had paid, then led the way back to the kitchen.

"Oh, this smells delicious. I didn't realize how hungry I am," she exclaimed as David set the extra-large box on the counter.

He laughed. "You'd better start grabbing because I'm famished."

"Maybe I should have ordered two."

"Nah, I don't mind sharing as long as you only take a couple of pieces."

With a scrunch of her nose, she piled slices on her plate.

His eyes widened in disbelief. "Wait a minute. I'm the big guy here."

Her mouth full, she grunted.

The conversation stopped until Tori groaned, "Okay, I give up. I can't eat anymore. You can have the rest."

"I wondered how long you were going to keep stuffing your face. Definitely unladylike." With a satisfying grin, he scooped her remaining pieces onto his plate.

Tori wrinkled her nose again as she shot him a look of disdain. "Sticks and stones and all that other nonsense." She leaned back. "Who do you think is behind this latest attack? Swanson?"

He swallowed a bite, wiped his mouth with a napkin, and said, "My money's on him. From what I've heard, he's still squawking about this place. The cave-in is his chance to prove the house and property are a liability."

"It's so frustrating. It's no wonder Elly didn't trust anyone when she went to Dan to get a new will."

"Ever get a chance to dig into those journals of hers?"

"No. But reading them has moved up on my to-do list. I might find something about our mystery man. The cufflinks alone indicate he wasn't some flunky."

"What about them?"

"Cartier, eighteen karat gold."

"You're right. There should be a record of his

disappearance, even if it was eighty years ago. Can I help?"

"You know a lot of people in this town. Start asking. If he lived here, there might still be family members. Stories get handed down through the family." Mimicking an old-timer's voice, she said, "You remember when my great granddaddy up and disappeared? Never did find hide nor hair of him. It was like he vanished off the face of the earth."

A belly laugh erupted. "Hey, that's pretty good," David told her. "I will. I'd start your team on it, especially Mia, since she seems to have a pipeline into most anything in Granbury."

He stood, picking up his plate. "Well, I hate to eat and run, but I've got an early morning meeting with a group from the power company." As he rinsed off the plate, he added, "I need to finish the report they expect to get."

Tori stood. "It never occurred to me that this business with the tunnel would cause you a problem."

Seeing the look of concern, he flicked a finger across her cheek. "It's not a problem and not something you need to add to all the stuff you're worried about. Don't think I don't see it, even with that stoic look you get."

She sighed. "If it were just me, it would be one thing, but I've dragged four other women into my schemes. I can't let them down." A sheen of tears sparked in her eyes.

"Hey, it's going to all work out." Placing his hands on her shoulders, he pulled her into his arms.

For a moment, Tori let herself sink into the comforting

feel of his arms. How easy it would be to shift all the problems onto his shoulders. She eased back. Wishful dreams, but the stark reality was that she was responsible. Her shoulders squared as she looked up at him.

David tipped his head back and laughed. "There you go, there's the look. Damn the torpedoes and full steam ahead." His hand lightly brushed her hair. "Don't forget. You're not in this alone. Okay, I'm out of here. I'll see you tomorrow."

She walked him to the door, waving as he climbed into his truck. Locking the door, she headed to the kitchen. Once it was squared away for the next morning, she stopped to look out the window. Reassured by the sight of the truck parked at the back of the property, Tori walked into her office. Back on the computer, she picked up where she had left off in the newspaper archives.

Two hours later and two more months crossed off, nada, nothing. Disheartened by her lack of progress, Tori tossed the pen she'd used to record her progress on the table. She rolled her head, working out the tension in her neck and shoulders. Her mind was beginning to feel frazzled, but she still wanted to make a stab at the poker chip. A myriad of sites and images popped up, but they were all new. Then she changed her search to vintage poker chips. *Ah*, Tori thought, *this is more like it*. Still, after clicking from page to page, nothing stood out to help her. Frustrated, she closed the computer.

Before heading to her bedroom, Tori wandered from room to room, envisioning how she could use each one.

She paused in the living room to stare at the large oil painting hanging over the fireplace mantle. Unsmiling, her great-grandfather exuded arrogance. Dark eyes under heavy black brows had a cold, calculating look. It wasn't hard to imagine Frankie pulling the trigger. But why? And why bury the man in the tunnel?

Her gaze shifted to her great-grandmother. Irene's hair was rolled on top, falling into soft waves around her face. Irene was dressed in a pin-striped suit with padded shoulders and wide lapels. The skirt ended at mid-calf. Her feet, crossed at the ankles, were shod in shoes with short thick heels. Unlike her husband, her face was unremarkable in appearance. It was easy to see Elly's distinctive features, as well as her own, came from Frankie's side of the family.

While she had learned a lot about Frankie's illegal gambling syndicate, she didn't know much about her great-grandmother. From the few records she'd found, Irene's family wasn't wealthy. Born in Iowa, her parents moved to Dallas, where Irene's father, a woodworker, built furniture for a local company.

Tori couldn't help but wonder how much Irene knew about her husband's criminal activities.

As she turned away, anticipation stirred as she thought about a long, relaxing bath. While she looked forward to the day she had a shower, there was something to be said about the luxury of a tub.

Tori cranked the handles on the large claw-footed tub. After dumping in bath salts, she breathed in the refreshing aroma of jasmine. Tossing her clothes into the small hamper, Tori twisted her hair into a knot on top of her head, holding it in place with a large clip. She eased into the hot water and slid down until her head rested on the edge.

Even though she didn't want to think about the day's events, she couldn't stop the shift of her thoughts to Farthing's visit. It didn't make sense. She hoped Dan could find out who was responsible. But would it make a difference at a hearing? Wouldn't they have to prove her property was dangerous? But how when there wasn't any evidence? Surely after hearing Dan's arguments, the city would be forced to reinstate the permit. That's what she had to keep in mind. Not let herself get discouraged.

Tori sank lower into the water, feeling the day's tension drain away. Her mind drifted to the mystery man. What was his connection to Frankie? There had to be one since he ended up dead and buried in the tunnel.

Tomorrow, she'd be back on the hunt, looking for answers. There was still a chance she'd come across a news article. Then a thought struck, and she sat up. Water droplets splattered. "My god, I'm an idiot." Why hadn't she thought of the one person who might have the answers—Ethel Morris, her grandmother's housekeeper.

Ethel lived at a senior citizens' apartment complex on the outskirts of Granbury. Every couple of weeks, Tori would stop by to visit. She loved to listen to Ethel's stories about the old days. Ethel's mother was the original housekeeper. A widow, she had been hired shortly after Frankie built the house. When Ethel's mother died, Ethel took over as housekeeper and lived in the house until a few months before Elly was murdered.

If anyone knew the mystery man's identity, it would be Ethel. Excited at the thought, Tori climbed out of the tub. Despite the enticement to visit the next day, she'd have to wait. With all the controversy swirling around the tunnel, it wasn't a good time to be gone.

She turned out the bedroom light, peeking around the edge of the drape. While the large lights were gone, a small one still lit up the area around the truck parked at the back of the property. Tori could see the guard seated in a chair, a reassuring sight. If someone slipped into the tunnel and was hurt, it would only reinforce the arguments about the liability of the property. Whatever it took, she had to make sure it didn't happen.

After sliding under the covers, it wasn't the problems with the tunnel, the building permit, or even the mystery man occupying her thoughts. It was how she had felt in David's arms. Feelings she wasn't ready for or even wanted to acknowledge. But as she drifted to sleep, Tori knew she couldn't control her dreams.

Chapter 9

After the early morning trek with coffee and breakfast croissants for the guards, Tori sat at the kitchen table. Over the horizon, the sun had started to rise, casting bright beams of light through the windows. She munched on a sandwich as she studied the to-do list on the tablet in front of her. At the top of the list, she added in bold letters—VISIT ETHEL.

Today, the most important task was a presentation to the city council. Tori didn't want to get caught by a short-notice hearing.

She stared at a new page, fingers drumming the table as she thought. Her mind was as blank as the page. What did she want to say? While she had a general idea of the points she wanted to convey, the words weren't there. How could she convince anyone the inn was good for Granbury if she couldn't figure out what to write? Why had she believed this would be easy. A groan rumbled.

This was ridiculous. She should be able to come up with a script. Okay, maybe this wasn't such a good idea. The ring of the doorbell was a welcome interruption. It was Carl, the security guard with the thermos. After another round of profuse thanks, he trotted down the steps, nodding as he passed Mia.

Her arms laden with books, Mia walked up the driveway. She called out, "Good morning."

Tori set the thermos inside the doorway, then rushed down the steps to help her.

"Good lord, did you buy out the bookstore?"

Mia chuckled. "Sample books for wallpaper."

With a resigned look, Tori said, "Dang, woman. I'm telling you, at times, you are downright uncanny. I planned to ask you about the wallpaper today."

Mia only laughed as she followed Tori inside, bumping the door with her hip to close it.

The books balanced against her chest, Tori reached to pick up the thermos. "Colt said there isn't any reason we can't go ahead with the walls and flooring. Later today, he's going to meet with us."

They dropped the books on the table as they passed the dining room.

After stashing her gear in the utility room, Mia asked, "Anything else happen last night?"

Tori slid onto the kitchen chair, glumly staring at the tablet. "Hmm … not really."

"What *are* you doing?"

"Writing a presentation in case there's a hearing."

Mia looked over Tori's shoulder. "Why is it blank?"

"I don't know what to say."

"I bet Tina can help. I know she had to design an

advertising campaign for a couple of her classes."

"Oh, wow, just wow. What else can she do that I don't know about?"

"When it comes to designs and advertising, she's the go-to person. She and Cammie are so excited." She laughed. "Last night, I got a phone call from both. I didn't think they'd ever hang up."

"Not half as excited as I am. It's a huge load off my shoulders."

With a glass of iced tea in her hand, Mia said, "Okay. I want to know about last night."

Puzzled, Tori glanced up. "What?"

"Wondering why there is a very large pizza box on the dryer. A lot of pizza for one person. I bet someone stayed. I'd also bet I know who it was."

Tori shot her a snarky look. "Pizza, nothing more."

The look Mia shot back said she didn't believe it. One eyebrow cocked up.

She rose, stepping around Mia to get to the coffee pot. "No big deal. We ate pizza, and then David left."

"Why do I have this feeling you are protesting a little too much?"

"Because you're a busybody, and you know it."

A roar of laughter erupted. "Got me there. Danged if I'm not. But inquiring minds want to know."

"In this case, inquiring minds aren't going to learn anything different." She decided it was a good time to change the subject. "We need to visit Ethel."

Mia immediately sobered. "We sure do. She might know the identity of our mystery man. Anything new on the tunnel?"

"So far, the reports from David's survey are good. There's nothing wrong other than repairing where the wall collapsed. To be on the safe side, Colt plans to put in a few posts for reinforcement. Another company will be here today for the second survey."

"Sounds as if progress is being made."

"We had an incident last night," Tori said. She explained about the reporter.

"Oh, that reminds me." Mia went back to the utility room. When she returned, she carried a newspaper. "I stuck this in my bag. You're the lead story again."

Tori glanced at the paper, *The Metro*. "Cripes. He managed to get a picture after all." Centered on the front page was a picture of her standing in the hallway, looking like a deer caught in headlights. "I've never seen or heard of this newspaper."

Mia snorted. "Nothing but a rag, a scandal sheet. They go for sensational headlines and are not concerned whether they are true."

"This one is a doozy, *Granbury Heiress Under Fire*." Tori's gaze quickly scanned the article. "The reporter states the city has halted all construction pending a hearing. Oh, no! This can't be right. She states, and I quote, '*the property could be declared unsafe and condemned.*' And, if that's not bad enough, there's a bit about the investigation into the identity of the murdered man."

Tori collapsed onto a chair, the newspaper trembling in her hands as fear rolled through her. With a stricken look, she stared at Mia. "No one has said anything about condemning my property. And this reporter makes it sound as if the man was just murdered, not that it happened years ago."

"Tori, don't panic. This is typical for *The Metro*, blow something out of proportion or even make stuff up."

"But Mia, they had to talk to someone. How would they know the construction had been stopped or about a hearing? *I'm* not even sure there will be one. Dan even said it was just a possibility."

"I wouldn't put much stock in the article. I think it's quite a stretch from a sinkhole in the backyard to a total condemnation of the property."

Fighting the nightmarish feeling, Tori said, "Maybe so, but someone is behind this. It has to be Judd." She crumpled the newspaper. "He's not going to get away with it."

Voices echoed from the front of the house. The rest of the team had arrived.

For a few seconds, Tori stared out the window at the backyard, trying to gather herself together. She didn't want anyone, including Mia, to know how the word condemned had affected her.

Heidi walked in, followed by Tina and Cammie.

"I saw the wallpaper books in the dining room. Is it next on the agenda?" Heidi asked.

"Yep," Mia said as the women brushed by her,

heading toward the utility room.

Once they dropped their bags and other gear, glasses were retrieved from the cupboard and filled with iced tea.

Heidi motioned toward the wadded-up paper. "I'd say there was more bad news."

With her emotions tightly suppressed, Tori downplayed the article. "*The Metro*, making something out of nothing." She looked at Tina. "I need help with my presentation. I'm drawing a blank on what to write."

A look of delight crossed Tina's delicate features. "Oh, what fun!"

Tori groaned. "She calls it fun."

With a quick laugh, Tina said, "Hey, it's not hard."

"Yeah, right. It's why I sat here this morning staring at a blank page, feeling like an idiot," Tori grumbled.

"What do you think about a video of the house?"

Tori perked up at the thought. "I like it."

"I'll jot down some ideas, and when you get a chance, we can talk about them."

"Music to my ears." Seeing Colt and his men milling around in the backyard, Tori said, "I'll be back," and dashed out the back door.

Outside, Tori raced across the backyard. When Colt spotted her, he stepped away from the group of men.

"Tori, what's got you in such a rush?"

"I need to talk to you." The looks of interest from three construction workers standing behind him had Tori tugging on his arm as she dragged him out of earshot.

With a concerned look, he said, "What's wrong?"

She told him about the newspaper article. "Colt, is there a chance the city could condemn my property?"

"They could, but is it realistic, no. Even if they tried, they'd face a lawsuit because there's no justification for a condemnation. But I don't like that a newspaper raised the issue. Where'd they get that idea?"

"Is there a way to find out?"

"Parker or Dan would know more about it than I would. I've heard reporters are notorious for not giving up their sources. I'd suggest giving Dan a heads-up about the article."

She glanced at her watch. "I'll call as soon as his office opens. Do you still want a meeting with us today?"

"Yes. I should be able to break away once David gets here along with the other engineering team." At the tight look on her face, he added, "Tori, try not to worry about what the article said. Let's see what Dan can find out and take it one step at a time."

"You're right. I went into full panic mode when I read it."

"Easy to do, but you've got a lot of help on your side."

She smiled. "Mia said the same thing."

"Hey, she's a smart woman."

Another group of men came up the driveway.

Tori said, "I'd better let you get back to work." She nodded to the new group as she passed them but kept going toward the back door. Right now, she wasn't up to making small talk.

The kitchen was empty. Tori grabbed the tablet from

the table and headed to the dining room. Mia was seated at the table with an open book in front of her. The others clustered around her.

Cammie said, "How can you decide? There are so many stunning patterns."

Mia chuckled. "Not any different than how you decide between all the pots and pans on the market." Spotting Tori in the doorway, she said, "We earmarked a couple for you to look at."

Tori moved to look over Mia's shoulder.

After flipping pages, Mia stopped at one with a paperclip. The color was a deep rose with embossed flowers. "How about this one for the dining room? It has an old-world look."

Tori studied it, then looked at the existing red wallpaper with similar flowers. "I like it better than this red. It's not so much in your face."

"It's what I was thinking, but I didn't want to influence you."

"Please, influence away. This is like writing advertising script. I know when I'm out of my depth. What does everyone else think?"

"We liked it," Tina said.

"One room down. Before I look at the rest, I need to make a phone call, then I'll be back."

Seated behind the desk, Tori laid the tablet down, then tapped the speed dial for Dan's office.

When she asked to speak to Dan, the receptionist said he'd just walked in.

A few seconds later, he came on the line. "Good morning. I hope a call this early isn't an ominous sign."

"It may be. Have you seen *The Metro* newspaper?"

With a somber tone, he said, "No. It's not high on my list of favorite papers to read. What have they printed?"

She explained what happened when the reporter showed up at the house, then what was in the article.

"I think the coffee shop on the first floor sells the rag. I'll get a copy. I certainly don't like the reference to the construction issues or the suggestion of condemnation of the property. Someone is feeding them information. I'll call Parker. Have him do some snooping. I'd like to find out who is behind this. What is the status of the survey?"

"David should finish today. So far, his findings indicate the tunnel is safe. Another engineering company is starting on the second one."

"Good. It may be overkill to get two surveys, but it would be nice to have the second one as our ace in the hole."

"Unless you have a reason why I shouldn't, I plan on doing a video if there is a hearing. I want to impress the city officials that the new inn is good business for Granbury."

"I like the idea. Hopefully, it won't be needed. Parker sent me the pictures of the poker chips he found. Any thoughts about them?"

"Mia suggested the mystery man might have been in the house for a poker game. Seems back in the day, it was a popular pastime for men at get-togethers. Still, why would the mystery man have them in his pocket?"

"An interesting question. The design, those lightning bolts, is certainly odd. I've been to a few casinos and have never seen any like these. And the only ones I've seen without the value of the bet stamped on one side are those your grandmother left you. It's certainly a puzzle. I have another call holding. I'll be in touch as soon as I hear from the city attorney."

Tori disconnected. As much as she hated to, the search for the mystery man's identity had to be put on hold. Finding out wasn't high on her agenda. The future of the Red Door Inn was on the line, and it was where she needed to focus her time. She had a long list of items to finish, and wallpaper was at the top.

As she stepped into the hallway, the doorbell rang. "I'll get it."

Leery from what happened the night before, Tori cautiously opened the door. Prepared to slam it shut, she peeked around the edge. Parker stood on the porch, slightly rumpled, with the inevitable computer bag slung over his shoulder. He appeared so mundane it was easy to discount his presence until you looked into his eyes. What he successfully hid in his demeanor was grit and determination. She wondered how many criminals had made the mistake of underestimating him.

His eyes gleamed with awareness as if he had discerned her thoughts. "Are you going to let me in?"

Tori laughed and opened the door.

"I heard you had a couple of intruders last night," he said, walking alongside her to her office.

"They didn't stick around after David and your security guard hustled them out the door."

"My man had gone around the back of the house and didn't see them drive in. By the time he got to the front porch, they were already inside."

"David answered the door, and they pushed their way in."

"I figured as much from your reaction. You need a peephole."

A frown settled on her face. "Dang. David said the same. I really don't want to cut a hole in the door."

"Then I suggest mounting cameras around the house. It would let you see anyone walking up."

Tori's eyes lit up with interest. "It's a great idea. Let's run it by Colt. If it doesn't interfere with the outside renovations, I'll do it."

They stopped in the dining room, where Parker greeted the four women.

From their reactions, it was obvious he was fast becoming a favorite visitor.

Mia said, "I'd offer sweet tea, but I know you prefer coffee. I just made a fresh pot."

He nodded.

"There are donuts and kolaches," Heidi added.

"Kolaches? Sausage?" Parker said.

Tori chuckled. "Part of Mia's attempts to indoctrinate me in Texas cuisine." She had learned one type of kolaches was dough wrapped around small sausages, then baked.

"I want to talk to Colt. Can I grab one later?"

Mia said, "The box is on the kitchen counter. Help yourself and to the coffee."

"Is it all right to leave my computer bag here?"

"Parker, you don't need to ask for permission. We consider you," Tori waved her hand at the other women, "as one of the group."

The women all nodded.

His eyes blinked with a stunned look before his cheeks turned rosy. "I … uh … thank you. I'll be outside." He set the bag on the table before rushing into the hallway.

When the back door closed, the laughter everyone had held back erupted.

Wiping her eyes, Mia said, "I think it's the first time I've seen Parker discombobulated."

As the laughter faded, Tori said, "I'd better see what's going on."

Chapter 10

Colt and David stood by a cluster of men near the tunnel entrance. Parker had joined them. Tori trotted up, stopping alongside David.

Turning toward her, David said, "I wondered how long it would take before you showed up."

Colt laughed. "This is her second trip."

David turned back to the group. "This is Tori Winters, the owner of the property. Tori, this is Mitch Lewis and Bob Granger. They own L&G Engineering."

The two men reached out to shake her hand.

Lewis, the older of the two, said, "We've heard a lot about you." At her wary look, he hastened to add, "I can assure you it was all very complimentary."

After a flustered thank you, Tori asked, "How long will your survey take?"

Lewis answered, "A few hours. Two of our men are in the tunnel. I should have a report to Colt in the morning."

"What about your report, David?" she asked.

"I have an engineer in my office working on it. It should be finalized later today."

She looked at Lewis and Granger. "Are you aware of David's findings?"

"No," Lewis said. "We thought it best not to discuss it, and David agreed. That way, we can testify we were not influenced in any way. Colt, we'll be in the tunnel."

The men headed toward the entrance. Instead of returning to the house, Tori moved a short distance away to watch. There was a steady stream of men in and out of the tunnel with various pieces of equipment. Most of the technical jargon didn't have much meaning, but still, she intently listened. When she finally strode to the house, she couldn't stop the flutter of apprehension. So much was riding on the surveys. What if they disagreed with David's conclusions? A thought she futilely tried to disregard.

A fresh aroma greeted her when she entered the kitchen, tantalizing her taste buds, even though she couldn't identify the smell.

Cammie stood at the stove, stirring a mixture in a large frying pan. "Everything okay? You were out there for a long time."

"Yes. The other company is doing their survey. What smells so delicious?"

Still stirring, Cammie shot a glance over her shoulder. "A basil and cream sauce. A new recipe I wanted to try. It's one I can serve over chicken or pasta. Today, it's pasta. This will be a good selection for the luncheon menu if everyone likes it. Easy to fix and serve."

Heidi, setting plates on the table, groaned. "I thought I'd lose weight when Mia quit the store." She waved her hand toward Cammie. "You wouldn't believe the amount of *real* butter and cream she used."

Laughing at Heidi's grumblings, Tori said, "Where is everyone else?"

"In the dining room. Mia is still immersed in wallpaper, and Tina is working on the video." Heidi pulled silverware from the drawer. "I offered my services to help our budding chef in the kitchen."

"Anything I can do?"

"Nope," Cammie said. "I'll holler when it's ready."

Tori wandered into the dining room and slid into a chair next to Mia.

She looked up from the books spread open in front of her. "I don't know what Cammie is brewing up, but it sure smells good."

"It's probably going to be delicious since she's got Heidi in an uproar, complaining about gaining weight. Any progress?" Tori motioned toward the books.

"I've got a selection for every room. Only need your seal of approval." She pulled a book toward her, opening to a page she marked. "What do you think about this one for the music room?"

Tori studied the cream-colored paper with delicate white and blue flowers for a few seconds. "I like it. It will make the room seem light and airy."

With a flick of her finger, Mia flipped pages. "How about this for the foyer?"

It was a slightly different version of the one for the music room. The difference was multi-colored flowers.

"What I liked about this one is the colors of the flowers compliment the stained-glass portal over the staircase landing," Mia told her.

"I absolutely love it."

Mia grabbed another book. "The living room was the most difficult. The existing gold wallpaper, in my opinion, is too heavy for the room and too overpowering with the dark furniture. I found two I thought would work." She turned to a page, then pulled another book toward her, opening it to the second selection.

Tori's gaze shifted between the two samples. In the first, the gold background was muted, with embossed gold swirls of leaves. The second was a light blue, with the same embossed swirls as on the gold one, but more delicate and multi-colored.

Mia anxiously watched Tori.

Tori jabbed her finger at the blue one. "This one. I think it complements the selections for the other two rooms and foyer."

Mia let out a sigh of relief. "It's my favorite, but I wasn't sure since it's such a dramatic change from the existing wallpaper."

"It's a good selection. Kudos to you."

"Well, it's not just me. Everyone chimed in. How are they progressing outside?"

"David is finished except for the report. I should have the report on the second survey tomorrow."

"It's progress."

A troubled look crossed Tori's face. "I suppose so."

Mia squeezed Tori's hand. "Don't get ahead of yourself. If trouble is on the way, it will get here without you reaching out to grab it."

From across the table, Tina said, "I've made a start on the video. Hopefully, it's going to help."

Tori smiled, reassuring Tina. "I'm sure it will. Tell me what you have so far."

"I want to start with a shot of the front of the house. The problem is the front yard is still ratty looking, but if we add pots of flowers on the porch and steps, I think we can dress it up."

Her hands fluttered in the air as if panning the room. "Then sweep inside with shots of the inside. Add music with an overlay of your voice, talking about the mystique and elegance of the house, making it the ideal place for group events, weddings, special venues, and fun weekends to enjoy the historic allure of Granbury. We don't want it to be long, maybe two to three minutes at the most. Long enough to demonstrate what the Red Door Inn can bring to Granbury. In your speech, we can add other details like tourism statistics, revenue, etc."

Stunned, Tori slumped back. "Tina, it's an awesome start. I think you've found your niche, advertising guru."

Encouraged, Tina leaned forward. "I think you can drive your point home by including an advertising plan for the inn. Here's another point you might want to use. There are several unique artists in Granbury. Offer samples of their work on consignment in the gift shop."

Heidi walked in. "I've been sent to tell you to get your

butts in there. Cammie is dishing up."

A mad scramble ensued as the three women jumped from their chairs to follow Heidi.

Cammie set a large bowl of pasta on the table. "What was going on in the dining room?"

Grabbing a can of Coke from the fridge, Tori said, "I've been blown away by wallpaper selections and Tina's advertising genius."

Once everyone was settled, the bowl was passed around. Tori scooped several spoonfuls on her plate, then leaned over to take a deep breath. "Oh, this smells so good."

When she forked up a bite, the creamy taste of basil, with a hint of lemon, burst in her mouth. Tori groaned with pleasure. She waved the fork in the air. "Oh! This recipe is a keeper."

From around the table, other groans of pleasure resounded.

"My gosh, Cammie. Why haven't you ever cooked this before?" Mia asked.

"I don't know. It never occurred to me."

Their forks suspended, four sets of eyes stared at Cammie.

"What?" she asked, taking a bite of pasta.

With a note of awe, Tori said, "This isn't a recipe you found?"

Still chewing, Cammie said, "Nope. Made it up."

Tori waved her fork in the air. "She made it up. Who makes up recipes?"

"Oh, come on guys. What's the big deal? It's a simple sauce, nothing complicated. No reason to make a fuss over it."

"You don't seem to understand. For the rest of us mortals, we rely on recipes," Mia said.

With a glum look, Heidi watched Mia scoop more pasta onto her plate. When Mia gave her a wicked grin and offered the bowl, Heidi muttered, "Some friend you are. I'm removing temptation," and stood, picking up her plate.

As Tori chewed, her gaze swung over the four women. A few months back, fearing for her life, she'd left Missouri with everything she owned packed into her car. On a wing and a prayer, she headed to Texas, all because of a vague phone call from Jonah Greer about an inheritance, which she didn't believe would amount to a hill of beans.

And now, she was surrounded by four incredible women, friends who'd become family. She had a fabulous home, a fortune in the bank, and a potential for a future beyond her wildest imagination. Tori swiveled her head to look out the window. Her eyes misted, the emotion threatening to overwhelm her. Beside her, she felt Mia's hand grip her shoulder. The woman was uncanny. She always seemed to sense when Tori's emotions threatened to get the better of her. She gulped.

Moving her hand away, Mia said, "Let's get the kitchen cleaned up, and then I'm back to the wallpaper."

"I've got it. This is my territory now," Cammie said.

Her spunk put a grin on Tori's face. How could she have ever thought Tina and Cammie were the two shy ones in the group?

"Even so, I'll help," Heidi said.

"Don't forget. We've got a meeting with Colt whenever he can break away." Tori tossed her can in the trash and headed to her office.

The ring of the doorbell had her turning around. "I got it," she hollered.

On the front stoop, Jonah Greer waited.

"Jonah, good to see you. Come on in."

He stepped inside, greeted her, then said, "I took a chance you might have a few minutes. I was in the area meeting another client."

"I'm glad you did, and yes, I have time." As they strolled to her office, she asked, "Can I get you a cup of coffee or iced tea? Though I have to warn you, it's Mia's tea and loaded with sugar."

He grinned. "Is there any other way? But, no, I'll have to pass. I only have a few minutes."

Settled into a chair in front of her desk, he adjusted his pant legs. "The house looks phenomenal. You've done a nice job with it."

"All the credit goes to Mia and her crew."

"I've heard you made some changes in their duties."

She never ceased to be amazed at how fast word spread on the Granbury rumor mill. "Yes. Red Door Inn is now officially a business. Mia is General Manager, Heidi, Director of Operations, Cammie, Culinary Director, and

Tina is the Advertising Director."

His head shook in amazement. "How astonishing."

"Cammie's cooking will make a believer out of you, and Tina will soon have a computer degree. Though, with her talent at graphic design, she's a natural for handling our advertising."

Uncomfortable, she didn't understand why she felt compelled to defend her team. Maybe it was because Jonah had been disdainful of Mia and her team's ability in the past.

He cleared his throat. "Well, yes, but that's not what I came here to discuss. I've heard some disturbing news. City officials are being pressured to condemn your property because of liability issues with the tunnel."

Her heart thumped, squeezing her lungs. Her worst fears had become a reality. What the news story had printed was true.

Tori leaned forward, her arms on her desk, as she vehemently protested. "How the devil can they possibly justify such an action? It's asinine. There isn't any danger. David conducted a structural analysis of the tunnel. He says it's safe."

"David could be considered biased."

"I don't believe he will take kindly to any suggestion questioning his integrity and professionalism."

Jonah frowned. "The difficulty is that perception can outweigh reality."

"Maybe so, but it's a moot point. I'm getting a second opinion from another survey company. They're outside right now. I should have both reports tomorrow."

A look of surprise flashed across Jonah's face that was quickly suppressed. "I'm glad to hear it."

"Who is applying the pressure? Judd Swanson?" Tori figured if anyone knew, it would be Jonah, considering the two men were close friends. They'd grown up together. "You, of all people, know just how fanatical he was to get his hands on my property."

His body tensed, though his tone was mild. "You don't have to remind me. I don't know who it is. But since the city attorney is involved, I felt compelled to warn you. Tori, don't get too far ahead with your plans for the house."

"Jonah! You and I both know there is nothing wrong with this house."

"I know. Still, you could be in for an uphill battle. One you might not win. If I can be of any help, let me know."

"I appreciate the offer. I can tell you, I'm not going down without a fight, even if I have to take this to court."

"I didn't think otherwise. How are you coming with your mystery man?"

Still fuming over what Jonah had told her, Tori said, "Thanks to the city, I haven't made much progress. Did you ever find anything in your records?"

"No, I haven't, but I'm still looking."

She opened the drawer and removed the poker chips, handing them to Jonah. "These might interest you. They were also found with the body."

As he fingered them, he said, "How very strange. An interesting design."

"Does it ring any bells?"

"No, can't say it does." He handed them back, then glanced at his watch. "I've got to go."

As they walked to the front door, Tori said, "Thank you for letting me know what you've heard."

"I'm very concerned about the city inspector's action. I also don't like how fast this has blown up. Typically, the city doesn't move fast on anything. But, for whatever reason, this is gaining traction." His face troubled, he trotted down the steps.

Shaken by his comments, she stood on the porch, watching him stride to his car. Who was behind this, and why? It had to be Swanson.

Chapter 11

Feeling unnerved, Tori slowly strolled inside. Should she call Dan to tell him about Jonah's visit? Since he planned to call after hearing from the city attorney, she decided to wait.

She poked her head into the dining room. Four women stared at her with similar expressions of concern. Of course, they would have heard, as close as the dining room was to her office.

Tori slid onto a chair. "Not good news. Jonah's visit sure backs up what was written in *The Metro*."

At the sound of the back door closing, she turned toward the doorway. David walked in with Colt and Parker behind him.

"Was that Jonah I saw driving out?" David asked.

Tori nodded. "He stopped by because of the issue with the city."

"And?" David said.

She looked at the dining room table piled with books and computers. "Let's take this into the library, where we have more room."

"Good idea. Got any iced tea left?" David glanced at Mia.

"Just made a fresh batch. I'll get it. Colt?"

"Tea sounds good to me."

"Parker, coffee?"

"You bet." He shot her a grateful smile.

In the library, the men eased into chairs.

Colt said, "I've always liked this room. It has a cozy air about it."

Mia and Heidi walked in, handed out the drinks, then turned to leave.

"Where are you going?" Tori asked.

Mia said, "We'll be in the dining room. Holler if you need anything."

Tori's eyes narrowed, realizing they thought they were intruding. "You are as much a part of this as anyone here. Let the other two know, then grab a seat."

Heidi walked out. When she returned, she had Cammie and Tina in tow.

Once everyone was settled, Tori said, "Jonah told me there's a push to condemn the property, and the city attorney is involved."

David cursed. Colt shot her a questioning look while Parker looked thoughtful.

"Who is Jonah, and what does he have to do with all of this?" Colt asked.

After hearing Tori's explanation, Colt said, "It's crazy. There is no justification to even consider condemnation. I've inspected this house from top to bottom. Something is going on behind the scenes we don't know about."

His face tight with anger, David said, "It's got to be Judd. He's wanted to get his hands on this property even before Elly was murdered."

Tori sipped, then set the cup on the small table next to her. "I asked, but Jonah said he didn't know. Judd hasn't said anything to him. But who else could it be?"

"Have you told Dan about Jonah's visit?" Parker asked.

"Not yet. I expect he'll be calling. I'll tell him then. I don't understand how the newspaper got ahold of the details so fast."

"I've got one of my men working on it," Parker said. "He has an in with someone at *The Metro*. Even if we find out, it may not help much. It could be some clerk passing on a tip."

Colt swallowed a swig of tea. "Parker mentioned the camera security system. It's a good idea since there could be more interest from the news media. The installation won't interfere with anything I'm doing to the outside of the house."

"Let's go ahead then," Tori told Parker. "What do you need from me?"

"Decide where you want the monitor. I'd recommend two, one in your office and the other in your bedroom. It's a wireless system, so it's not a complicated installation."

"Whatever you think is fine with me." She looked at David. "What about the second survey?" Tori couldn't hide the apprehension in her voice.

"Lewis said his men are on track to finish today. You'll have the report tomorrow. His preliminary assessment is the same as mine. The tunnel is sound. The problem was the hole dug into the side of the tunnel to bury the body. It created a weak spot in the wall, causing the cave-in."

Colt spoke up. "The two reports should be sufficient to stop any discussion of liability or the possibility of future cave-ins. If your great-grandfather hadn't decided to dig a hole and bury a body, there never would have been a problem."

"It's reassuring," Tori said. "Though, listening to Jonah, someone is pushing the city to take action."

"And it brings us back to why," David said, his tone grim. "I don't like how fast this has built."

Tori said, "Odd. Jonah said the same thing."

"Well, at least he and I agree on something."

Tori knew David still had hard feelings over Jonah and Linc's actions after Tori inherited the property.

"Jonah also said to expect a hearing, and I shouldn't get too far ahead with the plans for the house."

Her comment brought David upright in his chair. "What did you tell him?"

"I wasn't going down without a fight. I've already got a start." She waved toward Tina, who was sitting alongside Mia on the couch.

"Tina is taking over the advertising. She is working on a video I plan to use at the hearing. Tina, tell them what you have in mind."

Startled, Tina jerked. A red blush stained her cheeks.

She started to speak, then stopped to clear her throat. Mia's hand gently touched her shoulder. With a look of determination, she took a deep breath and began to explain. As she talked about the concept for the video and the points Tori would make during the presentation, her voice grew with confidence.

When Tina finished, Colt said, "A video is a great idea."

"Does anyone know when it might be scheduled? How much time do we have to prepare?" Tori asked.

"If we need extra time, I expect Dan will arrange it. He's not going to let them take any action that doesn't allow you a fair hearing," Colt said.

"That's a relief. Then how long will it take to repaper the downstairs, replace the flooring, and make the changes to the kitchen? I'd like to have as much done as possible before I do the video."

Pursing his lips, Colt stared off into space. After a few seconds, he said, "If I put men in different rooms and go to overtime, I can move fairly fast. I may need to hire some additional help since I need a crew working on the tunnel entrance and the reinforcement posts. I probably don't need to ask, but any issues with the cost?"

"No! I've got to convince the city officials!"

"Then I need the selections for the wallpaper, flooring and the list of new appliances."

"We've got the wallpaper and appliances but not the flooring."

"I have sample books at my office. I'll call Ben and

have him bring them here."

"I've wondered why we haven't seen him," Mia said.

"He's at the office, finalizing the paperwork for another project." He glanced around. "Here's the game plan. I'll start with the foyer, this room, and the living room. In here, I can work around the furniture since all I have to do is paint the ceiling and put in new flooring. But I'll need to move everything in the living room into the music room to make enough space for the men to work."

Raising his hand, David said, "I'll help."

"So will I," Parker said.

"Then let's get started." He pulled out his phone, calling Ben. After giving his foreman a list of items to bring to the house, he followed Tori to the dining room, where Mia and Cammie handed him their lists.

Over the next hour, the house was inundated with men as Colt issued orders to his crew and one to Tori about not using the front door while the men worked.

Mia and Heidi supervised moving the living room furniture to the music room, and not without difficulty, as both were overly protective of the antiques. Once the room was bare, David and Parker headed outside. David wanted to check on the survey team, and Parker wanted to examine the outside of the house for the camera system.

When Ben arrived, the team poured over the sample books of wood flooring, debating the merits of a light wood versus a dark look. Liking the parquet pattern in the foyer, Tori wanted to extend the design through all the rooms. They finally settled on a cherrywood style.

As Tori restacked the sample books on the dining room table, she eyed the tired looks. "Let's call it a day. Not much else any of us can do. Starting in the morning, we need to use the back door instead of the front."

They gathered their bags and headed out.

Tori grabbed a bottle of water from the fridge and re-treated to her office. It wasn't until near dark that Colt shut everything down, telling the men to be back early in the morning. Before leaving, David and Parker stopped by her office for an update.

"The second survey is finished. I'll have their report sometime in the morning. But it all still looks good," David told her. "I've got to go. It's poker night at my place. Parker, are you sure you don't want to come? We like to get fresh blood."

Parker laughed. "No, not my thing. Never could get into betting."

With a flick of his fingers to his forehead, David walked out.

"Tomorrow, a crew will be here to install the camera system. So, I'll be around most of the day if you need help," Parker told her. After retrieving his computer bag, he left.

The sudden silence in the house was disconcerting. Tori wandered to the front, staring at the clutter of ladders and drop cloths in the foyer. Doubts clouded her mind. Was she doing the right thing, pushing to get this done for a video?

With a sigh, she wandered to the kitchen. After

getting a sandwich and a can of soda from the fridge, she collapsed into a chair. As she chewed, the events of the day buzzed in her head. With all the activity, she'd been able to hold her fears at bay. But now, in the stark silence of the house, they reared their ugly heads, setting off a sickening feeling inside her.

What would she do if the city did condemn the property? Could she file a lawsuit? Would it stop them from tearing down the house? Questions with no answers, only a sense her world was about to unravel. Her appetite gone, Tori managed to choke down the last couple of bites by washing it down with the sharp tang of Coke.

Lamenting about what the city planned to do wasn't getting her anywhere. Tori's only solace was her office. With the furniture stashed in the music room, she couldn't get to the piano.

At her desk, she picked up where she'd left off with the research on the poker chips. Strolling through page after page of articles, one caught her eye. A four-year-old article detailed how Sid Jeffery used poker chips to trace the origin of illegal gambling casinos in the early 1900s. Fascinated, Tori read about how he used the archives of a company that manufactured most of the chips. Once he found the purchase order for the chip, he had a location and name for the casino and could backtrack the history. At the end of the article was an email address.

Tori pulled the chips from the drawer. After taking pictures with her phone, she transferred them to the computer, then attached them to an email with her questions.

Considering the article's age, she didn't hold out any hope. But still, it was worth a try. She hit send.

When nothing else popped up in her research, Tori switched to the newspaper. Finishing out 1939 with no luck, she shut down the computer, calling it a night.

As she snuggled under the covers, her thoughts twisted back to the disaster looming over her. She had to find out who was behind the threat. Drifting off, the question that clung in her mind was not who, but why?

Chapter 12

With only a sliver of light on the horizon, Tori carefully picked her way across the uneven ground. As she neared, the two men seated near the truck rose.

"Good morning," she called out.

Carl reached to take the box. "Miss Tori, you're up early as usual. We sure appreciate the fresh coffee and food." He set it on the table.

As the two men emptied it, Tori said, "I don't know how you stay awake all night. Before I moved to Granbury, I was a nurse and pulled a few all-nighters in the emergency room. But there was always a buzz of activity. Still, I never could get used to the change in hours."

Steve said, "It helps with two of us here. We keep each other alert." He handed her the empty box.

Carl opened the thermos. The aroma of freshly brewed coffee drifted in the air. "Smells good. We'll drop the thermos off on our way out."

With a cheerful goodbye, Tori headed back to the

house. Inside, she filled her cup and made another sandwich. As she ate, Tori studied the to-do list. In uppercase letters, VISIT ETHEL was still the first entry. Since the house would be crowded with construction workers and the tunnel was squared away, she and Mia should be able to leave for a few hours. Tori hoped the elderly woman could provide a few answers. She was certainly tired of reading news articles.

Tori scrolled down, pausing to study her list of shops on Granbury Square, including a charming bookstore, local wineries, a candy store, and a shop for custom-designed jewelry. She planned to visit each one to discuss consignment options for the inn's new gift store.

After visiting Ethel, there'd be enough time. But was it a good idea? Maybe it would be better to wait. Then anger sparked. Why should she? There was nothing wrong with her property. And she wasn't going to act like she had a problem. What better way to show it than to march into those stores and talk about her future plans.

With a new sense of resolve, she worked her way down the rest of the list before adding an entry to get boxes. By the time she finished, sunlight streamed through the window.

The back door closed. Mia's voice rang out. "It's just us." Heidi and Mia strolled in.

Mia set a thermos on the counter. "From one of the guards with his profuse thanks. Cammie and Tina will be late. They have a house to clean. It won't take them long." She pulled out a paper from her bag and handed it to Tori.

"You made *Metro's* front page again."

"Oh, great," Tori moaned as she scanned the lurid headline—*Drama Reigns at the Leichter Mansion.*

Heidi grabbed a couple of cups and filled them. "Refill?" she asked, glancing at Tori.

"Hmm … yes, please," she said, engrossed in the article. "This one is all about the identity of the victim and speculation about the pocket watch and initials. Jeez, they even know about the chips. How did they find out?"

"Has to be from the police department," Heidi commented.

"I suppose so," Tori said.

Mia plopped into a chair. "You never know, maybe someone will come forward who knows who this guy was." Before taking a sip of coffee, she motioned toward Tori's tablet with the cup. "How long is our list?"

"Some items crossed off, but more added. Today is probably a good day to visit Ethel." She explained about the stores, then added, "We need boxes to pack up the dining room, kitchen, and pantry. We can pick them up while we are out."

"They're in my car," Mia said.

Tori groaned. "Why is it that you *are always* one step ahead of me? A seriously aggravating trait."

With a mischievous gleam, Mia said, "Hey, when I'm good, I'm really good."

Heidi said, "Lordy be, don't get her started. You know how she delights in one-upmanship."

"Yeah, well, she did it to me again," Tori muttered,

crossing the entry off her list. "Since we've got boxes, let's start in the dining room. I'll check with Colt and find out when we need to clear out the kitchen and pantry. The visit with Ethel will have to wait. Maybe tomorrow."

The doorbell rang. Mia slid her chair back. "I'll get it." She paused. "I thought we weren't supposed to use the front door."

Focused on the paper, Tori murmured, "Only when men are working in the foyer. It's probably Colt or Ben."

When she returned, she said, "It's both, along with several of their crew."

Heidi said, "Mia, let's get the boxes."

They headed out the back door. Tori tossed the paper aside and rose, strolling to the front of the house. Several men clustered in the foyer. Ben stood off to one side, a phone to his ear.

Colt greeted her, but before she could say anything, Ben pocketed the phone and said, "Colt, we've got a problem. Max's wife called. He is in the hospital with a broken leg. While I was talking to her, Luca left a voicemail. I just finished talking to him. His house caught fire last night."

Stunned, Colt stared at him. "Anyone hurt?"

"No, everyone got out in time. A neighbor spotted the fire and called 911, then pounded on the door. The fire department managed to save most of the house."

"Does he need any help?"

"He's okay for now. They are staying with his parents. He asked for time off."

Colt nodded. "Tell him to take whatever time he

needs. What about Max? What happened to him?"

"Someone ran him off the road. The police think it was road rage. Losing them will put us behind."

"Do we have any applications?"

"Three came in yesterday."

"What do you know about them?"

"From my initial checks, they seem okay. Light to moderate construction experience."

"Call all three. We can use the extra man. If you can, get them here today. The faster, the better. I'll check with Max and Luca later."

Ben nodded. "Will do."

"Tori, did you need something?" Colt asked.

"Nothing that can't wait." She turned and walked away. Colt and Ben had enough to handle without her questions about the kitchen.

In the dining room, Mia and Heidi had cleared off a section of the table. As Heidi pulled out a glass from the hutch, Mia carefully wrapped it with paper before laying it in a box.

Mia looked up. "Everything okay?"

"I guess so." She relayed what had happened to the two men.

"How odd," Heidi observed. "What are the chances something would happen to two of Colt's crew?"

The ring of her phone stopped the discussion. She pulled it from her pocket and rushed into her office. "Good morning, Dan." She slid into her chair.

"How is everything at the house?"

"I'm going ahead with renovations that don't require a permit." She explained Colt's plans, then said, "All of this was planned once we finished with the new building and apartment. We just moved it up on the timeline."

"It's a good strategy."

"Dan, Jonah stopped by. He said there is a push to condemn the property."

"He's right."

The fear that had never gone away rose in her throat.

"It's why I'm calling. I've talked to Will Marshal, the city attorney. Because the city received complaints about liability issues and the tunnel's collapse, Marshal indicated he had no choice but to investigate. And yes, he made a comment about condemnation. I informed him there were no grounds for such an action, and if the city proceeded ahead, I would file for a restraining order. I have been assured the city has no plans to do so, though he did mention the possibility of an inspection. I told him we would cooperate. If they do, I plan on having an expert there to keep an eye on them."

"What about the hearing?"

"Marshal hasn't decided. I suspect it will depend on the outcome of their investigation."

She told him what Jonah said about fixing the house, then asked, "Dan, am I making a mistake by going ahead with the renovations?"

"No, not at all. You are entirely within your right to improve the property. How long will it take?"

"Colt wasn't sure. What about the inspection? Should

you delay it until he's finished?"

"No. It will demonstrate you're not trying to hide structural faults with cosmetic changes."

"Did you find out who lodged a complaint?"

"Marshal refused to tell me. He said it wasn't pertinent to the issue of liability." Anger tinged his voice. "I informed him it was entirely relevant as it spoke to motive. I'm letting it go for the moment, but I will find out."

"Hmm … Judd Swanson?"

"Could be. But let's not jump to conclusions until we know for sure. As soon as you have the survey reports, send them to me."

"I will. Did you see today's issue of *The Metro*? I'm the lead story again."

"Yes. I stopped in the coffee shop on my way in. Any luck on identifying the victim?"

"Not yet. Searching the news articles is a slow process. I haven't heard anything from the police either."

"All right. I'll be in touch."

After disconnecting, Tori rested her head against the back of the chair. Don't panic, she told herself. Dan didn't sound worried about Marshal's talk of condemnation or an inspection. Or was he putting on a good show for her? Jeez, she hated it when she started to second-guess herself. One step at a time. Right now, she needed to get the dining room squared away.

Cammie and Tina had arrived and were wrapping dishes as Tori walked in and greeted them.

Mia was stacking boxes against the wall. Hearing

Tori's voice, she asked, "Where do you want us to stash these?" When she turned and saw Tori's face, she said, "What's happened?"

"Dan called."

Everyone stopped.

After explaining, Tori added, "What am I going to get hit with next?"

Mia said, "It's certainly not good news. At least it sounds as if Dan is on top of it."

"He is. Dan's already put Marshal on notice about a restraining order. Stewing over it isn't going to change it one iota. Now, as for the boxes, the upstairs is out since we can't get to the stairs. Let's put them in my bedroom."

It was early afternoon before they finished. Tori said, "That's all we can do today. There's no reason for you to stick around. We'll only be in the way."

With a look of doubt, Mia said, "None of us mind staying."

The other three nodded their heads.

"I know. Mia, let's plan on visiting Ethel tomorrow. Unless Colt wants us to start on the kitchen, there's nothing we can do here. Heidi, if the three of you want to take the day off, you can."

As they left, Tori followed. She wanted to talk to Colt.

The backhoe operator was plowing a trench leading into the tunnel. Two of Colt's crew stood on one side of the machine and Colt on the other.

Tori stopped alongside him.

In a loud voice over the engine's roar, he said, "David called. He's got both surveys and is on his way here."

"I talked to Dan."

Colt's brow shot up.

Mindful of the men listening, she said, "When David gets here, can you take a few minutes for a meeting in my office?"

He looked behind her. "Here he comes now."

Tori turned. Something seemed to settle inside her. The apprehension faded at the sight of David loping across the yard with a file folder under his arm. The warm smile reached deep into his eyes. It added a sense of anticipation, a waiting. But for what?

Colt's voice broke into her musings. "I didn't expect you quite this fast."

"I'd already left when I called you. Any chance we can talk inside or is there too much activity?"

Tori's eyes sparkled as she gazed up at him. "My office is still good. All the work is in the front of the house."

"You two go ahead. Tori, ask Ben to come outside." Colt motioned with his hand. "He can keep an eye on this while I'm inside."

David stopped to pour a cup of coffee as they passed through the kitchen. Tori headed toward the front of the house, where voices rumbled. Ducking into the dining room to avoid the hallway, she weaved around the furniture in the music room, then strode into the living room. Ben stood in the arched doorway.

Two men she hadn't seen before ripped up pieces of

carpet, tossing them onto a pile against one wall. She wondered if they were the replacements. As she sidestepped around them, they gave her a long look.

In the foyer, the flooring was nearly gone, and ladders had been set near the front door. Two men stripped the old wallpaper.

"Ben, I'm relaying a message from Colt. He needs you outside. Are those the new men?"

He nodded. "Jack Crimshaw and Tommy Logan." He ducked around the ladder to get to the front door.

She turned and caught the men staring at her. Tori nodded with a friendly smile as she passed. One gave her a cheeky grin while the other shot her a contemptuous look. She kept going, though she felt they still watched her.

David was already in her office. He motioned toward the folder lying on her desk. "I made several copies."

Anxious to read the reports, the unsettling encounter slipped from her mind. While she didn't understand the technical references, she did garner both David and the other company agreed the tunnel was structurally sound.

Colt, followed by Parker, walked in. Colt settled into a chair, and Parker sat on the couch against the wall. She murmured a hello to Parker and kept on reading. When she finished, she handed the reports to Colt.

"I know you told me, but reading the official reports is reassuring."

David smiled. "With this evidence, it will be difficult to prove your property is a liability."

"Dan called and wants the reports. I'll send these to him. He talked to the city attorney." She relayed the details.

David said, "I know Will Marshal. Been involved with him on a couple of projects. I'm not surprised he raised the issue of an inspection. Marshal will make sure the city isn't liable for any damages. But with Dan involved, the city will tread lightly, especially once they see these reports. Don't forget, you have a lot of influence in this town."

"Hmm … not really. It's Elly's name that works magic, not mine."

David shook his head. "It's money that talks, not the name attached to it."

Colt, relaxed in the chair with one leg hooked over the other, said, "They're on shaky ground. The city inspector didn't do his job. Farthing didn't even attempt to investigate the accusations. He pulled the permit, and when he did, it put the city in the middle. I can't imagine the city attorney is too happy right now."

A troubled look settled on David's face. "I've thought about what Farthing did, and the more I've thought, the less it makes sense. I've dealt with him in the past and never had a problem. I wonder if it was his decision or if he was ordered to pull the permit."

An arrested look crossed Colt's face. "You could be right. Was it the city attorney?"

David shrugged. "If so, then whoever complained is talking to Marshal. Why else would he shield the person?"

Tori said, "When Linc stopped by, he had the same comment about Farthing."

"Well, I'm on a roll. Two areas now where the Greers and I agree."

Colt glanced at him. "Maybe it's why we haven't received an answer to Tori's application for a food service permit. With Marshal in the picture, Farthing may not have the authority to issue it."

At her look of distress, David said, "Tori, don't let this upset you. There's no justification for Marshal's actions, even more so now that you have the two surveys. Dan's not going to let them get away with this."

She nodded. "I know, but it's hard not to when I have no idea who and why someone is so set on condemning my property. Colt, Dan wanted to know how long it would take for the renovations."

"I'm still hesitant to give you a time frame. As you learned this morning, when I lost two men, there's always something that can go awry in construction."

"What happened?" David asked.

"Someone ran Max off the road, and he's in the hospital with a broken leg. Luca's house caught on fire."

Parker leaned forward with an intent look. "Any indication either was intentional?"

Startled, Colt glanced at him. "All I know is the police think Max's was road rage. I don't know about the fire."

Parker pulled the small notebook he was never without from his pocket. Tori had once asked him about it. He said it was part of a cop's gear. "Give me their full names."

After writing down the information, he said, "I'll follow up with the police and fire department."

Tori's concern edged upward. "What are you thinking?"

"Right now, it's just a feeling. It may not be anything." He slid the notebook back into his pocket. "By the end of the day, the camera system will be operational. The control system is already in place in the utility room. Tori, you'll have a monitor here and one in your bedroom. I'd like to install an alarm system, but it will have to wait until Colt is finished."

Parker glanced at his watch. "I'd better get outside. I want to keep an eye on the installation."

"Before you go, anything from the police about the murder victim?" Tori asked.

"Not yet. I still don't have an answer about the source for the newspaper, either."

"I need to get back outside," Colt said as he stood. "I'm hoping to get started on the posts today. Especially if we get hit with an inspection."

"Tori, do you need anything?" David asked.

When she shook her head, he added, "I need to get back to my office."

After David left, she scanned the reports into her computer, then attached them to an email to Dan. Tori added a few notes detailing the meeting before hitting send. She picked up her tablet only to lay it back down. The rumble of her stomach was a reminder to eat.

She remembered seeing a package of chocolate chip cookies in the pantry. After grabbing it and a can of soda, she settled in a kitchen chair. While she munched on cookies, Tori eyed the flurry of activity around the tunnel entrance. Men hauled wheelbarrows in and out. Like a line of ants, one went in, and another came out. Nearby a pile of debris slowly built.

She licked chocolate off her fingertips as her thoughts shifted to the surveys. Would the conclusions of two eminent engineering firms convince the city her property was safe? Would it be enough, or was there another agenda? One waiting to yank down her hopes and dreams.

Disturbed by the dismal thought, she cleaned up her mess, then idly made her way back to the office. At the corner of her desk, she came to an abrupt halt. An unsettling sensation rolled over her. The tablet had been moved. She'd left it in front of the keyboard, but now it was near the corner of the desk.

As she pondered the reason, she slowly dropped into the chair and pulled the tablet in front of her. A tap on the screen brought up the to-do list. Then she tapped the computer keyboard. On the monitor was Sid Jeffery's article about poker chips.

Footsteps echoed. Ben appeared, waving as he passed by, a reminder of who was in the house. If someone had been in her office, it had to be one of Colt's men. But why would one of them be interested in her tablet? It didn't make sense. Besides, she'd been in the kitchen. Surely, she would have heard if someone had walked into her office.

Then another alarming thought rose in her mind. Tori jerked open a drawer. With a sigh of relief, she picked up the poker chips. "This is crazy," she muttered. Still, to be on the safe side, she stuck them in her pocket, intending to stash them in the safe once Colt's men were out of the house.

Concerned about the whereabouts of Colt's crew, she strolled toward the front of the house. Men carted out bags filled with the old wallpaper, library and foyer flooring, and stacks of carpet through the living room doors that opened onto the veranda. It wasn't reassuring. With all the activity, it would be easy for one of the workers to slip away. But why? Since it didn't make sense, it had to be her paranoia. Nevertheless, she couldn't stop a sense of foreboding as she made her way to her office.

Intent on her research, her only interruptions were from Parker. First, he wanted permission to install the monitor in her bedroom. She told him to go ahead. It was nearly dark when he walked in with one in his arms.

She moved out of the way, relieved to have an excuse to quit. So far, she'd found nothing and wondered if it was a waste of time. Obviously, research was another area in which she didn't excel.

It only took a few minutes to set up the monitor. Once it was operational, Parker gave her a crash course on the new system, taking time to ensure she had no questions.

After he left, she wandered to the front of the house. The crew gathered their equipment while Colt and Ben stood near the doorway and watched.

When she walked up, Ben said, "I'll see you tomorrow," and left.

His eyes still on the men, Colt said, "Anything I can do before I leave?"

"No. Mia and I may be gone for a while tomorrow."

Once everyone was out the door, Tori locked it. In the kitchen, she poured the last of the coffee into a cup, washed the pot and set up the machine for the next morning. She grabbed a sandwich from the fridge, picked up the cup, and strolled to her office.

While she ate, she checked her emails. Nothing from the chip expert. Then she turned her attention back to the newspaper archives. Despite the frustration and lack of progress, she reminded herself that, if nothing else, she was tenacious.

The new monitor on the corner of her desk flashed, catching her attention. A truck pulled around the house to the back of the property. One of Parker's men had arrived. For a few moments, Tori played around with the cameras. Two were mounted on each corner of the house, one over the front and back doors, and two on the garage. She practiced moving them before resetting them to their original position.

Restless, she stood and heard the clink in her pocket, the chips. Tori pulled them out, studying the lightning bolts. What was the meaning? She'd found a lot of poker chips online. None were quite like these two. She'd take one with her to show to Ethel. In the meantime, she'd stash them in the safe.

Tori ambled along the hallway, careful not to trip over piles of old flooring. Flipping on the chandelier in the foyer, she slowly turned to stare up at the ceiling. The fresh coat of paint gave the room a light and airy look. While she could only envision the finished results, Tori could already see an improvement.

She walked into the library, where she twisted a raised scroll on the wall. A panel swung open to reveal the door to a safe. She spun the combination, laid the chips inside, then closed and locked the safe. Pushing the panel shut, she shut off the lights as she strolled to the kitchen.

For a moment, she paused to look out the window. The portable light was set up, and she could see the chair next to the truck. Tori switched off the lights and headed to her bedroom. After a quick bath, exhausted, she crawled into bed. As Tori slid into sleep, her last thoughts were about Ethel. Would she have the answers?

Chapter 13

Following what had become her morning routine, Tori fixed sandwiches and filled the thermos. Outside, a chill hung in the air and tendrils of fog slithered along the ground. The two men saw her coming, giving her a cheery hello. She was still amazed at how they could be so chipper after staying up all night. If it was her, she knew she'd be dog-ass tired.

For a few minutes, she stayed to visit, which delighted them. Both had worked for Parker since his retirement from the Fort Worth PD. Listening to their comments, it was apparent they had a lot of respect for their boss.

At the flash of headlights in the driveway, Carl said, "Early for someone to be here."

A tinge of worry flitted over her. He was right. "I'd better get back." She picked up the box and hurried toward the house.

The back door opened, and Mia stepped out. Her voice tight with strain, she said, "I was hoping you were up. I didn't want to call."

The distress on Mia's face when Tori reached the steps

deepened her trepidation. "What's wrong?"

"It's Ethel. She's in the hospital. Someone broke into her apartment and attacked her."

Tori cried out, "Oh no! How bad?"

"I don't know. One of Ethel's cousins called. Since I work for you, she wanted me to let you know."

"We need to get to the hospital, but I can't leave until Colt gets here."

"I called Heidi. She's on the way."

"Let me grab my bag. As soon as she gets here, we'll leave." She rushed to her bedroom with Mia close on her heels.

"Do you know anything else?" Tori swept up her bag and a light jacket.

"I asked, but Gloria, Ethel's cousin, didn't have any more information."

"Your car or mine?"

"I'll drive. I can get us there faster."

"I need to get my phone."

As they headed toward the kitchen, Heidi dashed in. Slightly rumpled, as if she'd thrown on her clothes, she asked, "Any more news?"

"No," Mia said.

Tori grabbed the tablet and phone lying on the table and stuffed them in her bag.

"Tori, anything I need to know?"

"No. When Colt gets here, let him know what's happened. One of us will call when we know something."

"Go. I've got this."

Tori hugged her, then raced out the back door behind Mia.

As soon as Tori hopped in the front seat, Mia backed out. "The medical center is located on the west side of town. At this time of the morning, there shouldn't be much traffic."

Tori buckled her seat belt. "Why would anyone break into her apartment?"

"A question I've been asking myself."

While she didn't break the speed limit, Mia zipped through intersections and around cars. Ahead a sign directed them to the parking lot for the emergency room. Mia parked, and they jumped out.

Rushing through the sliding glass doors with Mia beside her, Tori's gaze quickly scanned the room. It was empty except for a group of people huddled together in chairs in a corner. An older woman with short grey hair cried out, "Mia."

"Gloria," Mia exclaimed, hurrying toward the woman.

Tori hung back as the two hugged, then two other women and a man stepped forward, greeting Mia.

"Gloria." Mia turned, grabbing Tori's arm to tug her forward. "This is Tori Winters." Mia pointed to the other family members. One by one, she introduced them.

After Tori had greeted them, Gloria said, "Miss Winters, thank you so much for coming."

"Please, it's Tori. What's her condition?"

As Mia pulled two chairs closer, everyone sat.

Tears glistened in Gloria's eyes as her hands twisted

in her lap. "We're not sure. Ethel has a head injury and is unconscious. It's all we've been told."

"I'll see what I can find out." Tori rose and strode to the front desk. As a nurse, she knew the procedures.

At her approach, the nurse seated behind the counter looked up. "May I help you?"

Tori introduced herself, then said, "Can you provide any information about Ethel Morris?"

"What is your relationship to the patient?"

"I'm a close family friend, and I'm also a nurse. For many years, Ethel worked for my grandmother, Elly Leichter." Tori wasn't ashamed to drop Elly's name into the conversation if it helped get the information.

"Oh, I've heard about you. That's why your name is familiar. You're the granddaughter who inherited the estate. I do recall someone saying you had been a hospice nurse. Even though I'm not supposed to give out any details, I'll make an exception in this case. Due to a violent blow to the head, Ms. Morris has a traumatic brain injury, or TBI, and is listed as critical. We're waiting for the results of the CT scan."

"When can we see her?"

"Not until we stabilize her and know what's going on with her brain. The doctor knows the family is here, and he'll update you as soon as he can. And if I hear anything else, I'll let you know."

"Thank you. I appreciate your help."

Tori turned, walking back to the group. Several sets of eyes stared at her, all with hopeful expressions.

Mia leaned forward. "Well?"

"She's listed as critical and is still unconscious. They are waiting on the results of a CT scan. It will tell the doctor the severity of the injury to her head." Tori decided to keep the part about a violent blow to herself. It would only add to their distress.

"When can we see her?" Gloria asked.

"They don't know yet. All we can do is wait. Do you know what happened?"

"I got a call from the apartment complex manager. She told me someone had broken into Ethel's apartment. Ethel was hurt and on the way to the hospital." Gloria choked, unable to stop the tears. She pulled a tissue from her pocket, dabbing her eyes. "Why would anyone want to hurt her? She had nothing of any significant value in her apartment. It doesn't make sense."

Tori said, "No, it doesn't. I need to make a call. If something happens, I'll be outside." She slipped through the sliding glass doors, stopping on the sidewalk where she tapped the speed dial.

A sleepy voice answered, "Tori, what's wrong?"

"Parker, another incident. I'm at the hospital. Ethel Morris is in the emergency room. Someone broke into her apartment and attacked her. It's all I know."

"Is she the ex-housekeeper?"

"Yes. Mia and I planned to visit her today. We hoped she might know the identity of our mystery man. She lives in the senior citizen's apartment complex."

His voice alert and decisive, Parker said, "I'm on it.

I'll head to the apartments. What's her condition?"

"Critical."

"I'll be in touch."

His quick response sparked a new idea. She should put Parker on a permanent retainer. Then her thoughts shifted back to Ethel. Who else should she call? David. He would want to know. She tapped the speed dial.

"You're calling early," he said.

Not wasting time on pleasantries, Tori said, "Ethel is in the hospital in a coma."

His voice deepened with alarm. "What happened?"

After Tori explained, David said, "I can't get there until later today. I've got meetings I can't cancel."

"There's nothing you can do. I'll keep you posted."

When she walked in, Mia gave her a questioning look. "Parker?"

Dang, the woman was scary. "Yep, he's headed to Ethel's apartment."

Gloria asked, "Who is Parker?"

With a wry smile, Tori said, "Sometimes, I think he's a guardian angel. In reality, Parker Hayes is a private investigator who gets answers."

While they waited, Mia and Tori took turns making the trek to the cafeteria for coffee, soft drinks, and snacks. As minutes turned into hours, she got to know Ethel's relatives. It didn't take long to realize it was a close-knit family, and they had worshiped Tori's grandmother. The conversation was dotted with comments such as Miss Elly did that or Miss Elly said this. It only served to push at the ache of never having a chance to know her grandmother.

The swish of the sliding glass doors caused Tori to turn her head. Parker walked in. She jumped up and rushed toward him.

"Any change?" he asked.

"No. We're still waiting for the doctor."

He glanced over her shoulder at the group sitting behind her. "Do you want to hear what I found out before you talk to the family?"

"No. I'll introduce you. Then you won't have to go over it twice."

They walked over to the group.

"This is Parker Hayes, the private investigator."

Mia motioned. Tori turned to see a tall, thin man in blue scrubs headed their way.

"Are you Ethel Morris' family?" he asked.

Gloria stood. "Yes. How is she?"

"I'm Dr. Durbin. Ms. Morris is holding on, though she is still in a coma. The blow to the head resulted in bleeding around the brain, but we have it under control. She lost a considerable amount of blood. Of course, her age is a factor. But all things considered, she is doing better than I expected when she arrived. I'm keeping her on the critical list while we monitor her condition. She will be moved into intensive care. Once she's settled, I can let two people go in for a limit of five minutes."

Tori stepped forward and said, "I'm a friend of the family, Tori Winters."

"Miss Elly's granddaughter?" Dr. Durbin gazed at her with interest over the rim of his glasses.

Tori nodded as they shook hands.

"A fine woman. Didn't come any better. I heard you're a nurse."

The rumor mill was alive and well. "Yes. I worked in the ER, then switched to hospice. Is there anything else we should know?" Tori knew doctors had a way of glossing over facts to save undue stress for the family. She had just done the same.

His eyes twinkled with humor as if he knew what she was thinking. "Not right now. You've got the full gist of her condition. Any other questions?"

With a slight twitch of her lips at his abrupt manner, Tori said, "No, sir. Not yet."

The doctor nodded before walking away.

She looked at Gloria. "Since the doctor is allowing visitors, it's a good sign. Decide who is going to visit her. I expect they'll let you have another visitation later today."

Gloria turned to her relatives; gimlet-eyed, she said, "Miss Tori and I will visit Ethel."

"Oh, no," Tori protested. "One of you should go."

"You're family, and that's that."

Sterned-faced, Gloria turned toward Parker. "Now, Mr. Hayes, what did you find out?"

"Someone broke in through the sliding glass door to the patio. The resident in the adjoining apartment had taken her dog outside. I spoke to her. She said she saw a flash of light in Ethel's window, then heard a crash. She knocked on the door. When Ethel didn't answer, she called 911. While I was there, the detective assigned to the case showed up. Based on evidence at the scene, the intruder struck her."

Gloria, her face puzzled, asked, "Do the police know why? She didn't have anything of value."

Parker shook his head. "No, ma'am, though they believe the neighbor's swift action saved her life."

Gloria, trembling, dropped to the chair. "She would have bled to death before anyone would have known."

Tori sat beside her. Her hand reached for Gloria's, holding it tight between hers. "Don't dwell on it. She's alive and has a good chance. It's what we need to focus on."

Gloria gathered herself, her shoulders straightening. "It sounds like something Miss Elly would have said."

"I'll follow up with the police later today," Parker told them. "They might have more information."

After the family thanked him, Tori stood. "I'll walk out with you."

Outside, they lingered on the sidewalk.

"Tori, I don't like this. First, Colt's two men and now this. And you are the common link."

"You don't think it's a coincidence?"

When he flashed her a sardonic look, her hands fluttered in the air. "I know. You don't believe in coincidences. But if it isn't, then why?"

"I don't know … yet. When I stop at the PD to check on the break-in, I'll follow up on the accident and fire. Dealing with the camera installation yesterday, I didn't get a chance. Who knew about Ethel?"

Astonished, she stared at him. "Why, probably any-one who knew my grandmother. Ethel was the house-keeper for many years, and before that, her mother worked for my great-grandparents."

"Interesting. I didn't realize the relationship went as far back as your great-grandfather. So Ethel would have known Frankie and Irene?"

"Yes. Is it significant?"

"Could be, and then it could be useless minutia. I'm gathering details. Never know where they will lead." He turned and walked away.

Thoughts furrowed her brow as she walked back in-side. Was it possible these events were related?

Mia stood, walking toward her. In a low tone, she said, "What do you say we take a stroll to the cafeteria? I suspect more is going on than you want to say here." She turned to face the group huddled in the corner. In a louder tone, she said, "We're going to get a cup of coffee. Can we bring anything back?"

After everyone shook their heads no, Mia hooked her arm through Tori's. With a light tug, they walked into the corridor leading to the cafeteria.

"Okay, fill me in on your confab outside."

Tori didn't beat around the bush. "Three incidents, two involving Colt's men and now Ethel. Parker's con-cerned it all evolves around me. He's following up on the police investigations."

"Good, because the same thought occurred to me."

"But like I told him, it doesn't make sense."

"It may not to you, but I'd bet it does to someone," Mia said, a grim note in her voice.

They filled their cups from the large dispenser, paid, then sat at a table out of earshot of other people in the room.

A troubled look settled over Tori's face as she took a sip. "If all these incidents are connected, what about our visit?"

Mia drank her coffee as she thought. "No. I just can't see it. Who could have known we planned to visit her? We didn't even know until yesterday. While there could be a connection between the three incidents, it seems to be quite a stretch to think our visit is tied in."

"A good point." Tori took another gulp of coffee. "I have the survey reports showing the tunnel is stable. I sent them to Dan. It should change the city attorney's tune. Oh, there is something new in the house. The camera security system is in place. I have a monitor on my desk and one in my bedroom. When we get back to the house, I'll show everyone how to operate it."

A look of dismay crossed Mia's face. She whispered, "Oh, no!"

Tori shifted in her chair to see what Mia was staring at. Across the room, several women were getting ready to leave.

Tori groaned. "Maybe she won't see us."

Even as Tori spoke, an older woman, mid-fifties, turned. Like a guided missile, she headed straight to them. Attired in cream-colored, wide-legged pants, a matching silk blouse topped with a short dark blue bolero jacket, and the ever-present spike heels, her makeup and hair were perfection itself. Everything about Myra Swanson, right down to the blood-red false nails, bespoke money. Tori had met Myra and her daughter Carly not long after she moved into the house. Since then, she'd found them, including Myra's husband Judd, arrogant and, quite frankly, obnoxious.

Mia looked up, plastering a smile on her face as she greeted the woman. "Hello, Myra."

"Mia," Myra said with a condescending tone, though it was Tori that she stared at with an avid gleam. "Tori, my dear, I haven't seen you for a while." She pulled out a chair and sat, dropping the minuscule purse in her lap.

With a smile as phony as the one on Myra's face, Tori greeted her.

"What are the two of you doing here?" Her gaze shifted between Tori and Mia.

"Visiting a friend," Tori said.

"Really! I didn't think you knew that many people. Who is it?"

"Ethel Morris."

For an instant, a knowing look flashed in Myra's eyes. "I don't recognize the name."

As brief as it was, Tori saw it. Myra was lying. "Ethel was my grandmother's housekeeper."

"Oh. A housekeeper. How odd. Whatever interest could you have in a housekeeper? Well, it's not im-portant." She waved her hand in the air. "*You* certainly have been stirring the pot again. Such a run of bad luck. The catastrophe with your tunnel, a skeleton, and now having your construction permit revoked. Too bad you didn't listen to what other people tried to tell you. It does seem someone has stopped all your ludicrous plans to turn the place into an inn."

Tori relaxed against the back of the chair, a hand lightly clasping the cup. Her lips twitched with a mocking smile. "I wouldn't rush to any conclusions, Myra. As a matter of fact, renovations inside the house are underway. I don't need a construction permit. Once the remodeling is finished, I plan to open the Red Door Inn for small social, business and family events. I know you belong to several clubs. You might consider holding a meeting or event at the inn."

As Myra listened, her eyes widened with astonishment. "You can't possibly be serious. With everything that has happened, you are still trying to *rent* out the place?" With a spiteful smirk, she leaned forward and said, "I've heard the city plans to condemn the property. You will have wasted all that money. What a shame."

"If I were you, I wouldn't bet on it. Besides, I wouldn't refer to it as renting, but rather as providing a unique and elegant atmosphere for social and business events." She smiled again, baring her teeth. "I am curious, though, about this run of bad luck, as you called it. Would your husband have anything to do with revoking my permit? Judd has certainly been overzealous in his ambitions to get his hands on my property."

Myra reared back. "Absolutely not! It's your tunnel and property that are unsafe. The city has no choice but to act. That house should have been torn down years ago. It's old and in disrepair. Just because you fix up a room or two doesn't change anything. My husband did you a favor by telling you the house was a liability and someone could be hurt or killed. You wouldn't listen."

She stood, slinging the strap of her purse over her shoulder. "My dear. I'm sure you wouldn't mind a tip from someone far more knowledgeable and experienced than you. Considering how wealthy you are, you really should do something about your attire. Quite frankly, when I saw you walk in … well, you look like a reject from a second-hand store."

Tori gazed at her with a disdainful expression. "Unlike others," she paused, letting her eyes drift down Myra's body, "I don't see the need to flaunt my money."

"You have to know it really is off-putting to people."

"Not the ones who matter to me."

Myra sniffed. "I must be on my way, or I'll be late for my meeting with the hospital administrator. I'm in charge of a charity event to raise money for new hospital equipment. I'm sure I can count on you for a sizable donation."

She turned and walked away.

Her tone grim, Mia said, "Lordy be, after those snide remarks, the woman has the nerve to hit you up for money."

"She certainly does think a lot of herself. Despite her assertions otherwise, I still believe Judd's behind the city's actions." Tori thought as she finished her coffee. "Myra lied about not knowing Ethel. I saw it in her eyes. Why? It would seem to be unimportant, so why lie about it?"

"It's odd, but remember, this is Myra. I've known her for a long time. The woman has her own agenda, and there's no accounting for why she does something."

Tori shrugged. "You're probably right. Let's go."

When they entered the emergency room, nothing appeared to have happened. Seated, Mia started a conversation with Gloria. Tuned in with one ear, Tori pulled her tablet from her purse.

She opened it, and her to-do list appeared. One entry caught her eye. A shock of trepidation rippled through her.

Chapter 14

The entry read—VISIT ETHEL. Tori lifted her head, staring across the room but seeing nothing. Her hands trembled as she clutched the tablet to her chest. Was her earlier fear, right? Was Ethel lying near death because she planned to visit her? Unable to breathe, Tori lurched to her feet, stumbling toward the glass doors.

Behind her, Mia cried out, "Tori, what's wrong?"

She didn't hear. The doors swished, sliding open. Bile rose in her throat as she staggered outside, gasping for air.

Mia grabbed her shoulders. "Tori, what's happening?"

Tori's anguished eyes stared into Mia's. "My fault," she whispered.

Ethel's family had followed Mia out the door, clustering near her as they gazed with frightened looks.

Tori knew she couldn't let them know. Pulling on her strength, she said, "Everybody, I'm okay. Please go back inside," though she clutched Mia's arm to stop her.

Gloria said, "Are you sure? Can we help?"

"I'll be fine. I needed some air."

They slowly trailed inside, casting worried looks over their shoulders.

Mia pulled her down the sidewalk, out of view of the doors. "What's your fault?"

"Someone might have known I planned to visit Ethel."

"What! But how?"

Tori handed her the tablet. "My to-do list and the entry—visit Ethel." She took a deep breath and explained her suspicion that someone had looked at the tablet. "Then, I convinced myself it was my imagination. But was it? Is this why someone tried to kill her?"

"Tori, this isn't your fault. We don't even know if what happened to Ethel is connected. Why would it? Ethel had nothing to do with what's going on with the property. All you planned to do was ask about someone killed eighty or so years ago. It certainly makes no sense, even if someone snooped and spotted what you had written."

Tori took another deep breath, striving to stop the apprehension racing inside her. "I hope you're right. Otherwise, how do I live with myself?"

In Mia's no-nonsense tone, she said, "By putting the blame squarely on the shoulders of whoever was responsible."

Gloria stepped out. "Tori, the nurse says we can see her."

"Okay, but I'm not through with this," Tori said as she turned to head inside.

Behind her, Mia muttered, "I didn't think you were."

The nurse led Tori and Gloria along a hall to the

oversize double doors into the intensive care unit. After donning masks, they approached the bed.

In a low tone, the nurse said, "You can only stay for a few minutes."

Tori nodded as she gazed at the elderly woman. Her face was nearly as white as the bandages circling her head. Then her gaze shifted to scan the screens on the machines connected to the small, frail body.

On the other side, Gloria touched Ethel's arm, careful not to jiggle the needle inserted in the back of her hand or the tube leading from it. She whispered a few words of love before stepping back.

Tori leaned over Ethel. "I don't know if you can hear me, but this is Tori. There is nothing for you to worry about. I'll take care of everything." She lightly touched the back of Ethel's fingers. The nurse tapped her shoulder. With one last caress, a brush of her fingers over Ethel's cheek, Tori turned, following Gloria out the door.

Back in the waiting room, she stopped. "Gloria, I can't stay, but I will be back. If you need anything, you call. I'll take care of it."

Tears trickled down Gloria's cheeks. "You are so like your grandmother. Thank you."

After gathering up her purse and stuffing the tablet back inside, Tori said goodbye to the other family members before she and Mia walked out the door.

As they strode to the car, Mia said, "Well?"

"While she doesn't look good, her vitals are stable. It's a positive sign."

Mia slid behind the wheel. "Since you're a nurse, you'd know."

⊱✦⊰

The house was a beehive of activity, with workers tramping in and out as they hauled out the debris. When they walked around back, Colt waved to them from across the backyard as his crew carried timbers into the tunnel.

Inside the kitchen, Heidi, Cammie, and Tina were packing the contents of the cupboards.

After greeting them, Tori asked, "What's all this?"

With an air of excitement, Cammie said, "Heidi called us. Colt wants to get the cabinets painted and the new floor installed before the appliances are delivered." Then her look sobered. "How's Ethel?"

Tori brought them up to date, though she didn't mention her fears about what might have triggered the attack. Even so, there was considerable speculation about the reason.

Heidi finally switched subjects and motioned toward several stacks of boxes. "Where do we put them?"

"Wherever you can find space, garage, my office, and bedroom. Be sure to leave a path to the bed and bathroom. I'll be back to help. I want to check the rest of the house."

Dodging the hallway, she passed through the connecting rooms. Men were hanging the new wallpaper in the living room, and from the few pieces already on the walls, she loved it. She stopped in the archway to stare in amazement at the foyer.

"Oh, wow!" The parquet floor gleamed under the lights. But it was the new wallpaper that had her gasping with pleasure. Most of it was in place. Mia had nailed it. Light shining through the stained-glass portal had a tint of color that enhanced the flowers in the wallpaper.

Across the way, men were laying the new floor in the library. Ben stood near the doors.

"Ben, can I walk on it?"

"Sure, not a problem."

Though he had reassured her, she carefully stepped toward him.

He grinned. "Don't worry. You can't hurt it."

"Oh, my, gosh, it's beautiful. And the paint and wallpaper. Wow, oh wow."

His eyes crinkled with pleasure. "It looks nice to me as well. Whoever picked out the wallpaper did good."

"It was Mia. I'll pass on your comment."

"How's your friend? Heidi told us what happened."

"She's in intensive care, still in a coma. But the doctor is hopeful."

"Any idea what happened?"

"Not yet, but Parker is looking into it."

"Did Heidi tell you about the change in the kitchen?"

"Yes. The team is frantically getting it all boxed up. I'd better go help."

She picked her way back through the living room.

As she stepped inside the kitchen, she exclaimed,

"The foyer is unbelievable. Have you had a chance to look at it?"

Heidi said, "We took a peek, and you're right."

"Mia, you have to go look. Ben likes your selection of wallpaper."

Pulling her hands from the soapy water in the sink, she rinsed and dried them before darting out of the room. When she returned, her face glowed with happiness. She plunked onto a chair. "I was so concerned. What if it didn't work? But the wallpaper is gorgeous, and so is what is going up in the living room. And, the floor, oh, my gosh. It's all going to make this place shine. Visitors are going to love it."

The back door slammed, and Parker strolled in. He glanced toward the counter where the coffee machine had sat. He sighed but didn't comment, instead greeting everyone.

Mia chuckled. "Don't worry. It's only temporary. Colt is starting on the kitchen today. Would you like iced tea?"

At his wounded look, Tori laughed. "See, Mia. I'm not the only one who isn't a fan of all the sugar."

She glanced at Parker. "Let's go to my office. I suspect it's going to get busy in here."

"I'd like to talk to Colt. Instead, let's walk outside."

As they strolled across the backyard, he asked, "How is your friend?"

"Still critical and in a coma. Were you able to find out anything more?"

"While I was at the PD, checking on what happened

to Colt's men, I talked to the detective assigned to the case. Nothing new other than there were no fingerprints, which I found suspicious. Your typical, smash-and-grab type burglar doesn't usually think about gloves. It doesn't appear as if anything was stolen, but I can't say with any certainty. Here's another odd point. This is the first time an apartment at the center has been burglarized."

Her heart sank. Had Ethel been targeted? "I found something else, though I may be way off base." She went on to explain about the incident with the tablet. Then added, "At the hospital, I realized one of the entries was to visit Ethel."

Parker's eyes narrowed. He stopped a short distance from the men working on the tunnel. When Colt spotted them, he motioned for Colt to join them. At a half-lope, he trotted over, a questioning look in his eyes.

"Colt, what do you know about the new men you hired?"

"Only the basics. Why? Is there a problem?"

"It's what I want to find out. Tori, tell Colt about Ethel."

"The woman Heidi said was injured?" Colt asked.

"Yes." After Tori had filled Colt in on the details, Parker picked up the story.

"I talked to the detective handling the case. He doesn't have much to go on. The intruder got in through the sliding glass door. No prints, and not sure anything was stolen. There have been reports of petty thefts at the center, but there's never been a break-in. While I was at the PD, I looked into what happened to your men. The fire was deliberately set. The primary suspect is the owner, Luca Sanchez. He's the only one with a motive, the insurance policy."

Colt's head jerked. "I don't believe it. He's worked for me since I moved here from Houston. I've never had an issue with him."

"Maybe so, but from the arson investigator's position, he can't find a reason someone would burn down the house other than Luca. The accident investigator handling the Doyle incident has reclassified it to a hit-and-run. There was contact between the two vehicles."

"Do you think someone deliberately ran him off the road?"

Parker scuffed his boot on the dirt, then looked around. No one seemed to be paying any attention to them.

"I don't know, just connecting dots. Yesterday, Tori left her tablet on the desk, but she thinks someone may have looked at it."

Colt shot a sharp look at Tori, who nodded.

Parker continued, "On it is her to-do list. One of the entries was to visit Ethel, and now she's in the hospital. If it wasn't for a neighbor, she'd be dead. I don't like what's swirling around Tori. All this business with the building permit, the incidents with your men, and now a close family friend almost dies. It's why I'm interested in the men you hired."

His hand resting on his hip, Colt adjusted his

sunglasses. "I hired three. Ben handled the paperwork. To-morrow, I'll bring a copy of their applications. If there's a chance one of these guys is involved, I can let them go. It's not worth taking a risk."

Parker shook his head. "No. Right now, this is all conjecture on my part. Once I get the applications, I can get deeper into their backgrounds than you can. Let's wait, keep an eye on them, and see if anything pops up. I need to leave." He turned, heading toward the driveway.

As they watched him hurry across the yard, Colt said, "I wonder what he's up to." He shrugged, then added, "Before I leave today, I'd like a short meeting to update you on the progress."

"I'll be in my office."

Inside, she sidestepped a ladder, careful not to bump the man balanced on a rung with an open can of paint. She tossed him a quick smile. Not recognizing him, she wondered if he was one of the new hires.

As Tori walked into the kitchen, Mia said, "Tori, we're about done. Only a few boxes left to move. These are going in your office."

"Once you're finished here, you might as well take off. And the same for tomorrow. It doesn't look like we can do much for the next day or so." The kitchen already had an abandoned, bare-bones appearance.

Cammie and Tina each picked up a box, hauling it out the door. With a quick tug, Heidi tore off a stretch of tape, wrapping it over the top of a box on the counter.

"Mia, any word from the hospital?" Tori asked.

"Yes, Gloria called. No change." Mia picked up a box.

Tori picked up another, following her out the door. Inside the office, the boxes were added to a stack in front of the bookcase.

"Mia, I'd like you to stay for a meeting with Colt."

It wasn't the real reason she wanted Mia to stick around. Since she didn't know who was listening, Tori didn't want to talk about what Parker had discovered until Colt's men were gone.

With a thoughtful look, Mia nodded before she turned and walked out.

Settled in her chair, she picked up her tablet and activated it. She wouldn't make the mistake again of leaving it turned on. The chime of the phone interrupted her. A groan erupted at the sight of the caller ID. It was Jonah. *Dang*, she thought. *She should have called him about Ethel.*

"Hi, Jonah."

"Tori, I heard about Ethel. Why is she in the hospital?"

She went through the explanations again.

"Good lord, why would anyone break into her apartment?" Jonah exclaimed.

"I don't know."

"I'll call the police chief and see what I can find out."

Not wanting to tell him Parker was already on the case, she said, "A good idea. Thank you."

"What's happening with the house?"

"Nothing new, other than Dan has talked to the city attorney. No one is saying who filed the complaint. Did you ever find out?"

"No, I didn't. I can assure you that I would tell you if I knew."

Hearing his indignation, she rushed to reassure him. "I know you would, Jonah. I didn't mean to imply otherwise. It's just that even the city attorney is being tight-lipped. Seems to me a strange way to conduct business."

"If I do find out, I'll call you. Please let me know how Ethel is doing."

"I will."

Disconnecting, she laid the phone on the table. Even Jonah, with all his long-time links to the Granbury business community, didn't know who was behind the complaint. She wasn't sure why she found it ominous. What would prompt such a deep, dark secret?

Chapter 15

With a shake of her shoulders to shrug off the foreboding, Tori turned her attention to her emails. Still nothing from the poker chip guy. She did have one from Dan with the paperwork for the new company. It prompted an idea.

A quick tap on the speed dial and a woman said, "Archer Financial Services, how may I help you?"

"This is Tori Winters. I'd like to speak with Jeff."

"Just a moment, Miss Winters."

After the debacle with the CPA her grandmother had always used, Tori hired a new firm to help her oversee and administer the millions of dollars she had inherited.

Clicks echoed, and Jeff Archer came on the line.

After greeting her, he said, "Tori, from what I've seen in the papers, it seems the city has thrown some road-blocks your way."

"Then you know my construction permit was re-voked. Supposedly there is a complaint about the liability of the property. Dan is working on it. Even though I had to stop construction on the new building, I've shifted to the renovations inside the house. For most of those, I don't need a permit."

"A good way to use the time and not get off schedule," Jeff observed.

"I've also made a change to the opening of the inn. It's going to be two phases. Once the renovations are finished, I plan to open the inn for social and business events. When the permit issue is squared away, and I can complete the rest of the construction, I'll do a grand opening to officially open the inn for overnight guests."

"Hmm … interesting. I like the idea."

"Dan finalized the paperwork for the new company. It's signed and official. I'm sending you a copy."

"I'll make the necessary changes in your tax records and filings."

"Jeff, I need your help with something else. Ethel Morris was Elly's housekeeper for most of her life. She's in the hospital in a coma."

"Oh, dear. I hadn't heard. Is it serious?"

"Yes. Someone broke into her apartment. Ethel suffered a blow to the head. I don't know anything about her financial status other than the money Elly left her. Would you contact the hospital administrator? Have the hospital bill me for anything not covered by Medicare. And I want it on the QT. It's why I want you to call. I don't want the family to know."

His tone somber, he said, "I'll take care of it and have the bills sent to me. What else?"

"Credit cards for the business. I need one for myself

and one for each of the crew. Can they all be put on the same account?"

"Sure can. I'll set up a subaccount in each of their names."

After thanking him, she disconnected. The call, however, had started another train of thought, Ethel's apartment.

In the doorway, Heidi, flanked by Cammie and Tina, appeared. "We're on our way out."

"I need a favor."

"Name it, and we'll do it," Heidi said.

"Can you find out what's being done to clean Ethel's apartment? I know there are businesses that specialize in cleaning a crime scene. The carpet may need to be replaced."

"I'll contact the center's manager," Heidi told her.

Cammie spoke up. "Mia mentioned several members of the family are at the hospital. They need to eat. We can use my kitchen and fix several meals that can easily be reheated."

Tina said, "We can all pitch in and help. I'm not a great cook, but I can peel, chop, and mix."

Tori gazed at them, tears misting in her eyes. How did she get so lucky?

She gulped. "It's a great idea." Tori wouldn't insult them by telling them she'd pay for it. Instead, she'd find another way.

As their footsteps receded, she turned back to her computer and accessed the newspaper archive.

Mia strolled in, balancing two cups of coffee and a foil-wrapped sandwich.

"How did you fix a cup of coffee?" Tori exclaimed, breathing in the aroma of the rich brew.

"The coffee machine is back on the counter. I didn't figure it would cause Colt's men a problem. I put a box in your bedroom with coffee supplies, cups, and the thermos. There is also a stack of sandwiches in the fridge. Enough to tide you over until the kitchen is back in commission. Cammie made sure of it."

Mia set the cups on the desk and handed the sandwich to Tori. "You forgot to eat … again." She dropped into a chair.

Realizing she was hungry, Tori eagerly unwrapped a turkey and cheese sandwich, taking a huge bite.

"I called the hospital. No change," Mia told her.

She swallowed. "Thank you." Then she told Mia what the other three were up to. Tori took another bite. "This is so good. What the heck did Cammie put in the dressing?"

"I don't know. She's experimenting … again."

"Well, whatever it is, this needs to go on our menu." She took another bite. "I've got a feeling once the new kitchen is in place, we're going to be in for some treats."

"Did you know she ordered a mixer to make bread?"

"Did she really?"

"Yep. She said store-bought bread wasn't good enough for the inn."

With a note of awe, Tori said, "Freshly baked bread? Maybe I should have added a workout room for all of us."

"We may need it. You haven't seen her menu yet. She's added desserts, and not just for lunch, but for an afternoon tea service and even breakfast."

"You know what we need to do?" Excited, she crumpled the foil, pitching it at the wastebasket by the file cabinet. "Bingo!" she exclaimed as it landed in the container.

Then she looked at Mia. "Hire someone to help her. Cammie can't possibly cook everything by herself. She needs an assistant, maybe two, as we get rolling. Since you know just about everyone in town, start thinking about who would be a good candidate."

Mia took a swig of coffee. "Lordy be! She may never come back down to earth. Oh, I forgot to tell you. A box was delivered."

"Where?" Tori looked at the mound of boxes.

Mia chuckled. "The other side of your desk."

She peered over the edge, then reached down to retrieve it. After setting it on the desk in front of her, she pulled out a letter opener from the center drawer and neatly sliced the tape.

"Oh, yes." She removed four boxes and dropped the larger box on the floor.

"What on earth did you order?" Mia leaned forward to take a closer look.

Tori grinned at her with a mischievous look, handing her one.

"You didn't," Mia said, looking at the name.

"Yep. I ordered one for all of you."

Her no-nonsense tone snuck into her voice. "Tori—"

Tori's hand flashed, stopping her. "It's not a gift. You need it for your job. Tablets are a much easier way to keep track of the countless details for the inn than a pad of paper." She moved the other three boxes to the corner of the desk.

"I'm not sure I'm buying all the BS you're shoveling. But thank you."

Tori grinned. "Got something else to run by you," deciding this was a good time to change topics. "I'm thinking about talking to Parker about a contract to handle the security at the inn. What do you think?"

Surprised, Mia dropped the box in her lap, pursing her lips as she thought. "I think it's a dang good idea since I've been concerned about the valuable antiques you own from the get-go. Plus, I don't think it's a hard sell. Parker's already worked his way into our circle. Did you know he lost both his wife and daughter?"

"No. I didn't. He doesn't talk about his personal life, and I don't like to pry."

"One day, he commented to Heidi about how much she reminded him of his daughter. When Heidi asked, he said she and her mother had died several years back. Didn't say anything more."

"No wonder there are times he has such a sad look."

"Let me know how the conversation goes."

Footsteps sounded in the hall. Colt walked in, followed by David. Mia switched to the couch.

"My crew's done for the day," Colt said.

Engrossed in their conversation, Tori hadn't realized

there was no racket in the house. Everyone had left.

As David sat, he stared at the boxes stacked on the floor. "What's all this?"

"We had to clean out the kitchen, utility room and pantry. This is the overflow," Tori told him.

He motioned to the boxes on the desk. "And these?"

"Electronic tablets for the team."

A roar of laughter erupted.

Tori glowered at him. "What's so funny?"

"Four converts for to-do lists."

"Hey, I'll have you know, your good buddy sitting next to you uses one. It's where I got the idea."

Colt laughed. "She's got you there." Then he turned to Tori. "Do you mind if Ben sits in on the meeting?"

"Oh, my no. I should have thought of it."

He walked out and, a few minutes later, returned with Ben behind him.

After greeting everyone, Ben settled on the couch next to Mia. When she glanced his way, a smile lit his face. A tinge of pink stained her face before she looked away.

Interest stirred in Tori. Mia blushing? Before she could consider it further, her phone rang. It was Parker.

When she answered, he said, "Tori, is Colt still there?"

"Yes, he's in my office."

"Ask him to wait. I'll be there in about ten minutes."

With a thoughtful air, she laid the phone aside. "That was Parker. Colt, he wants you to stay until he gets here."

Mia rose. "I'll fix a fresh pot of coffee. I don't think I

can handle the sad, hound dog expression he gets as if he's been deprived. It's a look that he's really good at using. Anyone else?"

David and Colt spoke up, though they asked for bottles of water.

"Tori, I know you probably want coffee." Then she looked toward the couch. "How about you, Ben?"

"Yes, ma'am, coffee sounds good." His lazy smile popped out.

Tori watched in amazement. *Oh, my gosh*, she thought as Mia hustled out. *She's blushing again.*

Headlights on the camera's monitor caught her eye. She reached for the control. "Parker's men have arrived."

David rose, stepping around the desk. He studied the screen before asking, "How does it work?"

"I can see the entire house on split screens or an enlarged one." While she demonstrated, one camera picked up another image. "Parker's here."

"Nice system," David said, settling back into his chair.

Voices emanated from the kitchen. Mia's laughter tinkled in the air. Her eyes gleamed with humor when she appeared in the doorway, carrying the glass pot in one hand and two bottles of water in the other.

Behind her, Parker, his computer bag jiggling over his shoulder, gingerly balanced a large tray laden with cups, sandwiches, and napkins in his big hands. He eased it onto Tori's desk. With a sigh of relief, he grabbed the chair from in front of the table. He turned it to face the desk and dropped the bag on the floor.

"I didn't know if anyone was hungry," Mia said as she poured the coffee.

The men eagerly reached to grab a sandwich.

Parker mumbled, "Missed lunch. Sure appreciate this," taking a large bite. A look of awe crossed his face as he chewed. Before taking another, he motioned with the sandwich. "This is really good. What did you put in it?"

Mia chuckled as she plopped next to Ben. "If I told you, I'd have to kill you." Her laughter rippled. "I've always wanted to use that line." At Parker's baffled look, another tinkle of laughter erupted. "Really, we don't know. Cammie made the sandwiches, and she's not telling."

"You should put these on your menu." Then Parker looked toward David. "Didn't expect to see you here, but glad you are."

After chasing a bite of sandwich with a deep swig of water, David said, "Colt only mentioned a progress report. Evidently, this meeting is much more."

Tori cradled her cup in her hands. "Originally, it was. Though I suspect Parker is about to change it."

His tone somber, Parker said, "Yes. Here's what I know. I talked to the arson investigator. His prime suspect is still the owner because the only motive he has is Luca's insurance. The accident investigator believed the crash was road rage until he discovered there was contact between the two vehicles. It's now a hit-and-run. I talked to Max this afternoon. He swears the driver forced him off the road. On his way home, a truck came up behind him at a high rate of speed. The driver swung out to pass. Max didn't think anything was wrong until the driver steered toward him, clipping the side of his truck. The net result of both incidents is Colt hires new men."

He took a gulp of coffee. "Yesterday, Tori leaves her tablet on her desk, then believes it's been moved when she returns to her office. One of her infamous to-do lists is on it, with an entry to visit Ethel. Early this morning, someone breaks into Ethel's apartment. Had it not been for the presence of a neighbor who banged on the door, the intruder might have finished her off."

A chill rolled over Tori as she listened. "You think he meant to kill her? It wasn't to steal something?"

"The police believe it was a burglary gone bad. Ethel woke up and interrupted the thief. In light of what else has happened, we have to consider the reason was to kill her." Parker's gaze swept across the group. "Then add in what the city is doing. Are these individual, random incidents? Or are they connected? It's what's bothering me. They all center around Tori."

David's body tensed. He leaned forward. "I don't like the sound of it."

Parker gave him a determined look. "I damn well don't either. The problem is the motive. So far, I can't find one, though the issues with the city could be a rehash of her earlier problems. A way to force her to sell. It still doesn't account for the other incidents."

With a worried look, Colt said, "Ben, you interviewed the new men. Anything unusual?"

Ben thought before saying, "Nothing comes to mind."

Parker asked, "Did any of them seem unduly eager or pressure you to find out when they'd get hired?"

"All three did. Colt has built an outstanding reputation in the construction business. He pays well and on time, and is fair in his dealings with his employees. Their inquiries weren't out of the ordinary. It's usually one of the first questions I get asked."

"Are you sure I shouldn't fire them?" Colt asked.

Parker shook his head. "In my opinion, it's a bad idea for several reasons. First, I could be way off base here. I don't want to tamper with someone's livelihood unless I know more than I do now. If one of them is behind all of this, I would rather have him where I can watch him. Colt, you and Ben can help. Keep an eye on them, but not to the point it could cause suspicion."

Colt glanced at Ben as they both nodded.

Tori said, "You didn't mention the mystery man."

"He's what certainly doesn't fit, an odd piece of collateral damage. What started all this was the collapse of the tunnel. I hate to say it, but everyone needs to be alert. I can't rule out sabotage if a man has been planted inside this house."

For a moment, no one spoke, then Mia whispered, "Oh, my gosh!"

"It would seem to be a stretch, considering how many people are in the house or outside at any given time. Colt, I have a man on my staff with some construction experience. Granted, it was when he was younger. I'd like for you to hire him. It lets me put a man with your crew. Can you justify it without undue suspicion?" Parker asked.

"Easily, since we are working on multiple rooms and the tunnel."

"He'll be here in the morning. His name is Rob Barton."

David asked, "Where do we stand with the city?"

Tori said, "I don't know. Dan has the surveys, but he hasn't called."

"Still no idea, then, who is behind this?" he asked.

"None. Though we," she motioned to Mia, "ran into Myra at the hospital. She emphatically denied Judd had anything to do with getting the building permit revoked. But I don't think I can trust anything she says."

Parker said, "One of my men contacted a source at *The Metro*. It's a dead end. His source at the paper doesn't know how the reporter got the information."

Colt glanced at his watch. "Ben and I need to leave. We've got work waiting for us at the office." He stood. "Thank you for the snack. I agree with Parker. It needs to be on the menu."

The two men walked out, but not before Ben thanked Mia, giving her another warm look.

After they left, Parker rose, setting his cup on the tray. "Before I go, I'll be glad to take this to the kitchen."

Mia laughed. "No. I won't put you to work this time. I'll take care of it."

David said, "I've got a stack of paperwork at my office to finish. Anything happens, you call." He flicked a finger across Tori's cheek before following Parker out the door.

"They have a way of filling a room, don't they?" Mia

observed as they heard the front door close.

"Ben's rather good-looking, don't you think?"

As she put the cups and empty bottles on the tray, Mia muttered, "I suppose so."

"This from the woman who talked about how sexy he looked in a tool belt." Tori gathered up the napkins, dropping them on the tray.

"Well, it was an idle observation."

"Oh, is that what they call it these days," she said, a teasing note in her voice.

Mia straightened. "Whatever *are* you nattering about?"

"Oh, nothing. Just curious about the way he looked at you."

"He's only being friendly."

"Oh, you think so."

She hefted the tray. "Yes, I do. And don't go making any big deal out of it."

Following her into the kitchen carrying the glass pot, Tori said, "I wouldn't dream of it."

Mia muttered, "Yeah, in a pig's eye."

"What was that? I didn't quite hear you."

Mia ignored her, though the platter thumped the counter.

Laughing, Tori decided she'd given her friend a hard enough time. She set the pot on the counter, then leaned over the sink to look outside. A somber mood settled over her at the sight of Carl's truck parked near the tunnel's entrance.

Mia said, "I made a quick call to the hospital when I

got the coffee. There isn't any change."

With a heavy heart, Tori said, "It's not good."

They washed and left the cups on the counter.

Mia eyed the box of coffee supplies sitting on the kitchen island. "No reason we can't leave it here tonight. There are still sandwiches in the fridge," Mia told her.

"I'm good. For some reason, I don't seem to have an appetite."

"Not hard to understand with all the stress you're under. I'll see you in the morning."

"You don't need—"

Mia's hand shot upward. "Don't even suggest it. I'll be here, even if the rest of the team isn't." Then she reached for Tori, giving her a hard hug. "Try to get some sleep."

"I will."

After Mia left, Tori grabbed a bottle of water from the fridge and wandered through the house, weaving around stacks of flooring and bundles of wallpaper. In the foyer she stood, gazing at the phenomenal new look. It was perfect. How could anyone not be impressed? She peeked into the library. About half of the floor was finished. Stepping into the living room, she studied the walls and floor. In her mind's eye, she visualized the room with the furniture and drapes.

A sudden realization struck her. Everyone had agreed she could probably use the old drapes, but now, they had to go. She made a mental note—new drapes.

In her office, Tori settled into the chair and booted the computer. Interesting that Parker had referred to the mystery man as collateral damage. He was probably right. Still, it didn't stop her keen interest in finding the man's identity. She swallowed the last of the water, tossing the empty bottle into the nearby wastebasket. She picked up where she left off in the newspaper archives, slowly sifting through each article. After an hour or so, she shut it down. She couldn't stop thinking about Parker's comments.

On her tablet, she used the stylus pen to draw a circle. In the middle, Tori wrote her name. Around the outside, she added the points Parker made, tunnel, body, permit, fire, crash, new men, tablet, and Ethel.

She drew a line connecting the tunnel and permit. It made sense if someone was after her property. The collapse of the tunnel gave them a reason. Revoke the permit, stop the construction, and get the city to condemn the property. So, was it the reason for the fire and crash? Was it to force Colt to hire new workers who could sabotage the property and give the city more ammunition? Still, it would seem if someone wanted to cause more damage, it could be done without planting a man inside the house. Even Parker admitted it would be difficult with as many people in the house and outside at any given time. Then, there was the tablet and Ethel. Where did these two incidents fit into the picture? They didn't affect the outcome of the controversy with the city.

Weary from her mind running in circles, she saved the page, closed the tablet, then shut down the computer. As she headed to the bedroom, the stark, bare kitchen added to her melancholy. Would all of this be for naught? No, she couldn't let herself believe it. There were answers, and she was determined to find them.

Before sliding into bed, she studied the monitor. The only movement was the two guards. One walked around the corner of the house. The other stood near the truck at the back of the property. As she drifted to sleep, her thoughts reverted to Parker's ominous words. With all the security in place, how *could* someone sabotage the house?

Chapter 16

After a fitful night of tossing and turning, Tori finally gave up. She dressed, grabbed her cell phone, and walked into the hallway, only to stumble over boxes. Dang, she'd forgotten about them and hadn't turned on the hallway light. Not a promising start to the day.

The coffee machine was an invigorating sight. At least she'd have coffee, though there wouldn't be any sandwiches for the guards. Then she remembered there were still some in the refrigerator.

When the beep sounded, she poured a cup, drinking while she filled the thermos. By the time she was ready to walk outside, Tori felt halfway human. The bracing cool morning air bolstered her quick steps.

The two men waited, waving as soon as they spotted her. Despite the disarray in the kitchen, she was glad she didn't disappoint them. Though she did say after greeting them, "These aren't the breakfast croissants. The kitchen is out of commission for a couple of days. These were made yesterday. Don't feel you have to eat them."

Carl said, "Oh, no, ma'am. I'm sure they'll be fine. This is a real treat since we usually don't even get coffee on an assignment."

She visited for a few minutes as they poured the coffee and sampled the sandwiches.

"Why these are downright tasty," Steve exclaimed.

Carl, his mouth full, grunted in agreement.

She'd have to remember to tell Cammie, though she did feel a tinge of chagrin. They'd never enthused over her sandwiches. But then, cooking had never been her forte.

Trotting back to the house, she filled her cup before heading to her office. Settled in her chair, Tori took a sip as she waited for the hospital to answer. The no-change response wasn't what she hoped to hear, putting a damper on her feelings.

She opened the tablet to access her latest list. She needed to follow up on the dishes, tableware, and glassware. Did they get ordered? Then a thought struck. What if she had Heidi oversee all the ordering? Once the inn was up and running, Heidi would handle the day-to-day operation. Until then, she didn't have much of a role in the activity. Another entry, talk to Heidi.

Next, she added drapes, another topic she knew nothing about. But then, her ignorance wasn't something new. Ever since she had arrived in Granbury, it seemed her life was more about what she didn't know than what she did.

A tap on the doorjamb broke into her musings. Colt stood in the doorway with a file folder in his hands. "The men are on their way in. Anything happen?"

"No, quiet night."

"Good." He stepped over to hand her the folder. "For Parker, when he gets here. I'll be outside if you need me." He walked out.

Before dropping the folder on the desk, Tori glanced through it. A stapled set of documents for each man included an application, a copy of the driver's license and the background check results. She scrutinized each picture. Randy Martell was the man she saw on the ladder in the utility room. Jack Crimshaw and Tommy Logan were the two men in the living room. Logan had been the one with the contemptuous expression. While inexperienced, her scan of the background check didn't raise any red flags. Did one of them break into Ethel's apartment and attack her? Or was it one of the other men on Colt's crew? A shudder rippled through her at the thought. Obviously, she couldn't trust any of them.

Mia's voice, then Parker's, gave her spirits a boost. With a smile, she picked up the folder.

Leaning against the counter, Parker sipped from a cup in one hand, then bit into a donut in the other. Next to him was a large box filled with a variety of pastries and donuts.

Mia unloaded a sack of groceries. "I stopped by the store on my way here."

Parker swallowed. With a sheepish look, he nodded toward the box. "I couldn't resist. Once a cop, always a cop."

"Well, I'm going to join you." Tori laid the folder on the table, reached for a donut crusted with cinnamon, and took a large bite. "Oh, this is good." She filled her cup before sliding onto a chair.

Parker sat across from her.

She pushed the folder toward him. "Colt dropped these off. Do you have a few minutes?"

As he dusted the sugar from his fingers, he shot her a quick glance. "Sounds serious. What happened?"

She smiled. "Nothing. I have an idea I want to run by you. Would you consider taking on the Red Door Inn as a permanent client, handling whatever security we need?"

Instead of taking a sip from the cup, he lowered it while studying her with a thoughtful air. Then he looked at Mia, who smiled and nodded.

"Mia's been concerned about the antiques I own, some of which will be displayed in the museum. Besides, we've gotten used to you being here and would like to keep you around."

With a hopeful tone, Mia said, "I'll keep you supplied with coffee."

His deep voice rumbled with laughter. "You don't need to bribe me. I just hadn't got the yes out. It would be a pleasure to continue working with all of you. You are an exceptional group of women."

"Welcome to the family," Tori said. "Send me a contract along with any recommendations."

"I'll need to look at your blueprints. I know you are replacing the guest house, but I don't know the specifics. It would also be helpful to know more about your plans for this place. And I need an inventory of the antiques, descriptions, and value. I'll also take pictures."

"Blueprints are in my office. We'll sit down whenever you're ready, and I'll go over my vision for the inn. As for the antiques, Mia is the expert."

Mia said, "I'll start making a list." Then a look of horror crossed her face.

Tori felt a jolt of fear. "What? What's wrong?"

"Did you hear what I just said? I need to make a list. My god, I've succumbed to the addiction of the to-do list. I've become … a list maker." Then a belly laugh erupted.

Tori gave her the stink eye. "My god, you scared the bejesus out of me."

"I'm sorry," though her chortles said otherwise. "I just couldn't help myself."

Despite the scowl on Tori's face, Parker joined in the laughter.

"Parker, are you sure you want to become part of this madness?" Mia asked. "This could be your fate, a list maker."

Still laughing, he said, "I hate to tell you, but I already am."

With a triumphant gesture with her hand, Tori said, "Hah! Just proves I'm right. Here's the expert admitting to making lists."

"Please, do not encourage her," Mia said. "We'll never hear the end of it."

His eyes still alit with humor, Parker said, "It's not often I'm taken by surprise, but the two of you managed it." He polished off the coffee. With the folder in his hand, he stood. "Uh, I'd better get to work."

After he left, Tori and Mia looked at each other.

Tori said, "I think we overwhelmed him … again."

Mia, who still hadn't stopped laughing, said, "I know we did. We should order a second coffee pot. Between the two of you, we'll need it. So, what else is on the agenda for today?"

Tori said, "New drapes. The old ones have got to go. Against the new wallpaper and flooring, they will look horrible."

"I had the same thought after looking at the changes. I'll do some research today. We'll need to measure all the windows. Are you going to do the same upstairs?"

"Yes."

Ben appeared in the doorway, followed by two men. "We're ready to get started in here. As soon as we finish the ceiling, the cupboards are next."

Mia said, "I'll wash the coffee pot, and then we'll be out of your way."

"I'll be in my office." As she walked out, Tori casually glanced at the two men. One was Martell, but she didn't know the other. Was he Parker's man?

Hearing the chime of her phone, she rushed toward her desk. She didn't want to miss the call if it was the hospital. It was Dan.

"How is the renovation going?"

"Moving right along. What's finished is beautiful. Colt's doing a fantastic job."

"I knew he would. I got a call from Parker. He told me

about Ethel Morris. How is she doing?"

"I checked this morning, and no change."

"If there is anything I can do to help, let me know. Parker also brought me up to date on the other incidents. He's worried, and so am I. Since I haven't received a call from the city attorney, I suspect I'm being stonewalled. I'm headed to court. If I haven't heard from him by the time I'm back in the office, I'll contact him."

"Dan, I approached Parker about taking on the security for the inn. He said he would."

"Excellent. Considering the valuable antiques, it's the right move. Once I talk to Marshal, I'll call you." He disconnected.

Mia appeared in the doorway, her new tablet in one hand and a tape measure in the other. "I'm starting on the windows. I'll do the upstairs first."

"I want to check on the tunnel, then I'll be up to help."

When she strolled outside, Tori didn't see Colt. A tinge of fear that something else had gone wrong had her picking up her pace. She stopped near the edge of the large, sloping hole. Wide planks had replaced the ladder. The sight of it atop the nearby pile of debris triggered unwanted memories. The warm sunny day couldn't stop a shiver that rolled over her. It was all in the past, but would she ever be able to forget?

Colt's cheerful expression as he climbed out helped ease her tension.

"I wondered how long it would take you to check on the progress. Want to see what we've done?"

Repressing another shudder, she said, "Yes. I would."

"I'll go first, then ease your way down. It's not as tricky as it looks."

Thankful she had on boots, she followed, sliding and stepping until she was on solid ground. Positioned along the tunnel wall, small portable lights eradicated the dense darkness.

Colt pointed as they walked. Large wood posts, sunk in concrete, supported a new cross pattern of beams across the ceiling. Set flush to the sides, the posts still left ample room to walk.

"It's the last one." He pointed to the men at the opposite end of the tunnel, where it connected to the room under the house. "Then I'll add lights on the ceiling. No more flashlights."

He grinned down at her. "As soon as I'm finished, David and G&L Engineering will examine it. If it passes inspection, they will add an addendum to their survey. It's additional proof the tunnel is stable."

"Wow! You told me what you planned, but I didn't envision this."

"Building the staircase will take a couple days and another couple for the new building. I want to get it in place as soon as possible. I don't want the tunnel to fill up with water."

Colt had recommended building a small structure to protect the entrance and keep out unwanted visitors.

"Ready to go back up?' he asked.

"I've seen all I need to. It looks good."

Tori slowly climbed up the planks. Atop, a man held out his hand to help her step onto the ground. She flashed him a smile and a thank you. It wasn't until she walked off that Tori realized she'd been in the tunnel and, for the first time since her brush with death, hadn't been afraid.

Feeling good, she made her way back to the house. Easing around the ladders, she headed upstairs, where she found Mia in the master bedroom.

"Write this down," Mia said as she carefully positioned the retractable measuring tape at the upper edge of the window frame.

As Mia called out numbers, Tori entered them on the tablet lying on the dresser.

Punching the button to retract the tape, Mia asked, "Everything okay outside?"

Excited, Tori said, "Mia, it's amazing. Somehow, I thought it would be a row of posts down the middle, but it's not. You've got to go look. We need to reconsider the tours. With the lights and new staircase, it will be a one-of-a-kind experience."

"When we get through here, I will."

Tori followed her to the next room. While Mia measured, Tori wrote as they chattered about the changes to the inn. With both of them working, it didn't take long to finish.

Tori said, "I want to look in the attic. We've never done much up there."

"Since we can't do anything downstairs, this would be a good time to prowl around."

At the end of the hall, Tori flipped the light switch for the short staircase leading to the attic. Behind her, Mia said, "What did you and Colt decide to do about blocking this entrance?"

"This was one of the structural changes, even though I don't plan on using the attic. He's adding a door."

At the top, Tori moved aside to let Mia enter the room. Sunlight streamed through portals. Still, Tori turned on the light to erase the shadows. Boxes, cast-off furniture, and trunks filled the two rooms.

"I wonder if Miss Elly ever threw anything away."

"I imagine a lot of this predates even Elly," Tori mused, tugging on a trunk to move it away from the wall.

"It will take days to go through all of this. It really needs to be cleared out before we open the inn."

"I know, but when? None of us have the time right now. Even if we did, we can't haul anything out of here until Colt's finished with the lower floor." Tori flipped back a trunk lid, staring at the pile of old clothing inside.

As Mia wandered around, she said, "We're going to need help getting some of this stuff down the stairs. You might consider hiring firemen to do the heavy work."

"A great idea. Oh, Mia, look at this old lace." She gently lifted a folded blouse, laying it aside. "This is a treasure trove under our noses."

Mia knelt beside her. Tori lifted more clothes, then a stack of doilies.

A squeal erupted from Mia as she carefully picked up one of the crocheted pieces. "These are gorgeous. Look at the intricate pattern. We can use these in the inn. I wonder who made them."

"We may never know." Tori's hand swept under the remaining stack in the trunk before she replaced what she'd removed.

"Are you looking for something?" Mia asked.

"Diaries. I found several of Elly's journals in the secret room. I also have the one her mother wrote that I read sometime back. Irene doesn't mention the mystery man in it. There might be more up here."

Mia stood, moving to a stack of boxes in the corner. One by one, she looked inside, marveling at the old books, bric-a-brac, and other collectible items. "You have enough stuff here to open a store."

When interest sparked on Tori's face, Mia hurriedly said, "Lordy be, no! Just forget I said anything. You have enough on your plate."

Tori let out a chuckle. "Don't worry. But it's worth thinking about."

Mia groaned.

"I'm just saying, we can't use any of this in the house or add it to the museum. What if we had a small retail store on the square." Ignoring the mutters and groans, she added, "Great advertising for the inn. Too bad I don't have a ghost. We could add the inn to the Granbury ghost tours."

Another moan erupted. "Tori, you are always the one to say, take it one step at a time. *Forget* … the attic for now."

Tori stood. With an amused glance at Mia, she dusted

her hands and clothes. "Okay. I will, at least for now."

Mia muttered, "Thank you, Lord, for small favors."

Tori headed to the stairs, glancing over her shoulder. "What did you say?"

"Hmm … nothing important."

With a smile, Tori said, "Let's see what's happening downstairs and discuss the type of drapes we want in each room."

On the way down, Mia stopped to pick up the tablet and tape, then followed Tori to the lower floor.

As Tori stepped off the stairs, Ben stood by the door. "You've got a visitor on the front porch, a reporter from *The Metro*. She's insistent about talking to you. I wasn't sure what to tell her."

"Cripes. I'm not talking to a reporter. I'll get rid of her."

"If you don't want to talk to her, I'll handle it," Ben said. "Step into the library so you're out of view."

Mia, hearing the conversation, had stopped on the staircase.

From inside the doorway, Tori intently listened as Ben opened the door.

"Miss Winters is unavailable. Please leave."

An angry voice replied, "What's she trying to hide?"

Tori recognized the voice. The same reporter who had pushed her way into the house.

"No comment," Ben said.

Another voice said, "Ma'am, you've been asked to leave. This is private property, and you are now trespassing. I won't hesitate to call the police."

Tori smiled at the angry thump of footsteps on the porch, though the reporter had the last word. Before Ben shut the door, she shouted, "Tell Miss Winters she won't like my next article. She has no one to blame but herself."

When Tori walked out, Ben grinned at her. "They can be pests at times."

Mia stepped into the foyer. "What could she possibly print now?"

Though Tori laughed and said, "Whatever it is, I bet it's a doozy," she couldn't help feeling troubled by the encounter.

"Good thing Parker has one of his men here," Ben observed before walking into the living room.

Tori's phone rang as they settled at the dining room table. When she answered, Dan said, "I talked to the city attorney. A team of inspectors will arrive in the morning to examine the house and tunnel."

"Tomorrow! That's all the notice I get?"

"I don't like it either. Marshal didn't ask. As he said, his call was a courtesy notification. This is your decision. If you want to delay, I'll tell him, but I don't recommend doing so without a good reason. I don't want to give the impression we have something to hide."

His comment was eerily similar to the one from *The Metro* reporter. What did the woman know? In a forceful tone, she said, "Then, I'll be ready."

"Good. An inspector from a Fort Worth company will be with me to keep an eye on the city officials."

Her gut twisted. "Why are they doing this? It seems excessive. I can see the tunnel, but why the house? This is my home. They don't have a right to come tromping through it."

"As for the why, I don't know. The city attorney isn't cooperating. He just said a team would be at the house. But when you decided to turn your home into a business, that gave them the right to inspect. I need to speak to both David and Colt as soon as you can get them together. I'll be in my office the rest of the day. Let me know when, and my legal assistant will set up a face-to-face call. Tori, don't worry. Marshal doesn't have a leg to stand on; he just doesn't know it yet." He disconnected.

Tori laid the phone on the desk.

"Okay, what's going on?" Mia asked.

"A team of inspectors from the city will be here in the morning to inspect the house and tunnel."

"Did Dan say why?"

She looked at Mia with a look of dismay. "He doesn't know. He said not to worry. Yeah, right, when even my house is threatened. How can I not worry?"

Mia said, "It would be unnatural not to. But you have a lot of people in your corner. You're not alone."

Mia's words sank deep into her mind and emotions. She wasn't alone. Something she had to remember. Those days were long gone. The kernel of anger slowly built, pushing aside the fear. She'd be damned if she let anyone destroy what she now had. She'd find out who was behind this and stop him, no matter what the cost.

Chapter 17

ori tapped the speed dial. When David answered, she said, "I talked to Dan. The city attorney called to tell him a team of inspectors would be here in the morning. He wants to set up a conference call with you and Colt this afternoon."

"What time?"

"Whenever you can get here."

"I've got a meeting about to start. It shouldn't take long. I'll get there as soon as I can. Don't worry." He disconnected.

Tori grumbled, "Now David's telling me not to worry. I'm glad everyone is so confident."

Mia chuckled. "I'd say the same, but you'd bite my head off if I did."

"I need to tell Colt."

She jumped up and raced out, intending to use the back door, only to turn around and head to the front. The kitchen was blocked with ladders.

As she charged outside, the more she thought, the madder she got. Still fuming, she saw Colt look her way.

She waved, and he headed toward her.

"I hope whatever put that look of irritation on your face isn't directed at me."

"No, it's the city attorney. A team of inspectors will be here in the morning." She explained about the conference call.

"Whenever you're ready, give me a high sign. And, Tori, don't—"

Her hand flashed in the air, stopping him. "Please do *not* tell me … don't worry."

A slow grin crossed his face. "Okay, I won't."

Mia was still seated in front of her computer when Tori entered the dining room. She plunked into a chair, her legs stretched out in front. "You know what?"

Mia cocked an eye toward her.

"This is a crock. The dang city attorney assumes he can tromp through my home any old time he wants to and doesn't even have to ask if it's okay. Instead, give her a courtesy call, but make sure she doesn't have time to hide anything. Wasn't it big of him? Okay, two can play this game. I'm not going out of my way to make it convenient for them. The kitchen is blocked. You can't get to the back door, and I plan to make sure it stays that way. Same with the hallway. If anyone complains, well, it's their problem, not mine."

Mia chuckled. "I wondered how long it would take to get your dander up."

"Well, they did it."

"Dare I make a suggestion?"

Tori grinned. "Okay, what's rolling in your head?"

"Let's clean where we can. Even though we did the upstairs a few days ago, we should hit it again. And then spiff up the downstairs. The living room is close to being finished. The library, foyer and living room need to shine when the inspectors walk in."

Tori straightened. "You're right. Give them a taste of what this place will look like when it's finished."

"I didn't want to call the team until we talked."

"Go ahead." Tori stood, walking through the music room to the living room. She stopped in the doorway and watched the men put up the last wallpaper strips. Two others were laying the flooring. If they could finish, the furniture could be moved back into the room, and the drapes hung. She wished she had new ones, but the old ones would have to do. At least they were clean.

Mia stepped alongside her. "They're on the way. Heidi is getting what we need since all the cleaning materials are boxed up. I'll start vacuuming upstairs."

"I'll help."

"No, you need to stay down here. Until Heidi gets here, it's about all I can do."

Footsteps echoed behind her. It was Ben. "I've been in the kitchen. Is there a problem?"

She tilted her head to look up at him. "City inspectors will be here tomorrow. We've decided to clean where we can, starting with the upstairs. We don't want to get in your way."

He eyed the living room. "If my men stay late, we can

finish this room. I'll clear it with Colt, but it shouldn't be a problem."

Tori breathed a sigh of relief. "I was hoping you could. The foyer, library, and living room are my *wow* factor." Her eyes narrowed as she looked across the room with a steely determination. "When they walk in, I want to blow them away. Make them realize who and what they are messing with. This isn't some old rundown house. *This* is the Leichter mansion."

A look of respect sparked in his eyes. "Don't worry, we'll get it finished."

Though she cringed at the 'don't worry' comment, she said, "We've got a game plan."

Following Mia's advice, Tori headed to her office. In the doorway she paused, looking at the clutter of boxes and blueprints spread across the table. Not much she could do here. Her phone chimed. With her thoughts on the room, she pulled it from her pocket, idly glancing at the caller ID. It wasn't a number she recognized.

"Hello, this is Tori Winters."

"This is Sid Jeffery. You sent me an email about the poker chips."

Anticipation sparked as she dropped into her chair. "Thank you for calling. Are you familiar with the chips?" She laid the phone on the desk and tapped the speakerphone.

"No. Never seen these before. But that's the case with most of the chips I research. Where did you get them?"

She chuckled. "You're probably not going to believe

this, but in a tunnel, along with a skeleton."

His voice rose with excitement. "Really! Wow! Do you know who the person was?"

"It's a mystery. I don't, and neither do the police."

"The police? Why are they involved?"

"A bullet hole in the skull. All that's left is the skeleton, remnants of clothing, a pocket watch, and these two poker chips."

"This is very intriguing. How old is the skeleton?"

"Best estimate is eighty or so years. I mentioned Frankie Leichter in my email."

"Yes, I'm familiar with Leichter. I've done some research on his casinos."

"In 1938, he built a house in Granbury, a town south of Dallas. He added a tunnel."

"Not surprising. Leichter did the same with a couple of his casinos. So, you're guessing Leichter killed the guy, then buried him in the tunnel. How are you connected to all this?"

"Frankie Leichter was my great-grandfather. I own the property. The body was found when a section of the tunnel collapsed."

"How about that! All these years, a body's been buried there, and no one knew it. How can the poker chips help?"

"I'm not sure. Other than the pocket watch with the initials DK, it's the only other lead I have to help identify the man."

"After I got your email, I did some research. Leichter

ordered the chips from a New Jersey company in December of 1940. This is where it *really* gets intriguing. Something I've never come across."

Another tug of excitement shot through Tori.

"Most casinos ordered chips in the tens of thousands. In fact, over the years, Leichter ordered 580 boxes, equating to about 58,000 chips, for his gambling syndicate. Occasionally a casino owner would order smaller quantities of a specific design for personal use. Leichter ordered 2000 chips with the lightning bolt design on one side and twenty-five on the other. And none in smaller values, a one, five or ten. Did he run poker games at his home?"

"I don't know." Tori's thoughts shifted to Ethel. She would know.

"If he did, the chips would likely have been used there, especially since the value is so high. These were high-dollar games, probably with affluent individuals who might not want to be seen in a casino. What's intriguing are those lightning bolts, another oddity. Chips from the illegal gambling era typically had initials for the casino name or owners. Leichter had several other patterns, all with initials for different gambling cohorts. One pattern had RD for the Red Door Casino."

"Yes, I have three chips with RD on the front."

"My first impression when I saw the picture you sent was a relationship. Silent partners didn't always want their initials on a chip. It might be the case with three bolts, a partnership with three individuals. Leichter only ordered 250 chips with the bolt design on both sides. This is very odd, something I've never seen before. I don't know how they were used. The bolt design certainly links the two chips. I'm still digging. I'll let you know if I come across someone with the initials DK."

"I'd appreciate any help you could provide. My grandmother left some journals. I'm hoping I might find a clue there. I'm also checking the newspaper archives. From what's left of the clothing and an expensive set of cufflinks, it's obvious he was affluent. Someone like that just doesn't disappear. If I find a name, I'll let you know."

"I'll be in touch. This is fascinating, absolutely fascinating. Thanks for contacting me."

Pleased, she disconnected. There was a possibility Sid would come up with something. While solving the riddle of the mystery man wasn't high on her priority list, it still nagged at her. Surely, the man had a family. Even after all these years, there could be relatives who would want to know. Case in point, her discovery she had a grandmother, one she knew nothing about.

The sound of the front door, followed by Heidi's voice, broke into Tori's thoughts. As she stepped into the foyer, footsteps clattered on the stairs as Mia trotted down.

Her arms filled with cleaning products, Heidi said, "Okay, we're here. What's going on?" Behind her, Cammie and Tina were similarly loaded down.

"Tomorrow morning, city personnel plan to inspect the house and tunnel. Mia and I feel it would be helpful to showcase the house where we can. Let's set everything in the dining room. It's the only place in the house with any room."

Mia spoke up. "We need to clean upstairs. Then once the construction crew is out of the way, we'll do the rooms down here."

The women grabbed rags, polish, and other cleaning paraphernalia before trotting up the stairs.

The doorbell chimed.

Ben hollered, "I'll get it."

As she passed through the music room, she wondered if Ben was staying close to the front door in case another reporter showed up.

David greeted Ben as he walked in. He looked around. "This is amazing! What a difference." Hearing the vacuum cleaner upstairs, he pointed. "What's going on up there?"

Tori poked her head out of the music room doorway. "The team's cleaning. Come on back to my office."

When he walked in, Tori said, "I'd offer you something to drink, but the kitchen is shut down."

"I'm good." He settled into a chair, crossing one leg over the other. "Okay. Where do we stand with this senseless visit tomorrow?"

Seeing his disgusted look, she grinned. "Dan's waiting to set up a conference call." She picked up her phone and tapped the speed dial. When Colt answered, she said, "David's here."

"On my way."

She disconnected, laying the phone aside. "I don't

know much more than what I told you on the phone. Dan plans to have another inspector with him to keep tabs on the city inspectors."

"Does Marshal have the surveys?"

"I don't know."

Colt loped into the office, dropping into a chair. After greeting David, he said, "The last post is almost finished. Is there any chance you can get Granger or Lewis back today for the addendum we talked about?"

In response, David pulled out his phone and tapped the screen. When the call was answered, he said, "This is David Tucker. I need to talk to either Mitch or Bob." His fingers impatiently tapped his knee. "Mitch, it's David. Can either you or Bob run the second survey this afternoon? Colt will be finished with the reinforcements. The problem is the city is sending out inspectors tomorrow. It would be helpful to have your follow-up analysis before they arrive."

He listened, then said, "Come on around to the back. We'll be waiting." He disconnected. "Both will be here in about an hour."

Colt nodded his head in approval.

"I'm going to call Dan. He wants a face-to-face."

When the receptionist at the law firm answered, Tori asked to speak to Dan. When he came on the line, she tapped the speakerphone. "Colt and David are both in my office."

"I'll get the call set up on my end. Are they using a computer or their phones?"

Her eyebrow twitched upward as she looked at them.

David said, "Phone."

Colt said the same.

Dan said, "I'll text the link. How about you?"

"I'd prefer my computer."

"Be watching for an email." He disconnected.

David said, "You still haven't told me why everyone is cleaning."

"We're getting the house ready for the inspection. Once Colt's men are gone, we'll start on the rooms downstairs. I want it to shine for tomorrow."

"It should set them back on their heels," David said.

"I hope so."

Two phones chirped. Once they clicked the link, each greeted Dan.

Tori opened her emails, spotting the one from Dan. Within seconds, his face appeared on the screen.

Not wasting time on pleasantries, Dan said, "Here's where we stand. The city attorney and two inspectors will arrive tomorrow morning at about 10 a.m. I plan on arriving an hour or so earlier. I want to examine the tunnel and discuss any last-minute strategy. An inspector, Edgar Henley with Holcomb Engineering, will be with me. I want an independent expert to watch the actions of the city's inspectors. David, I would also like you to be there."

Colt asked, "Do the inspectors work for the city?"

"I don't know. Marshal hasn't been forthcoming with any information. We'll find out tomorrow. I've read the surveys. If they had waited, all of this could have been avoided. But they didn't, and I still don't know who is pushing their buttons."

Not only did Dan's voice radiate anger, but it was clearly visible on his face. Since meeting him, this was the first time she had seen a visual display of emotion.

"The way Marshal has handled this is totally irresponsible and, in my opinion, defamatory. A point I plan to make tomorrow. To date, the city's actions have caused undue financial harm and stress for Tori and her plans for the Red Door Inn. Even the newspapers claim the property is unsafe, which can impact future business."

Her heart lurched. She hadn't considered the damage from the newspapers.

Colt asked, "What about my men? Do I pull them off the job for tomorrow?"

"Absolutely not. Marshal didn't give Tori the courtesy of asking when it would be convenient. If I had said no, Marshal could claim she wasn't cooperating or trying to hide something. Keep your men on the job. If it causes a problem, I don't care. Also, I'll make it clear that parts of the house are off-limits, namely your living quarters, Tori. Another point I plan to make. This is Tori's home."

Reassured Dan had supported her decision to keep Colt's men in the house, she asked, "What about my team?"

"They should be there since they are an integral part of the plans for the inn. Tori, I want you to take an active role tomorrow. Introduce them and their responsibilities."

A rap sounded on the door jamb. With a questioning

look on his face, Parker stood in the doorway. Tori motioned for him to come in.

"Dan, Parker is here," Tori said.

"Good. I planned to call him."

"Parker, grab a chair and sit next to me. Dan should be able to see you."

Once Parker was settled next to Tori, Dan said, "Parker, since you're taking over the security for the inn, I'd like you to be at the house tomorrow. I'll let Tori fill you in on what's happening. Tori, introduce him along with the rest of your team. Colt, where do we stand with the tunnel?"

"Last support post is going into place. David and the other company are running a second assessment this afternoon. If they are satisfied, they will issue a supplement to their reports."

"I'll need copies, but you can give them to me in the morning. Does anyone have a question?"

David asked, "Does Marshal have the first set of surveys?"

"Not yet. Anything else?"

When no one said anything, he added, "I'll see you in the morning." Dan's face disappeared.

David glanced at his watch. "Lewis and Granger will be showing up at any time. We'd better get outside."

Parker said, "I'm going with them. I want to look at the tunnel, then you can get me caught up, Tori."

She followed them out the door. The hallway was still blocked, so Colt turned toward the dining room. Not wanting someone to overhear, she followed them outside before saying, "Colt, hold up a minute."

All three stopped.

"Colt, can you keep the hallway blocked tomorrow? Like Dan said, let's not make this easy for them."

His eyes sparked with interest. "Sure can. Since all you wanted was to finish the living room, I can stop the work for today and send the rest of the men home. In the morning, I'll make sure the hallway is still blocked, and I'll do the same in the kitchen. It will force them to go out the front and around the house to get to the back door. What about the wine cellar?"

"I don't see any reason to deny them access. And to get into the tunnel, let's make them walk the planks instead of using the staircase." She chuckled. "It should be interesting to watch."

His boyish smile erupted. "Ma'am, I never suspected you had such devilish depths."

Back inside, Tori trotted upstairs to talk to her team. In the hallway, she hollered, "Everyone, gather around." From the various rooms, the team members emerged.

Mia said, "From your malicious look, I suspect you're up to no good."

"I think we can serve up crow on the menu by the time Dan gets through with Marshal." Tori quickly filled them in on the pertinent details. Their laughter erupted when she reached the part about Marshal and his entourage walking the planks to get into the tunnel.

"Oh, this may be good after all," Heidi exclaimed.

"Okay, let's get this place squared away," Mia said.

"What can I do to help?" Tori asked.

"Nothing until we get downstairs."

"Except for the men in the living room, Colt's crew is leaving. I'll be in my office."

She trotted down the stairs, plotting her strategy. While she had more questions than answers, there was one point of which there was no doubt. She wasn't going down without a fight.

Chapter 18

As she stepped onto the floor, Parker strolled into the foyer. He said, "Colt did a heck of a job on the tunnel. David and the other engineers are crawling all over the inside. From the comments, they're impressed."

"Yes. It wasn't what I expected. Let's get a cup of coffee and talk. With Colt's men gone, I can use the kitchen." She hollered up the stairs. "Mia, where did you stash the coffee machine?"

Footsteps echoed, and Mia leaned over the rail. A knowing look crossed her face when she saw Parker. "I moved it to your bedroom along with the box of supplies."

With the hallway empty of workers, they stepped around stacks of flooring to reach the kitchen.

Parker said, "This new floor looks good. Classy. So, tell me what's happened. From what little I heard, I gather the city is showing up tomorrow."

"Yes, they are." Tori retrieved the coffee supplies from her bedroom. While the coffee brewed, she talked.

After she finished explaining, Parker asked, "Still no idea who is behind this?"

"No, not a clue. Did you find out anything about the three men Colt hired?"

"Not yet. My people are still digging into their backgrounds."

"I'm curious. How many people do you have working for you?"

"Full-time, seven. Part-time, another ten or so."

"I had no idea your business was so large."

"In addition to the security protection, I handle cases for insurance companies, false injury claims, accidents, and some criminal and civil investigations."

The machine beeped. Tori poured two cups, handing one to Parker. They each sipped, sighing with pleasure.

"We can leave it set up. Let's go to my office."

"What time do you want me here in the morning?" Parker asked, easing onto a chair.

"Dan plans to be here around nine, so sometime before then."

"I talked to Andy Rodriguez today. Nothing new about the mystery man. In fact, he's closing the case."

"What about the watch?"

"Since it was found on your property, he'll return it to you, along with the cufflinks."

"I talked to a man in Houston about the poker chips." She filled him in on the details.

"Since the chips weren't ordered until December in 1940, it narrows down the time frame." Parker finished the coffee. "I need to make a run to my office. I'll be back in an hour or so. I'll put the cup in the kitchen."

She followed him into the hallway to check on the progress upstairs.

Ben still stood guard at the front door.

As she approached, a clatter sounded on the stairs as the four women trooped down. Mia brought up the rear, carrying the vacuum cleaner.

Ben rushed forward to take it. "Where do you want me to put it?"

With a smile, Mia said, "If you are finished in the library, we'll start there."

As he strolled into the room, Mia glowered at the women, who all avidly watched.

Oblivious to the bit of byplay, he said as he set the machine near the doorway, "We're almost finished in the living room. Is there anything I can do to help you?"

"Thank you, Ben, but we've got it," Mia said, casting another dark look toward Tori and the other three women, who all now had broad smiles.

Holding back a laugh, Tori asked, "What can I do?"

"Nothing," Heidi said. "We know what we're doing and can do it a lot faster."

Tori's lips twitched with a wry smile. "In other words, stay out of your way."

"Yep, you got it," Heidi said with a chuckle.

At odds with the lack of something to do, Tori decided she might as well work on the research for the mystery man. As she accessed the newspaper archives, she thought about the time she had wasted searching 1939 and 1940. Tori picked up where she had left off. One by one, she clicked on dates. It was as if the man had never existed. Frustrated, she logged off and picked up her phone. The answer at the hospital was the same, no change.

Idly, she scrolled through the lists on her tablet, stopping at her drawing. Leaning back, she studied it. What was the connection? There had to be one. Something niggled in her mind, a whisper, a hint. What? Straining to think didn't help.

"You look deep in thought." David stood in the doorway.

"Hmm … trying to figure out what connects all of this." She laid the tablet aside. "What's the verdict?"

"Good. Even though the posts weren't needed, they add additional support." He settled in the chair. "Mitch and Bob were very impressed. I'll have their report later today. Once I get back to my office, I'll type mine and make copies of both reports. I'll bring them with me in the morning. Where'd Parker go?"

"His office. He'll be back."

"Smart move to bring him on board. He's a good man and a definite asset. I don't know how anyone wouldn't be impressed with your accomplishments."

"David, you know it's not just me."

"I know others have played a role, but it all starts with you. I've told you before you are an amazing woman. Once we get by all this, I'm taking you to dinner, the theater, the works. I'd like to see you again in the fabulous gown you got from Mia's friend. Maybe erase some memories of the last time you wore it."

"Oh, yes, Myra's dinner, the party from hell as I now call it."

"Well, you did make it interesting when you proclaimed you planned to turn the house into an inn. And, here you are, about to make it a reality."

"It is unless someone can stop me."

David leaned forward. "I can't envision it. Not the redoubtable Tori Winters." The warm look in his eyes was both unsettling and enticing.

David eased back at the sound of Colt's voice.

"I'm done outside." He dropped into the chair.

Still tingling from the emotions David had elicited, she forced herself to pay attention.

"Before Granger and Lewis left, I had a word with them. They are quite impressed with the modifications to the tunnel and won't have a problem saying so, even if this goes to court."

Ben walked in. "Colt, the wallpaper in the living room is done. The floor will be finished in another thirty minutes or so." With a chuckle, he added, "By the time Mia and her team are finished, I don't think there will be a speck of dust left. Mia borrowed a ladder and is cleaning the chandelier. I offered to do it, and all I got was a look of disbelief. She did say I could clean the portal over the landing. I did, then it had to pass Heidi's inspection. They're worse at barking orders than my drill instructor during Marine boot camp." He turned and walked out.

Colt said, "Ben and I are going to stick around, help move the furniture and hang drapes."

"I can stay too," David said.

Tori looked at the monitor. "Parker pulled in. I've got to warn him Mia is on the ladder."

As she passed Mia, she looked up and grinned. Drill sergeant was a perfect comparison.

She stood on the porch for a moment, relishing the light breeze on her face. Parker spotted her and waved.

"Are you coming inside?"

"First, I want a short meeting with my men."

"If you come in the front, be careful. Mia's on a ladder cleaning the chandelier."

Inside, she stopped in the archway to the living room. The sight was unbelievable. The soft elegance of the new wallpaper accented the gleam of the wood paneling, and the parquet floor was nothing short of stunning. The room glowed with a warm ambiance.

Two men knelt, adding the final pieces to the floor butting against the doorway into the music room. As she watched, they stood and stretched.

One turned to Ben, who stood nearby. "We're done."

"Okay, you're out of here. I'll see you in the morning."

The men gathered up their tools, nodding to Tori as they passed. Once the door closed behind them, Tori stepped into the room, spinning on her toes. "It's fabulous, absolutely fabulous."

Heidi, Cammie, and Tina walked in. Each turned to gaze around.

"It is," Heidi exclaimed.

Tina said, "This is going to be an awesome picture for the video."

"Let's get it cleaned," Heidi told them.

Mia crawled off the ladder. "Ben, would you move the ladder so I can clean the light fixtures in the living room?"

While the four women worked, Tori wandered over to look at the library. The furniture was still in disarray, but the wood paneling and floor gleamed.

"Mia. Are you done in here?" she asked in a loud voice.

"Yes."

David walked in. "Are you ready to move the furniture?" With the three men helping, getting the room squared away didn't take long. Heidi and Tina went upstairs and hauled the drapes back down. Colt and Ben handled hanging them.

With the library finished, they started moving the furniture from the music room into the living room. Parker arrived and pitched in.

As David and Parker picked up the sofa, straining to carry it through the doorway, David moaned, "My god, what is this thing made of—steel?"

Mia squealed, "Be careful! Don't bump the legs."

David muttered, "My back may never be the same, and she's worried about the dang leg."

Colt, his hands resting on his hips, stood in the middle of the room and chortled. "Hey, old buddy, getting wimpy, are you?" he said with an emphasis on old.

David grunted. "You try picking this thing up."

"I did when we moved it into the music room."

Once it was on the floor, David said, "Tori, please tell me you won't move this monstrosity again."

Another squeal from Mia erupted. "Monstrosity! That's a Duncan Phyfe couch."

"I don't care if it came over on the Mayflower. It needs to stay put. Tori, tell her."

She laughed. "It's not up to me. It's Mia's bailiwick."

Once the room had been arranged to the satisfaction of all the women, something else David moaned about, the men helped hang the drapes.

Once the last fold had been twitched into place, Mia said, "Okay. All that's left is the music and dining room. We can handle it."

Colt asked, "Are you sure?"

"Yes." She looked around. "We're almost ready for tomorrow."

Once the men were out the door, Mia said, "The other two rooms won't take long. What about your office?"

"It's good as it is. You cleaned it a few days ago."

While Mia and Heidi cleaned the music room, Cammie and Tina did the dining room. Chattering as they worked, Tina asked, "What are you going to wear tomorrow?"

Gathering up papers she'd left on the dining room table, Tori stopped. Her brow wrinkled. "I don't know. I hadn't thought about it. What about all of you?"

Mia stopped in the doorway between the two rooms,

a rag in her hand. "What do *you* want us to wear? This is your show."

"Hmm … you know what this reminds me of? Another conversation we had about Myra's dinner party. I want you to wear what's comfortable. This isn't about how we dress but who we are." She paused before saying, "It goes for me as well. I'll be wearing jeans, a t-shirt, and my boots. It's who I am."

Mia chuckled. "I'm good with it. Jeans and a t-shirt."

Tori carried the stack of papers into her office. Spotting the boxes with the new tablets, she picked them up. This was a good time to hand them out.

As they gathered in the dining room, Tori gave one to Heidi, Tina, and Cammie. "I expect these will make keeping track of the pesky details to run this place easier." As Heidi started to thank her, Tori flashed her hand in the air. "No thanks needed. Just consider it part of your job."

At last, Mia and Heidi were satisfied they had done all they could. Along with Cammie and Tina, they picked up their belongings and boxes of cleaning materials, telling Tori they'd see her in the morning.

Locking the door, Tori leaned against it, gazing around. The change was unbelievable, beyond what she had expected. The living room needed a large area rug, but it could wait. The library, more books. Turning off the lights behind her, she wandered into the kitchen to look in the fridge. It was still stocked with sandwiches. Tori grabbed one and a bottle of water.

Seated behind the desk, she unscrewed the cap and

took a deep swig before she unwrapped the sandwich. As she munched, she turned her attention to the newspaper archives. Might as well spend some time researching.

By the time Tori finished six more months, her mind was frazzled from reading the articles. She made one more call to the hospital, only to hear there was no change. Discouraged, Tori crumpled the wrapper, tossing it at the wastebasket. She missed. Dang, she must be more tired than she realized.

Rising, she stepped to retrieve the ball of foil from where it had landed near the window. When she bent over, a piece of metal protruding from under the edge of the desk caught her eye. Something she didn't remember seeing or feeling before. Curious, she dropped the foil in the wastebasket, then crouched to look under the desk. It was a square object, about half the size of a credit card.

Puzzled, Tori stared at it. What was it, and how long had it been there? Surely, one of the crew should have seen it since the desk had been polished many times. She reached to remove it so she could examine it. Then a horrifying thought flooded her mind. She snatched her hand back. Was it possible?

She sat back in her chair. Fingers pounded the keyboard as she typed listening devices into her computer. Multiple images popped up. One looked like what was stuck to her desk. *Oh, my god,* she thought.

Panicking, she didn't know what to do, remove it, call the police? Stop it, she told herself. One step at a time. First, she had to find out if she was right. Tori took a picture with her phone, then texted Parker — *is this what I think it is?* — and added the picture.

His response was immediate—*where did you find it?*

Desk

Leave your office, then call me.

How far did she have to get away from it? Not wanting to take a chance, she turned on the front porch light and stepped outside. Tori sat on the step and tapped her phone.

"Where are you?" Parker asked.

In case one of the guards walked up, she kept her voice low. "On the front porch. Is it a bug?"

"Yes."

"What do I do? Remove it?" She could feel the panic rising.

"No. Not yet. Where is it on your desk?"

"Under the edge near a corner."

"I suspect it was planted by one of the three men Colt hired. The question is, when? What did someone hear? Unfortunately, there's no way of finding out. In the morning, I'll bring a device to sweep the house to make sure there isn't another one. Don't talk to anyone in your office; be careful what you say in the hallway."

"Parker, why would someone plant a bug? What could I possibly talk about that someone would want to know? This business with the city certainly isn't a secret."

"I don't know. I'll see you in the morning."

Tori disconnected. She waved at Carl walking up the driveway before turning to go back into the house. Fear and outrage tugged at her as she locked the door. Her office, even her life, had been invaded. But who was the threat, and why? While her thoughts raced with questions, she didn't have a single answer.

In her office, Tori knelt, staring up at the device. Who was on the other end? What did they want? Her fingers itched to rip it from the desk and stomp it into pieces. Though it was still early, she couldn't stay in the office, knowing someone was listening. Tori shut down the computer, then flipped off the lights as she walked out.

Too restless to go to bed, Tori sat on the piano bench and pulled off her boots. After adjusting the bench, she positioned her feet on the pedals. Her shoulders back, her spine straight, Tori began to play. Music had always been her refuge, even as a child. Memories of the day a used upright piano was delivered rose in her mind. She'd been about ten. She'd taken to learning as a duck takes to water, sitting for hours, practicing scales. A metronome sat atop the upright. The tick, tock of the long metal arm kept her timing on track.

Her mother declared Tori had a natural talent. It wasn't until high school others echoed her mother's words. Her first job was playing for weddings, birthday parties, and funeral services. When her mother became ill, fighting a cancer she couldn't beat, Tori played for her. The music seemed to ease her mother's pain.

Tori's fingers segued into one of her mother's favorites, *Unchained Melody*. Her strong alto voice soared as she sang the mournful words.

Her father had been an Army Captain. During her parent's separations, the song became a way of communicating their love. When he was killed in Afghanistan, the song took on new meaning for her mother.

After her mother died, she had to sell most of the furniture, including her beloved piano. The day it was hauled out the door was a painful reminder of all she had lost.

Tori truly believed her music was in the past until she walked into the house she inherited and saw the magnificent baby grand piano. She also discovered another link to the grandmother she never knew existed … a love of music.

As the last note died away, she sighed, slid off the bench and picked up her boots. Closing her bedroom door, she flipped the deadbolt lock. Though she had to wonder at the precautions. Two guards, locked doors, and a camera system, all to keep someone from breaking in. But then, they didn't have to. Someone was already inside, listening.

Chapter 19

She'd set the alarm for what was, even for her, the wee hours of the morning. While she was more meticulous in her morning ritual, makeup and hair, she still dressed in blue jeans, a t-shirt, and boots. Tori wasn't out to impress anyone. She'd let the house do it.

She studied the refrigerator contents, none of which piqued her appetite. Her stomach was a rolling ball of nerves.

The sight outside the window did nothing to ease her anxiety. A fog had settled in, obscuring even the illumination from the guard's portable light. A bleak and dismal start to her day.

While Tori waited for the coffee to brew, she hunted down a box, then retrieved the thermos where Mia had stashed it in her bedroom. The thermos, along with sandwiches and cups, went into the box.

With it clutched under her arm, she eased her way down the slick back steps. Her flashlight, casting a hazy glow across the ground, did little to break up the murkiness. A figure, waving a light, strode out of the mist.

"Miss Tori, what are you doing out here? This isn't a good time to be traipsing around."

"I know, Carl. But I didn't want to miss bringing the coffee and sandwiches."

With a gruff tone, he said, "We didn't figure we'd be seeing you this morning. Here, let me have that." He reached for the box tucked under her arm. "You get on back to the house. It'd be real easy to twist an ankle, or worse, in all this fog."

As she turned, he stepped alongside her.

"Carl, I'll be okay."

"Don't hurt to make sure."

She gave up protesting. When Tori opened the door, he turned, disappearing into the murky haze.

Inside, Tori shook off the chill that had seeped through her clothing. Cradling a hot cup of coffee in her hands, she headed to her office before she remembered. Someone could be listening, even if she was only on the computer. Her gut clenched. Still, she didn't have an option.

Settled behind her desk, she took a sip of coffee before setting it near the keyboard. Trying to divert her thoughts, she scooted her tablet in front of her. When Tori activated it, the page with the drawing, the circle with her name in the middle, appeared.

She picked up her cup, taking a swig while she stared at the screen. What was it about the drawing that bothered her? What was she missing? Tori took the last swallow, setting aside the cup. She added a word to the outside of the circle—bug.

After she changed pages, she studied the latest to-do list, where she'd made notes about the upcoming inspection. Her phone chirped, her text alert. It was Parker—*at front door, don't want to ring doorbell.*

When Tori opened the door, Parker walked in and lifted a finger to his lips. She nodded in understanding.

He set the computer bag on the floor, then pulled out a device about the size of a cell phone. His finger pushed a button, and a light blinked with a steady pulse. He walked into the library. With a slow pace, he waved the device at the walls and baseboards. He pulled the drapes aside to scan the window frame before moving to the furniture. It was a slow, methodical search. When he finished, he flashed a thumbs-up before moving into the foyer, where the scan was faster.

By the time he finished the living room, the sun had risen. While he scanned the music room, Tori kept an eye on the driveway. Before her crew walked in, she wanted to alert them. Seeing Mia's car pull to the curb, she stepped outside. The fog had dissipated, and the early morning smell lightened her mood.

Arms loaded with sacks, Mia walked up the driveway. Spotting Tori, she said, "It's a beautiful day." As she neared the steps, her smile slipped, overlaid by concern.

"Someone planted a bug in my office."

Dumbfounded, she stared at Tori. "What! How?"

On the street, the rest of the crew emerged from their cars.

"I'll wait until everyone gets here."

At the sight of the women on the porch, the three women picked up their pace.

Heidi, with her long-legged stride, was the first to reach them. "What's wrong?"

"Someone bugged my office."

Exclamations resounded. Heidi's voice won out. "What did you do?"

"I found it last night. Since I wasn't sure what it was, I took a picture and sent it to Parker. He's already here, running some type of bug finder in all the rooms."

"Where is it?" Mia asked.

"Under the edge of my desk."

The door opened, and Parker walked out. He grinned at them. "Good news. I didn't find any more. I examined the one in the office. It's a voice-activated, wireless device. Whoever put it there didn't do a good job, and that's why you spotted it, Tori. Probably in a rush and slapped it on. We need to get rid of it without raising any suspicions. Where is your vacuum cleaner?"

Heidi answered, "It's upstairs."

"Once we go inside, we're going to play out a scenario. Here's the script."

As they intently listened to his instructions, wide grins spread across the women's faces.

Tori walked in, heading to her office, where she settled in her chair.

Mia's voice echoed, "Tori, where are you?"

"Office," she shouted.

Mia walked in, followed by Parker. "Well, are you

ready for the city personnel to arrive?" Mia asked.

"Yes, though I'm not worried. Where is everyone?"

"Since we didn't get a chance to finish last night, Cammie and Tina are cleaning the dining room. Heidi went to get the vacuum cleaner. I'm doing this room. I want to polish your desk."

"I'll get out of your way," she said, though she didn't move.

Mia leaned a hip on the desk as she kept up a stream of conversation about patterns for drapes.

Wheels rattled as Heidi walked in, pushing the vacuum. "Morning, Tori." After plugging it in, she flipped the switch. A dull roar filled the room as she shoved it close to the desk.

"Tori, move your chair?" Heidi said in a loud voice.

Parker walked around the desk. Dropping to one knee, he reached for the device and twisted. He dropped it, then stomped on it. With a pleased look, Parker picked up the larger pieces.

As he looked at each woman, a grin split his face. "Well done. Heidi, please do the honors and clean up the remains."

Heidi zipped over the small bits, then turned off the machine.

Tori said, "What a huge relief, knowing it's gone. Do you think he will plant another one?"

"Could, especially if whoever was listening believes our little charade. But … we have the advantage. We know. Until we get this stopped, I'll be running sweeps."

Mia said, "Well, I've got good news to cheer everyone up. Before I left my house, I called the hospital. Ethel is still in a coma, but her condition has improved. They are moving her to a private room."

Another surge of relief rushed through Tori.

With a thoughtful look, Parker asked, "They're moving her today?"

"Yes," Mia said.

The doorbell rang. "I'll get it and give Cammie and Tina the all-clear," Mia said.

Colt and David's voices rumbled in the hallway. As David walked in, a look of surprise crossed his face when he spotted Parker. "I thought I'd be the early one."

Parker said, "We had a problem. Tori found a listening device stuck to her desk."

Colt's voice, as he strode into the room, overrode David's curses. "I take it you dealt with it."

"Yes." He held out his hand with the pieces he picked up. "The rest Heidi took care of."

David's hand raked his hair. "We need to talk about this, but we can't now. Colt's men are on the way in."

Tori said, "You're right. It will have to wait."

"Colt, will the new men be in the house?" Parker asked.

"No. They'll be outside, waiting for the inspection to finish, so we can get back to working on the entrance. I figured having them inside the house while the inspectors were here wasn't a good idea."

"Good thinking." Parker glanced at his watch. "Dan's

probably on his way. I need to call him, give him a heads-up on the bug."

"I'll take the vacuum back upstairs," Heidi said.

"I'll do it for you," David said. "Where do I stash it?"

"Thanks. The closet in the master bedroom."

Colt headed outside, followed by Parker. David left with the vacuum cleaner, and Tori followed Mia and Heidi into the kitchen.

They began unloading Mia's sacks. Sandwiches and containers of potato salad and coleslaw went into the fridge.

Tori watched, thankful for Mia's foresight.

"There's also donuts and cookies," Mia said.

After filling her cup, Tori poked around in the sacks, pulling out a package of chocolate chip cookies. Opening it, she grabbed one and took a bite. "Oh, these are good." She licked a glob of chocolate off her finger, then popped the rest of the cookie in her mouth.

"As much as I hate to ruin this healthy breakfast you're eating, I picked up the latest edition of *The Metro* while I was at the store." Mia pulled the paper from her oversized tote bag, handing it to Tori.

She groaned as she read the headline—*Leichter Mansion On The Chopping Block!* As she read, the madder she got. "For cripes sake! Where do they come up with this garbage? Listen to this. '*According to an unnamed source, the Leichter mansion is scheduled for demolition. Today, city officials are scheduled to meet with Tori Winters, the heiress to the Leichter fortune, to finalize the demolition schedule. The house, in serious disrepair, and the collapse of a tunnel connected to the house have caused grave concerns in the community, forcing the city to take action.'"*

Livid, she threw the paper on the counter. "I bet this is the reporter who showed up here. It's exactly what Dan was afraid of. Stories like this could affect the inn." Fuming, she stomped out.

Cammie and Tina were seated in front of their laptops in the dining room. Pushing back her anger, she asked, "How is it going?"

Cammie exclaimed, "I've got a list ready to order whenever you have time to look it over."

"If we can't do it today, we will tomorrow." It was a reminder she still hadn't talked to Heidi about taking over the ordering.

Tina piped up. "I have the layout ready for the video. Plus, the artwork is done for the menus and business cards. I'm working on the flyers to send out."

"What do you want us to do today?" Cammie asked.

Tori thought, a plan gelling in her mind. "Stay here, keep working on your projects."

She walked into the music room, closed the connecting door, then did the same with the doors on the living room side. Tori was staging her presentation.

The doorbell rang. On the porch stood Dan and a burly man with a rugged face, each holding a briefcase.

She greeted them, motioning for them to come in.

Dan stopped; his astonished gaze flashed around the foyer. "This is absolutely stunning. What a difference."

His companion said, "I've heard about the house but certainly didn't expect to see this."

Dan said, "Sorry, I was taken aback by the changes you've wrought. This is Edgar Henley, our independent inspector. He's with Holcomb Engineering. Ed, this is Tori Winters, owner and driving force behind the renovations."

Tori, lightly blushing from Dan's comment, shook Ed's hand. "Nice to meet you. Would you like a quick tour? Do we have time, Dan?"

"Yes, that's a good idea. It will help Ed get familiar with the house before the city personnel arrives."

Tori said, "Let's start with the library."

While Ed prowled the room, Dan pulled Tori to the side. "Parker called about the listening device. Let's talk about it later."

Tori nodded as Ed strode toward them.

"Impressive, Miss Winters."

"Please, it's Tori." She led the way upstairs.

Ed intently studied each room, tapping walls and examining the flooring, ceiling, and window frames. The staircase leading to the tunnel had him muttering in amazement. In the attic, he paid close attention to the ceiling. Once he'd seen enough, they returned to the first floor.

Colt's men had arrived. Two men were already at work in the hallway. Tori led the way through the rooms. Ed followed the same pattern as he had done upstairs as they passed through each one.

Her crew was seated at the table when she reached the dining room. After the introductions, she showed Ed her office, where he closely studied the blueprints.

In the kitchen, two men were occupied with ripping up the flooring, while a third painted the ceiling in the utility room. Ed looked around, then backed out of the room. "I'd like to walk around the outside."

Tori and Dan followed the man's slow pace as he examined the foundation, porch, and roof.

When he stepped back, his head tilted to look up at the turret, Tori said, "The roof is new. Colt McLean, the contractor, had it replaced before starting the construction for the new building."

Opening the back door, she said, "On this side are my living quarters, which are off-limits for the inspection."

She motioned for Dan and Ed to precede her into the pantry, closing the door behind her. "Only a few people know how to access the staircase, and it's how I want to keep it." She pulled a shelf away from the wall, activating a hidden lever to open the door. The two men followed her down the stairs.

Ed stopped, staring in amazement. "How many bottles are here?"

"Taking an inventory has been on the back burner, so I'm not sure."

Ed strolled around the room. His sharp gaze didn't seem to miss much. "Absolutely amazing."

Tori opened a door, flipping on the light switch. "Furnace, air-conditioning, hot water heater and electrical."

Inside, Ed spent several minutes before walking out. Dan asked, "Seen enough, Ed?"

"Yes." Ed walked out, dusting his hands.

"Tori, let's go to your office and talk strategy."

They circled around, entering the front door where the two men retrieved their briefcases. They weaved through the rooms. When they reached the dining room, Colt, David, and Parker had joined the four women seated at the table.

After the introductions, Tori asked, "Dan, any problem if we stay here? I'd like to include my team in this conversation."

"If you're comfortable with it, so am I," Dan said, dropping onto a chair. He set his briefcase alongside him.

Ed sat next to him.

David picked up two stapled sets of papers from a stack in front of him, handing them to Dan. "My supplement and the one from Granger and Lewis on the additional modifications to the tunnel. I have additional copies if you need them."

Dan quickly scanned them. "Keep them for now. I'll see how this plays out before I decide to give Marshal a copy of the reports. I do plan to tell him what we have."

"Dan, did you see today's *Metro*? I'm front-page news again."

"Yes, I did. Between the city's unwarranted actions and the newspaper articles, we have a solid case for litigation. Another point I plan to make. Ed, what's your opinion of the house?"

"A few areas need repair, the porch, a couple of outside light fixtures, outside paint, and of course, the rooms that still need new wallpaper. I didn't see any structural issues that would justify the property's condemnation. No water or dampness in the rooms under the house, which is usually the case in old houses like this. Even the heating, air conditioning system, and hot water heater are up to date. This house appears to be in exceptionally good condition for its age."

David said, "I was raised in this house. Over the years, there have been several renovations. The wine cellar is one, and the kitchen. I know Elly had some of the electrical wiring and plumbing replaced."

Ed said, "Quite frankly, I'm shocked at the city's response."

"You are echoing our sentiments," Dan said. "*The Metro* article mentioned grave concerns in the community. I haven't been able to find out who or why. However, I believe this visit by the city inspectors will be as enlightening to them as it has been for you. It's going to be interesting to see their response."

With a wolfish grin, he added, "Will Marshal will be between the proverbial rock and a hard place. Nowhere to go. If he tries to move forward with the condemnation, I can crucify him in court. If he doesn't, he's caused unwarranted financial damage to Tori's new business. He and the city could be on the hook for the damages."

Hearing Ed's opinion was a huge boost to her

confidence. Some of the tension faded. "Dan, if you're agreeable, this is what I want to do." Tori outlined the steps she'd formulated.

Dan grinned. "It's your show. I don't have a problem with any of it. But are you certain you want to meet them outside by yourself?"

"Absolutely. I want Marshal and his personnel to understand who they are dealing with up front."

Dan's eyes sparked with approval as he said, "We'll wait inside. Does anyone have any questions?" He glanced around the table at Tori's team. All stared back with a look of determination. The doorbell rang. He looked at his watch. "Showtime."

Chapter 20

Even after the doorbell had rung a second time, Tori waited until everyone was in place in the foyer. Before she opened the door, Tori gave them one last glance. Mia was right. She wasn't alone.

Tori took a deep breath, willing her heart to slow, then pulled the door open enough to slip outside, forcing five men to step back. She immediately recognized the one in front from his picture on the city's website. Will Marshal, slightly overweight and balding, was in his late forties. He held a briefcase in one hand.

His eyes raked over her hair pulled back in a ponytail, t-shirt, worn jeans and boots. While he still smiled, the look in his eyes perceptibly changed, becoming dismissive. "Are you Miss Winters?"

She hooked her thumbs in the front pockets of her jeans. "Yes."

He extended his hand. "I'm Will Marshal, the city attorney."

Though she glanced at it, she didn't move. "I recognize you from my research."

Startled, Marshal quickly pulled his hand back. "Well then, I assume you know we're here to inspect the house and property."

"Yes. Please introduce me to these men."

"Wouldn't you prefer to go inside?"

"Not until I know who is walking into my home," she said, emphasizing home.

He shrugged. "This is Murray Sadler, building manager. Carter Evans and Dale Miller, two independent inspectors I hired to ensure impartiality, and Lane Watkins. He'll record the proceedings." He motioned to the video camera the man held.

After nodding to acknowledge the introductions, she said, "No. He won't."

"Uh … won't what, Miss Winters?"

"Take pictures or record the inspection."

With a condescending tone, he said, "Miss Winters. There is nothing to be concerned about. The video is as much for your benefit as it is for us."

Tori snapped back. "Mr. Marshal. This is my home. I will not allow any pictures or recordings. In fact, I see no reason for Mr. Watkins to be here."

She looked at Watkins. "Please leave."

Marshal blinked in disbelief.

Tori stared back with a hard look. Refusing to give an inch, she waited.

"Lane, wait in the car," Marshal finally said.

Tori turned, opening the door. With a graceful sidestep, she twisted to watch the men's reaction as they stepped inside. The daunting group facing them triggered a look of surprise that quickly morphed to shock as their eyes flicked around. Marshal looked upward at the magnificence of the chandelier with an expression of disbelief.

As Tori closed the door, she wondered what he had expected—cobwebs, dirt, dilapidated walls, and floors? She stepped around the group to face them. Unable to resist a subtle taunt, she said, "The chandelier is an original Waterford. As you can see, it's in excellent condition, worth around twenty thousand dollars. A smaller version is in the dining room. I would say this foyer rivals the one in the historic Granbury Opera House."

Marshal's lips thinned as his gaze shifted to the people in front of him. Behind him, Sadler's eyes darted everywhere but at her. Dumbfounded, the inspectors slowly looked at the ceiling and walls.

Tori motioned toward each individual as she made the introduction. "Mia O'Brien, General Manager, and Heidi Grant, Director of Operations for the Red Door Inn, LLC. Parker Hayes, Hayes Security and Investigations, head of security for the inn. David Tucker, CEO of Tucker Engineering, Colt McLean, CEO of McLean Construction, Edgar Henley, Holcomb Engineering, the independent inspector we hired and my attorney, Daniel Foote, who you already know." Even to her ears, it was impressive. She looked at Marshal. "Please introduce your men."

In clipped tones, he rattled off the names before stepping toward Dan. "We already have a problem, Dan.

Miss Winters has refused to allow a video recording of the inspection."

Before Dan could respond, Tori moved closer, forcing Marshal to look at her. "Mr. Marshal, this is my property … my home … my decision. It isn't up for debate. Now, shall we proceed ahead with the inspection?"

Stymied and not bothering to hide his displeasure, Marshal said, "Carter, you take the upstairs. Dale, you start down here. Once we're done inside, we'll examine the tunnel."

Tori angrily jabbed her hand to stop the men. "Mr. Marshal, you seem to have difficulty understanding your position in *my* home. You are not in charge of this inspection. I am. I have graciously acceded to your request. One, which I would add didn't have a semblance of courtesy for my convenience, to conduct … what can only be termed as an unwarranted, ill-advised inspection."

Her voice vibrated with anger. "I resent your intrusion. This is private property, and you will adhere to my terms. I will conduct you from room to room, providing full access to the house except for my living quarters. Your inspections will be overseen by Mr. Henley and my attorney. If you have questions, you will direct those questions to me … not my attorney. Your decision and this inspection are costing me time and money. You've made a serious mistake. One I won't forget. Have I made myself clear?"

Marshal's head drew back as his shoulders straightened. Resentment flashed in his eyes.

Tori brushed past him. "We'll start with the library." She slid the doors open.

The inspectors whipped out notepads and pens before striding into the library, followed by Marshal and Sadler. They came to an abrupt halt to stare at a room lit by the morning sunlight streaming through the windows. After a quick glance at each other, the inspectors walked around, scrutinizing the ceiling, baseboards, window frames and tapping the walls, much as Ed had done. They even examined the wall outlets and lights. They moved furniture to look underneath as if hoping to find some hidden flaw. One even lifted the cushion on the bench in the curve of the turret. From the doorway, Dan and Ed kept an eye on them.

Once they finished, Tori said, "Upstairs next." Earlier, it had been agreed that Mia would participate in the inspection. Everyone else would wait in the dining room.

In the master bedroom, Tori said, "Miss O'Brien is an expert on antiques. Mia, please tell them about the etagere." She pointed to the eight-by-five-foot mirrored display case with elaborately carved individual holders for objects down each side.

Mia stepped forward. "It is an original Alexander Roux, dating back to 1850 or thereabout. Value is approximately $35,000."

Forced to listen to Mia's enthusiastic and detailed description of the other antiques and their values, Tori grinned at the irritation on Marshal's face. Though he rigidly stood on one side of the room, he refused to look at

Mia. Instead, he focused his attention on the inspectors. Sadler couldn't stand still, continually shifting his feet.

As they moved from room to room, Mia continued her lengthy descriptions while the men searched.

In the attic, the two men prowled, closely studying the ceiling as they had in the other rooms. She figured they were looking for water damage or cracks. Next, she opened the door under the staircase. After the trek down and back up, the inspectors' notepads and pens disappeared. She hadn't seen them write a single note. Marshal's face had settled into rigid lines, his jaw tightly clenched.

Before they headed down the stairs, she asked, "Any questions, gentlemen?"

No one answered.

Downstairs, Tori walked into the living room, explaining the renovations. Mia again pointed out the antiques. The inspectors did much the same as in the other rooms, only in less time, as if they were simply going through the motions. With a flourish, Tori slid open the sliding doors. While the music room didn't have the sparkle of the living room, it still had a quiet dignity.

Dan stepped alongside Tori. "There is a feature I'd like to point out about this room. The acoustics are phenomenal. Tori, would you mind giving us a demonstration?"

Surprised, she stared at him. He motioned toward the piano.

While she removed her boots, she said, "The piano

was purchased in the early 1940s for my grandmother Elly Leichter. I've been told it was shipped from New York." She spun on the bench, positioning her feet on the pedals.

For a moment, she paused, considering which piece to play. Then her inner demon beckoned, and her fingers struck the keys for the *William Tell Overture Finale*. It had always been a favorite with the children at birthday parties. It was the theme song for the Lone Ranger. When she finished, a brief silence filled the room, then loud applause from the inspectors and Dan and Ed. Tori noticed, though, Marshal and Sadler were less than appreciative.

His eyes twinkling with humor, Dan said, "As you have heard, Miss Winters is a very accomplished pianist."

Tori laced her boots, saying, "Shall we continue?" She slid open the doors leading to the dining room.

Inside, Cammie, Tina, Heidi, Parker, David, and Colt were seated at the table.

"Gentlemen, this is Cammie Dodd, Culinary Director for the inn, and our Advertising Director, Tina Lopez. We're using this room for a temporary office."

The inspectors didn't bother to examine the room.

She stepped into the hallway and then into her office. She waited for everyone to enter before saying, "Blueprints for the new construction and the renovations are on the table if you would care to examine them. Which, by the way, were approved by your office, Mr. Sadler."

Sadler's eye twitched as he stared over her shoulder.

Her gaze shifted to Marshal. "The 2,500-square-foot

building, the construction you stopped, Mr. Marshal, will house the office for the Red Door Inn, a gift shop featuring products from local artists in the Granbury area, and a museum. A two-bedroom apartment will be added to the garage. Any questions, gentlemen?"

No one spoke up.

"Since the kitchen is being renovated, we'll have to go out the front door and around to the back. Mr. Evans, Mr. Miller, I am sure you will want to examine the outside."

With difficulty, she didn't smile at their disgruntled look.

At a pace much faster than Ed's earlier, the two men circled the house, barely glancing at the roof or foundation. Inside, they casually glanced at the utility room but perked up when she said, "I'm sure you'll be interested in the wine cellar."

More interested in the wine than in the cellar, Tori answered the two men's questions. By the time they had finished, Marshal's lips were a thin line. If possible, his jaw even more rigid.

When they walked outside, David and Colt joined them.

Tori said, "Do you have any questions about the house?" When no one answered, she said, "Then Mr. McLean will show you the tunnel. He and Mr. Tucker will be able to answer any questions."

Marshal headed toward the sinkhole. Like a drowning man grabbing a rope, he exclaimed, "That certainly looks dangerous." As they stopped near the sloping entrance, he eyed the planks with suspicion. "Are you certain this is safe?"

"Absolutely," Colt said.

As they had prearranged, David stepped up, explaining why the tunnel collapsed.

Marshal looked at him in disbelief. "You expect us to believe this was caused by someone digging a hole in the side of the wall?"

"Yes, I do. Before Mr. McLean started the demolition, he examined the tunnel to ensure there weren't any structural problems. Since the hole had been covered with wood, no one knew it was there."

"Well, if it happened once, it could happen again," Marshal growled. His eyes flashed with satisfaction. "This by itself is enough to establish the property is unsafe."

For the first time, Dan spoke up. "I wouldn't rush to such a conclusion just yet. Mr. Tucker, a well-qualified engineer, has surveyed the tunnel, including seismic readings. I have his report indicating the tunnel is structurally sound."

"It's only one opinion. I don't mean to disparage your report, Mr. Tucker, but you are, after all, associated with this property."

Dan held up his hand. "I have a second report from G&L Engineering confirming Mr. Tucker's survey. There is one additional point, as you will see when we get into the tunnel. Mr. McLean has installed support beams along the tunnel walls, despite both surveys indicating such action was unnecessary. After the installations, Mr. Tucker,

Mr. Granger and Mr. Lewis reexamined the tunnel. I have their addendums to the original report addressing the additional structural support. Quite frankly, Miss Winters has taken every possible step, and more, to ensure the tunnel is safe."

Despite the hot sun, Marshal's face had a sickly hue. He looked like a man who had just been cut off at the knees.

Tori sidestepped down the planks. It didn't take long to walk the length of the tunnel. Neither the inspectors, Marshal nor Sadler, were inclined to tarry as they quickly and silently strode back to the entrance. After walking out of the tunnel, Marshal pulled Sadler and the two inspectors to the side. From the angry gestures and taut faces, it was apparent the inspectors weren't happy.

Ed stepped closer to Dan and Tori. With a low tone, he said, "Marshal's got a problem. I've overheard some of the comments between Miller and Evans. Like me, they spotted minor issues but nothing to justify condemning the property. They don't understand why there was even an inspection in the first place. Their reputations are on the line, and they don't appreciate Marshal's misrepresentation of the condition of the house and property."

Finally, Sadler and the two inspectors headed toward the driveway.

Marshal stepped toward her. His manner stiff, he said, "Miss Winters, I'd like to meet with you and Dan before I leave."

"Let's go to my office," Tori said.

Marshal never said a word as they worked their way back to the front of the house. Inside, he grabbed the briefcase he'd left in the foyer. The hallway floor was finished, and the men were gone, so they had a direct path to her office.

Marshal closed the doors before taking a seat. Uneasy, he shifted in the chair. He cleared his throat as he shot a sharp look at Dan, sitting relaxed, then at Tori.

Seemingly as unperturbed as Dan, none of the anxiety crawling inside her showed on her face while Tori waited.

Marshal cleared his throat again before saying, "I've certainly been blindsided by this from the start. First, my sincere apologies, Miss Winters. After the tunnel collapsed, I was informed, by a very credible source, that your grandmother had allowed the house to deteriorate to the point it was in serious disrepair and, along with the tunnel, represented an immediate and dangerous liability. If you were allowed to proceed with your plans, someone would be injured or killed. Your ignorance and gullibility in refusing to recognize the dangers created an untenable situation. It's obvious none of it was as represented."

Dan's calm demeanor shifted to anger. "Who was your informant?"

"I'd rather not say. There is no reason to make a bad situation even worse. The question now is how to resolve this?"

Gimlet-eyed, Dan leaned forward. "We can both agree that you and the city have a problem. Your actions and the damaging information leaked to the news media will have a detrimental impact on the financial success of Miss Winters' inn. Then add the stress she's experienced. My client has ample grounds for a lawsuit."

A look of vexation crossed Marshal's face. "Dan, a lawsuit isn't going to solve anything. I think we can both agree to that fact as well."

"No! I don't. A lawsuit will rectify the damage your precipitous and unwarranted actions have caused Miss Winters. In court, we can prove beyond any doubt there was a conspiracy afoot to defraud my client of her property. The publicity alone will go a long way toward eradicating the damage Miss Winters has experienced."

Marshal tensed. His eyes flashed. "Strong, provocative words. You can't prove it."

Dan's lips curved in a smile that never reached his eyes. "I think we both know I can. Why else were you out here this morning, ready to crucify Miss Winters? I'd be willing to bet that in your briefcase is a signed condemnation order you planned to hand her before you walked out the door. A decision was made before you even conducted a semblance of an investigation. If this goes to Court, I'll subpoena every record the city has in connection to Miss Winters' property … and your employees. You won't be able to deny it."

Marshal stirred in his chair, though his gaze stayed locked on Dan's face.

If Tori hadn't been acutely aware of every change in the man's demeanor, she would have missed it. Fascinated by Dan's legal machinations, Tori's anxiety eased. He had Marshal on the ropes and wasn't giving an inch.

The intensity of Dan's voice deepened. "You revoked her permit without warning. You didn't ask if today was convenient. You show up to inspect her home with less than twenty-four hours notice. Then, you plan to film the proceeding. The only reason was to document what you believed you'd find. I heard what you said on the porch. It wasn't to her benefit. It was additional evidence you planned to use if she tried to obtain an injunction or filed a lawsuit. Your apology doesn't eliminate the damage you've done, but a lawsuit will. I won't have any problem proving my accusations. Someone played you. I intend to find out who and why. In the meantime, I'd like to hear how you plan to fix this if you want to avoid a nasty litigation."

Tori wasn't surprised to see a look of relief flicker across Marshal's face. Dan had handed him a way out.

"Miss Winters, tomorrow, you will receive an official notification advising your permit has been reinstated. I will issue a press release that after an investigation, my office ascertained the allegations regarding the liability of your property were unfounded."

Dan said, "Add an apology to Miss Winters for the damage the accusations caused, along with a statement regarding the inaccuracy of the recent news reports."

Marshal grimaced. "Going for the throat, are you?"

Dan didn't bother to answer, just smiled with a wolfish look.

"I will include an official apology and refute the news

reports. In return, I want a written release that Miss Winters will not file a lawsuit."

"Will, you are in no position to make any demands. My client isn't signing anything."

Before Marshal could protest, Tori leaned forward. "I applied for a food service permit. Sadler's department has refused to issue it. In your official notification, add confirmation the permit has been granted. In addition, I want your written assurance that I will receive the city's full cooperation in issuing future permits or the required inspections as part of the construction process."

She gave him a piercing stare. "I don't plan on taking any further legal action. But if I encounter any more roadblocks from you or other city personnel, I won't give you a second chance. Next time, I will file a lawsuit. Here's something you need to consider. The Red Door Inn is good business for Granbury. This isn't your typical B&B. My great-grandfather's legacy, a notorious reputation, and an eighty-year-old murder mystery add a unique twist that will draw in the tourists."

For a moment, he stared at her. "It certainly was a mistake to underestimate you, Miss Winters."

"Why, thank you. I'll take that as a compliment."

Dan grinned, this time with humor. "If you'd asked, I could have told you."

Marshal stood, picking up his briefcase. "I won't say it was a pleasure. I did, however, enjoy your performance, even your choice of music. The Lone Ranger?"

He started for the door, then stopped. "I'm curious

about the name, Red Door Inn."

Tori chuckled. "Red Door was the name of my great-grandfather's casino."

"Ah. An inn named after a gambling casino and the Lone Ranger. Why do I feel as if I walked into a well-laid trap?"

Tori said, "Next time, you might want to check your sources before you rush to a judgment. Besides, I had … how did you put it … a very credible source tell me, 'he doesn't have a leg to stand on, he just doesn't know it yet.'"

With a mocking glance at Dan, Marshal said, "I wonder who it could have been." He tipped his fingers to his forehead. "I predict your inn is going to be a roaring success. I truly hope that the next time we meet, it will be under more favorable conditions. I can show myself out, albeit with a limp." Despite a troubled expression, he chuckled as he walked out, closing the door behind him.

Tori said, "I could almost like the man if he had handled this differently. I noticed he didn't deny having the paperwork in his briefcase."

"He's a decent lawyer with a good reputation, which makes his actions even more suspicious. Someone with a strong influence was behind this. Does Swanson have that kind of clout?"

"I'm not certain. Maybe."

"Until we find out who it is, this isn't over." A grim look crossed his face. "The bug in your office confirms my suspicions there's more to this than what happened with the city. Do you have any questions before I leave?"

"No, I don't."

Tori opened the door. Everyone was clustered in the hallway.

Mia, an anxious look on her face, asked, "Well? What happened?"

"The construction permit has been reinstated."

"Then why aren't you jumping for joy?" she asked.

"I don't think it has sunk in yet."

Dan smiled at Tori. "We got past one huge hurdle today. I need to get back to Fort Worth." He shot a glance at the group. "Each of you was an invaluable asset. Thank you."

Ed waited in the foyer. Before he walked out, he shook Tori's hand. "This was a genuine pleasure. Once the inn is open, I'm making a reservation. I know my wife and I will enjoy spending a weekend here."

After she closed the front door, relief overwhelmed her. Tori leaned against it. Her eyes closed as the tension faded away.

"Tori, are you alright?" Mia asked.

Opening her eyes, Mia stood in front of her, frowning with concern. Behind her, the hallway was empty.

Tori smiled. "Absolutely. Where is everyone?"

"David, Colt, and Parker headed outside, talking about the tunnel. The team is in the dining room."

"Is there any coffee? I sure could use a cup. Even better would be a glass of wine, but it will have to wait."

"I figured you would. A fresh pot is ready, though

Parker has already made inroads on it. I swear he'd probably go stark-raving mad if he was deprived of his coffee. The pot is in the dining room. I had to move it with what's happening in the kitchen."

Laughing, Tori swung her arm around Mia's shoulder. "Come on, and I will tell everyone of the dastardly deeds we foiled today."

Chapter 21

*T*ori stopped in her office to grab her phone and saw she'd missed two calls from Jonah. Dang. She was surprised Jonah or Linc hadn't been pounding on the door, wanting to find out what was happening.

Just as the thought occurred, the doorbell rang. Tori stepped into the hallway and saw Linc charge inside, barely slowing to say hello to Cammie, who held the door open.

When he spotted her, he rushed along the hall, saying, "What's been happening here, Tori?"

"Calm down. It's all been fixed."

"Dad and I had to be in court this morning and didn't see the paper until we got back to the office. Is it true? Is someone coming out from the city to condemn the property?" He followed her into the office. "We can make some calls and see what we can learn. Dad didn't want to interfere until we had a chance to talk to you."

"Linc, sit down, and I'll explain, though I appreciate your concern and offer to help. It means a lot."

Exasperated, he dropped into a chair.

"Will Marshal, the city attorney, has already come and gone. After inspecting the house and tunnel, he reinstated the permit."

Linc stared at her with a stunned expression. "That's it?"

"Yes. How could there be anything else? You know there's nothing wrong with my property. And now, so does Marshal."

His stunned look turned to one of suspicion. "Why do I believe there's a lot more to it?"

Smiling, she shrugged.

"Okay. Now, I do know there's more."

"There really isn't." There was no point in talking about all the nitty-gritty details. "In the morning, Marshal is releasing a statement admitting there aren't any problems with my property." She added with an air of self-satisfaction, "There's a reporter at *The Metro* who will have egg all over her face."

"What about the tunnel since it did collapse? Dad mentioned surveys."

"Colt repaired the hole that caused the problem. I have two engineering surveys, one from David and another company in Fort Worth, stipulating the tunnel is safe. To make sure, Colt installed a few support beams. Hard for the city to argue otherwise with that type of evidence."

Footsteps echoed in the hallway. David walked in, followed by Colt and Parker.

Linc looked at them. "David, it sounds like you and Colt were the day's heroes. Tori was telling me about the tunnel. Hello, Parker. Looks like you've become part of her entourage."

Did she detect a snide tone in his voice? No, it was probably her imagination. Linc still smiled with that same easy grin.

David grinned at her. "Nah, it was all Tori. She trounced the enemy."

"Humph … I knew you weren't telling everything, Tori," Linc said.

"It's not important. All that matters is the construction is back on track," she said.

"I guess that's my cue to leave. I'll catch you later, Tori. Maybe I'll get to hear what *actually* happened."

It wasn't her imagination, a definite snit. "I'll walk out with you." As they stepped into the hallway, she said, "Before you go, let me show you the changes to the house."

After viewing the living room and library, his attitude appeared somewhat mollified, his smile genuine when he left. Entering the dining room, everyone was waiting for her.

Mia said, "Okay, we've waited long enough. What happened?"

Tori laughed. "It was rather anticlimactic. Dan did a heck of a job whittling him down. Marshal was under the impression the house and tunnel were in bad shape. Once he found out otherwise, he reversed his position. He'll issue a statement tomorrow." She looked at Colt. "We won't have any further issues with permits or inspections, including the food service permit."

Parker asked, "Did you find out who's pushing the issue?"

"No. Marshal wouldn't say, but Dan is still concerned."

"I am too. The issue with the city may be squared away, but the answer to what's been happening isn't. I've got to get back to my office. I'll see you later."

"Parker," Tori said.

He stopped.

"Thank you for staying."

He smiled. "Anytime. It was a real pleasure to hear you play." He walked out.

David said, "I have to leave as well. I'll stop by tomorrow to check on how everything is going."

"What I said to Parker is ditto for you."

Tori turned to her team. "There's no reason for you all to stick around. Let's take a couple of days off. We're in good shape."

"Tori, would you mind if I visited a few stores on the square? Start spreading the word about the plans for the inn," Tina asked.

"Not at all. It's a great idea. Until all of this popped up, I planned to do it myself."

Cammie piped up. "I'd like to go with you."

The two walked out, talking about whose car and what time, with Mia and Heidi close behind.

Tori said, "Come on, Colt. I want to see what Mia meant with her comment about the kitchen."

Stopping in the doorway, she exclaimed, "Oh, my, gosh." Except for the refrigerator, the room was gutted, no stove, dishwasher, or sink.

"The new appliances will be delivered today."

"Good lord! The refrigerator. I need to clean it out."

"Don't worry about it. I'll have one of the men move everything to the new one. Though, it probably won't be organized to your satisfaction."

With a sigh of relief that it was one task she didn't need to handle, she said, "It won't matter. I've got a feeling Cammie will rearrange it anyway."

After Colt left, Tori wandered to the front of the house to check on the progress of the music room, where men had started to strip the wallpaper.

The doorbell chimed, not once but a persistent three times. At the sight of two women standing on the porch, Tori barely restrained a groan, instead forcing her lips into a smile.

Myra brushed past her, followed by a slim, older woman Tori didn't recognize.

Intent on watching Tori with a malicious gleam, Myra never looked around. "Oh, my dear. I've heard the awful news. You can't imagine my distress. I had to come. This is Liz Talbot, the mayor's wife."

Tori nodded, extending her hand. "Tori Winters, nice to meet you."

Still eyeing her like a cat watching a mouse, Myra added, "They are new to the area and never knew your grandmother. I assured Liz that you wouldn't mind her seeing the house before—"

When her companion gasped, Myra finally stopped talking to look around. Stunned, her eyes widened, and her jaw dropped open.

Amused, Tori said, "Before what, Myra?"

"It … it gets torn down." Her hand fluttered in the air. "Good lord! Whatever have you done? Why would you waste money … on all this?"

"For the simple reason, the house isn't going to be torn down."

"Oh dear, I have been precipitous, haven't I?" she said, though her eyes glowed with satisfaction at being the bearer of bad news.

"I can assure you there isn't a problem with the city."

Myra said, "How horrible. Since you haven't been no-tified, I hate to be the one to tell you. I have it on good authority the city plans to condemn the property."

"Myra, the city attorney, Will Marshal, just left. The house isn't going to be torn down. In fact, Mr. Marshal re-instated my building permit, and I'm back on track with the construction. And, just who is your good authority. I'd be interested to find out who was the instigator of these malicious rumors."

Myra's face went slack with disbelief, then her lips thinned, and her eyes flashed with loathing. Just as quickly, she suppressed the emotion as she glanced at Liz Talbot standing in the archway to the living room.

The brief glimpse of hostility raised the hackles on Tori's neck. While Myra was spiteful and petty, Tori was stunned by the woman's animosity.

Lowering her voice, Myra hissed, "Not everyone is a fan of your present endeavors. As to who, I don't see that it's relevant. Besides, it's your tunnel that has caused all the problems for everyone."

"Yes. It's a pity the city didn't bother to investigate the unwarranted allegations. It would have solved all those problems."

Though Myra's nostrils flared with anger, before she could respond, Liz Talbot walked up. Her eyes narrowed as she looked at Myra.

Tori wondered if the woman had heard the byplay between her and Myra.

With a gracious smile, her face relaxed as she turned to Tori. "Miss Winters, I am so glad there is no truth to the dreadful rumors running amuck. As Myra said, we are new to Granbury. Nevertheless, we have heard a lot about your grandmother and this house. May I go into the library? I love books, and the room is very appealing."

After hearing Liz's comments, Tori was certain the woman had heard. And judging by the sour look on Myra's face, Myra also knew it.

"Please, it's Tori, and yes. I'd give you a tour, but as you can tell, I am in the middle of renovations."

"The chandelier is gorgeous. Is it Waterford?"

"Why yes, you have a good eye."

"Antiques are a hobby of mine."

"I'll have to introduce you to Mia O'Brien, General Manager for the Red Door Inn. I am turning the house into a B&B. Mia is the resident expert on antiques."

"I'd love to meet her. The inn sounds fascinating, and I would like to hear more."

Tori and Liz strolled into the library as they talked, leaving Myra with a bug-eyed look before scuttling after them. After discussing the various antiques, they moved to the living room. Tori explained about the work in progress as the workman gathered their tools and left. Liz was particularly taken by the oil painting and listened intently to Tori's explanation of her great-grandparent's history.

As they wandered across the room, she stopped in the doorway to the music room.

"What a beautiful piano."

"From what I have been told, my grandmother loved to play it."

"Do you play?" Liz asked.

Before she could answer, Myra, who stood next to Liz, said, "I'm sure it takes an accomplished pianist. Don't you agree, Tori?"

With an amused look, Tori said, "Yes, it would."

By the time Liz was ready to leave, Tori had found an ally. Much to Myra's chagrin, Liz promised to help spread the word about the inn.

Despite her sickeningly sweet voice when she said goodbye, Myra gave Tori a spiteful look as she stepped past her.

Tori stood in the doorway, watching them walk to their cars. She couldn't suppress a sense of foreboding from Myra's reaction.

After a quick exchange of words, Liz, who had parked behind Myra's car, pulled out. Tori started to close the door, then stopped. Myra stood by the open car door, looking toward the back of the house. With an annoyed look, her gaze darted toward the front door. Wondering what Myra was up to, Tori quickly closed it and dashed to the window in the library.

She brushed the drape's edge aside. "What the—" she muttered. Tommie Logan had walked into view, stopping in front of Myra. The foreboding she already felt deepened. Why would Myra talk to one of the construction crew, particularly Logan? It was certainly out of character.

Whatever he said had the woman furiously gesturing with her hand. Even from Tori's position inside the house, she couldn't miss the incensed look on Myra's face. Logan didn't like it either. His body tensed as he leaned forward. His finger jabbed, stopping just short of her chest as if he was telling her what to do.

With another angry motion of her hand, Myra tossed her bag into the car and hopped in. Logan had to step back to keep the door from hitting him as she slammed it shut. Tires spun as she hit the accelerator to back out.

His hands fisted on his hips, Logan watched her drive off, then turned to stare at the house. From the ugly look on his face, Tori was thankful he couldn't see her.

Shaken by what she'd seen, Tori slowly walked out of the room. Why would Myra even know Logan?

Colt's voice broke into her musings. He'd stepped out of the kitchen. Motioning, he said, "Take a look."

While she had been occupied with her visitors, Colt had been busy. "Oh, my. Cammie may never come back to earth." While it was the same kitchen with old cupboards, the new paint and flooring accented the new appliances and granite-style sink with brass fixtures.

Colt's fingers trailed over the counter. "I still think you should let me replace the countertops. You're going to use the kitchen as is for several months. It won't take long."

"As good as this looks, you're right."

"Do you want to pick out a pattern?"

"No. I'll let Cammie decide."

Ben walked up. "Well, what do you think?"

"I love it."

"Colt, anything else before I leave?" he asked.

"No, I'll be right behind you. See you in the morning, Tori."

She walked with them to the front door, making sure it was locked after they left. Slowly meandering through the rooms, she turned off the lights, letting the day's tension fade. In the kitchen, she stood, reveling in the changes. What an amazing difference. She grabbed a sandwich and bottle of water, then headed to her office.

She eyed the stack of boxes. They had to be unpacked, but not tonight. She settled in her chair and eyed the computer. The research could wait. Instead, Tori propped her feet on the corner of the desk. After opening the bottle, she took a deep swallow, then munched on the sandwich as she thought. The day's events rolled in her mind.

Whatever satisfaction she'd felt from the rout of the city was overshadowed by Dan's comments and the ugly scene with Logan and Myra. Dan said it wasn't over, and he was right. She shoved the last piece of sandwich in her mouth, then picked up her tablet, scrolling through the pages until she reached the drawing.

She studied the words around the outside of the circle and her name in the center. For a moment, she hesitated, then added Myra to the list. All the new entry did was add more confusion.

One set of events, the tunnel and permit, were undoubtedly connected. The second set, fire, accident, new men, bug, tablet and probably Ethel were connected. Then there was the body … no connection to any of it. Parker had referred to it as collateral damage because the hole where it was buried was the culprit, triggering everything. And now, she had Myra and Logan to add to the mix.

Her fingers tapped the arm of the chair. The niggling feeling tickled in her mind. What did it all have to do with her? A new thought buzzed. Maybe it wasn't. Was all this connected to the house itself?

Tori erased her name and wrote house, then studied each piece of the puzzle. She could draw an arrow from the tunnel and permit to the house in the center of the circle. Marshal had said he didn't receive a complaint until after the tunnel collapsed.

If someone … dang. Tori was tired of thinking of this person as a nebulous, vague entity. Right now, she'd call him X. If X used the tunnel to get her property, why plant a man inside the house? Why the bug? What did X hope to hear that he couldn't find out from the city personnel? X certainly had a direct and powerful inroad there, so how did any subsequent incidents connect to the house? Much to her dismay, they didn't. And the attack on Ethel even less. Tori couldn't link any of the pieces other than the tunnel and permit. The substitution didn't change a thing.

She turned her thoughts back to the scene with Logan and Myra. How did it fit in? What was behind it, and did it have anything to do with X? She straightened. Her feet hit the floor. Could Myra be linked to the permit? As a new hire, Logan was linked to the other events. Was Myra the connecting link between the two sets? Nothing said X was a man. Myra? No! Not possible. This was a woman who never had a thought for anything other than her social status and attire.

Social status, the words stuck in her mind. To Myra, it was all important. But would she be willing to kill to protect it? Myra had a single-mindedness that, at times, was scary. As much as she would like to cast Myra as the evil doer, X, even to her untrained investigator's mind, there were too many loose ends. Even the permit was a stumbling block. Would the city attorney have reacted as he did to a complaint from Myra? Considering X's actions to date, there must be a powerful motive, and Tori didn't believe it was social status.

Cripes, her brain was a chaotic jumble of endless questions and no answers. All she was doing was running in circles, going nowhere. No wonder she envisioned

Myra, of all people, as the mastermind. Time to put it aside and let her mind clear. She'd come back to it later. Laying the tablet aside, Tori turned her attention to the computer and picked up where she had left off with the newspapers. It didn't take long for her interest to fade. Exhausted, she needed to shut it all down.

Turning off the lights, Tori headed to her bedroom, though she did stop to admire the kitchen again. While it wasn't what she had planned for the new inn, it was a step forward.

After locking her door, she filled the large bathtub with water. Too tired to wash her hair, she piled it atop her head. While she wished for a glass of wine, she settled for a cold bottle of water. With everything still packed, Tori didn't have the energy to hunt down the corkscrew.

Sliding under the hot water, she breathed a heavy sigh of relief. A major setback had been overcome. With the city's threat eliminated, it was full steam ahead with the renovations. Tori chuckled as she thought about Marshal's reaction as she escorted him through the house. As she discovered, he had expected to see the place in a state of decay. His 'credible source' had certainly led him down the garden path. This was one day Tori didn't think he would forget any time soon.

Then there was Myra. Despite her resolution to push aside her worries, her thoughts shifted to the scene on the driveway. As it replayed in her mind, her sense of satisfaction faded. Today, she won a skirmish, not the war. Tori moaned. Cripes, another annoying metaphor, but how true. As satisfying as today had turned out, she couldn't get complacent. The danger still existed. X lost today, but what about tomorrow? Even the hot water couldn't stop the chills racing over her skin.

Who was X? She had to add Myra as a possibility. After all, Judd was still her top suspect. Was Myra the brains behind him? The notion seemed so ridiculous she almost laughed. But then she couldn't deny the ugly scene between Myra and Logan, or the look she'd caught on Myra's face. She had no doubt that Myra wouldn't hesitate to discredit or even try to destroy Tori's dream for the house.

What could X hope to gain? How could she find the answers when she didn't have a single clue about X's motivation? Or did she?

An unbelievable thought had Tori sitting upright, sending water droplets flying. Was that it? Why hadn't she thought of it earlier? The exhaustion vanished. Energized, she scrambled out of the tub, grabbed the towel, and quickly dried off. After pulling on her nightshirt and underwear, she raced out of the bedroom. Her hand smacked the light switch as she darted into her office.

She picked up the tablet and quickly erased house in the center of the circle. Then Tori wrote another word. Slowly, one by one, she drew an arrow from the words around the outside of the circle to what she had written. Wild and implausible, it all seemed to fit. "Oh! My! God!" she muttered.

Chapter 22

arely able to contain her impatience, she was dressed before the sun had peeked on the horizon, even though she had to wait to make a call. Tori had spent half the night working and reworking her new theory, searching for holes.

Flipping on the kitchen light, she took a moment to gaze in delight at the new appliances before filling the coffee machine.

Once the coffee was ready, she filled the thermos, grabbed a couple of sandwiches from the new refrigerator, dropped them into a box, and headed out the back door. Buoyed by a sense of well-being, she stood on the back porch, breathing in the cool night air. Waving the flashlight's beam across the ground, Tori carefully strode across the yard. Not a hint of moonlight broke the heavy darkness between her and the small circle of illumination from the portable spotlight near the tunnel's entrance. Carl saw her coming and headed toward her.

"Good morning. Everything is still packed. These are sandwiches from yesterday."

"They'll do just fine. I was surprised to see the light in the kitchen. It's earlier than usual." He reached for the box and set it on the table. Over his radio, he said, "Breakfast has arrived." The radio crackled as Steve responded.

"Can you stay a bit and talk?" Carl asked as he pulled a chair around.

Tori did, enjoying the visit with the two men. When she stood to leave, the sun was rising. Some of her nervous energy had dissipated. It was a good start to the morning.

As she walked away, Steve said, "She's just like her grandmother, Miss Elly. She wasn't high in the instep either." His tone was low, and Tori was sure she wasn't meant to hear, but the sound carried in the quiet of the early morning air. Warmed by his words, she trotted inside. She filled a cup and walked to her office.

Eagerly, Tori studied the drawing, looking at the connections with a fresh eye. She still couldn't find a flaw in her reasoning. The notation about Ethel had her checking the hospital, but no change.

It was still too early to call Parker. Instead, hoping some physical activity would ease her jumbled nerves, Tori hauled a box from the office to the kitchen. It felt good to unpack it, moving the contents to the cupboards and drawers. The heavier boxes with canned goods went to the pantry, where she restocked the shelves.

Intermittently, she glanced at her watch, willing the hands to move faster. When Colt walked in, it was a welcome distraction.

He eyed the empty boxes piled near the back door.

"You've been busy. Do you need any help?" He helped himself to the coffee.

"I've got it. I needed something to keep me busy."

Her tone must have alerted him. Taking a swig of the hot brew, he studied her over the rim of the cup. "What's going on?"

"Nothing I'm ready to talk about. At least, not until Parker gets here, though it does involve Logan. I'd still like to keep him out of the house."

"It won't be a problem."

"Now that we have the permit reinstated, when do you plan to start back up with the construction?"

"I've got to reset the schedule. I need to finish the music and dining room, plus the entrances for the tunnel. I should be able to at least continue with the demolition. That excavator sitting idle is costing money."

Voices echoed outside. Colt's crew had arrived. "I'll have one of the men get rid of the boxes for you." He finished the coffee and set the cup in the sink before walking out.

She glanced at her watch again. Anticipation surged as she hit the speed dial.

Parker answered on the second ring. "I didn't expect to hear from you this early. Something happen?"

"Maybe, maybe not, but I need to talk to you."

"I'm almost to my office. Let me get a problem squared away, then I'll head your way."

She went back to unpacking. When Parker walked into the kitchen, Tori was on the last box.

He stared in amazement. "Wow! What a change. Has Cammie seen it?"

"Not yet."

"I'd like to be around when she does." He zeroed in on the coffee machine. "Ah … coffee." He poured a cup. Leaning against the counter, he eyed her. "For someone who should be riding a high over yesterday's rout of the city attorney, you look like a frazzled cat on a hot wire. What's up?"

"Well, thank you for that inspiring description."

He grinned and took another sip of coffee.

"Let's talk about it in my office. Do you have your debugger with you?"

His eyes narrowed. "I do."

Colt walked in. "Parker, saw you drive in. Any news?"

"Yes, there is."

The two watched as Parker swept the room. "It's clean." Still, being cautious, he closed the doors before settling into a chair. "Someone tried to get into Ethel's room last night."

Tori gasped. "What! I called this morning, but the nurse didn't mention a problem. How do you know?"

"After Mia told us she was being moved, I put a round-the-clock guard at the hospital. It's impossible to access intensive care, so she was safe there. A private room isn't as secure. Last night, a man dressed in scrubs and pushing a cart attempted to enter Ethel's room. The guard became suspicious, and when he stopped the man, he bolted down the stairs and got away. It's why I had to stop at my office. A detective was waiting."

A sick feeling roiled inside her. If it hadn't been for Parker's foresight, Ethel could have been killed. "Why didn't you tell me?"

"You've had enough on your plate without adding another worry. Besides, it was a hunch on my part, a precaution."

Colt asked, "Any idea who it was?"

"No. The man was wearing a cap, mask, and gloves."

Tori cleared her throat and picked up her tablet. "Maybe what I've come up with isn't so far-fetched after all. I've been playing around with ideas about the motivation behind what's been happening."

Before handing it to them, she said, "Something else happened yesterday that might have some bearing on all this." She explained about the scene between Myra and Logan.

With an arrested look, Parker said, "Since her husband may be involved, it certainly moves Logan up the list of suspects. An interesting turn of events. I wonder what they were discussing." He took a sip of coffee.

"I might have a reason." She handed the tablet across the desk to Parker as she explained her drawing and how none of the events were connected until she made one change. Colt scooted his chair, leaning forward to look at it.

Her nervous tension built. Neither of them said anything. Was all this her wild imagination?

Then Parker looked up, a gleam of excitement in his eyes. "I think you're onto something."

In disbelief, Colt said, "All of this happened because of a skeleton in the tunnel?"

Parker said, "Can you print this for me?" He handed the tablet to her.

Tori accessed the print function, making two copies. She rolled her chair backward, where the printer sat on a small table behind her. Picking up the sheets of paper, she glanced at the drawing and the word written in capital letters—BODY—in the center of the circle. She passed them across the desk.

Parker set his cup down, reaching for the paper. For a moment, he scrutinized it, then mused, "The body was the catalyst, not the tunnel collapsing. Someone wants to know what you are doing about it. How? Get rid of two of Colt's crew to force him to hire replacements. Plant a man inside to keep an eye on your activities. A bug to listen in on your conversations. Stop your visit to Ethel to ask about the mystery man. And now, another attempt to silence her. It all makes sense, even if we don't know the why." He tapped the paper. "Could Myra be the mastermind, who you are calling X?"

Frustrated, Tori shook her head. "That thought has been driving me crazy. I just can't picture her having the clout to pressure Marshal, let alone doing all the rest."

"It wouldn't be the first time a woman was the power behind the scenes. Judd could still be the instigator with the city, and Logan is doing her dirty work."

"The city is the one flaw in my theory. Why the push?" Tori said.

Parker picked up his cup and took a swallow, his gaze thoughtful as he studied the drawing. "Distraction, smokescreen. Direct your attention elsewhere. Keep you busy. How much time have you spent researching the mystery man?"

"Hit and miss when I had spare time. And you're right, there's not been much. Besides, I didn't figure finding out was a high priority."

"If X had been successful in getting the city to condemn the property, it would certainly push your search to the back burner. You'd be too busy with a lawsuit to even think about who this guy was. It also bought X time to devise a permanent plan."

Tori wasn't sure she liked the word permanent since X had tried twice to kill Ethel.

He shook the paper. "We need to change the focus of our investigation. It's imperative we identify the body. Where do you stand on the newspaper archives?"

"I still have several years to go. I'll work on it today. What about Logan?"

"I need fingerprints. Something I planned to discuss with you and Colt today. I brought the equipment with me." He stared at the drawing. "While it looks like Logan is the inside man, I still need to get the prints for the other two. Colt, where are they?"

"Logan and Martell are outside working on the tunnel entrance. Crimshaw is with your man in the music room."

"I wonder if he's touched any of the furniture."

Colt said, "Ben would know." He tugged the phone from his shirt pocket. When Ben answered, he said, "Come to Tori's office."

After Ben walked in, Colt explained about the finger-prints.

Ben said, "Crimshaw helped move the furniture from the music room to the living room this morning."

Parker said, "Can you give the men a break and get them out of the house?"

"Yes, I can."

"Wait until I get to the living room," Parker told him.

Once the door closed behind Ben, Colt asked, "What about the other two?"

Parker's lips pursed as he thought. "Tori, I bet Mia's got a pitcher of tea in the refrigerator."

Puzzled, she looked at him. "Yes, she does. Why?"

"You're going to take iced tea to the men outside. I can get the prints off the glasses Martell and Logan use."

Colt said, "Parker, since the plan with the city failed, any ideas about what X may try next?"

A worried look settled over Parker's face. "Consider-ing how fast X reacted after the body was discovered, I'd say X is desperate, even irrational, making him or her all the more dangerous. Something's driving X hard. Tori could be the next target."

The furrows in Colt's brow deepened as he cursed. He rose and handed her the drawing. "I'll keep an eye on Logan." He walked out.

After the door closed, Parker said, "Short of kicking the entire crew out of here, it's going to be difficult to protect you. Until we figure out who is masterminding these attacks, you should consider stopping the construction."

Though fear stroked her, Tori gave her head an emphatic shake. "No. I'm not letting someone scare me or force me to stop what I've started. Believe me, Parker, I understand more than anyone I need to be careful."

"I didn't figure you'd take the easy way out. Come on. I want to find that piece of furniture."

"If it's any help, all the furniture was polished before Marshal showed up."

"That's good to know. I won't have to deal with a multitude of prints." He followed Tori out the door.

In the living room, Ben stood near the doorway to the music room, keeping an eye on the men. Two of Colt's regular crew stripped wallpaper while Barton and Crimshaw ripped up the old carpet.

Parker and Tori strolled into the living room, commenting on the changes.

Ben stepped into the music room. "Take a break. Be back in thirty minutes."

The men slowly meandered their way outside.

Once they were gone, Ben motioned toward a table amidst several other pieces of furniture near the wall.

"I'll get my kit. I left it in the utility room. Tori, let's start on getting the prints for the other two men."

In the kitchen, Tori intently listened to Parker's instructions. After he left carrying a small case, she pulled glasses from the cupboard, lining them up on the counter. Tori wiped each glass with a towel before setting it in a box she retrieved from the utility room. Next, she partially filled several plastic jugs with ice, then added the tea.

Looking out the window, she nervously eyed the men as they worked on the new steps.

Parker walked in, setting his case on the kitchen island.

"Did you get them," she asked.

"Yes. Are you about ready?"

Flustered by the unexpected anxiety, she said, "I hope this works." Tori set the containers in the box. "What about their gloves? Should I say something about them?"

"No. Just pass out the glasses with a friendly smile. Though, I expect they'll remove them. If they don't … well, let's not cross that bridge until we get there."

With a moan, Tori thought, *another disquieting metaphor*.

"I'd offer to carry it, but it's better if you do, less suspicious. Keep your eye on which glass each man uses."

"Will do," she said, with more confidence than she felt.

Carrying the box, she picked her way across the ground, musing over what a pleasant day this would be if it wasn't for the dark cloud hanging over her. Parker would never have said what he did about X if he wasn't convinced. He wasn't the type to exaggerate.

David came around the corner of the house, catching up with her.

"I thought you'd be knee-deep in reports or meetings today," she said, hiding her pleasure at seeing him.

"No, it's a light day. What have you got?"

"Mia made an abundance of iced tea. I thought Colt's men would like a glass."

"Let me carry it."

Not wanting to let David handle the box, she said, "I'll hand out the glasses. You take a jug and pour."

She stopped alongside Colt. "How's it going?"

"Look for yourself," he said.

Tori peered into the hole to see a series of steps angling toward the bottom.

"I'll pour the concrete for the pad later today. Once it sets, I'll start on the building over the opening."

Tori pushed the box toward him. Colt reached inside to pick up a glass. With a smile and cheerful hello, she moved from man to man. Alongside her, David filled the glasses. When Tori stopped in front of Logan, her anxiety spiked. He hesitated, giving her a sharp look, before picking up the glass. Martell was the last man. She hid her relief behind another bright smile. Both men had stripped off their gloves.

While she waited to collect the glasses, she talked to Colt and David, primarily about the tunnel. It didn't take long. The men gulped down the tea and asked for a refill. Once they finished, she let them set their glasses into the box, noting which glass was which.

Several of the men thanked her before she turned to walk back to the house, though Tori didn't miss Logan wasn't one of them.

Parker opened the door.

Behind her, David greeted him as he walked inside. "Wow, what a facelift." His gaze darted around the kitchen.

As Tori set the box on the counter, Parker said, "The men are still outside. Did you have any trouble?"

"No, I didn't. I got them." She identified the two glasses the men had used.

Bewildered, David said, "What's going on?"

"Fingerprints." With a paper towel, Parker reached into the box. He picked up each glass by the edge and set it next to the case.

With a grim look, David said, "Why do I feel there have been new developments?"

"I'll let Tori tell you. I need to get these lifted and get back to my office."

Fascinated, David and Tori watched while he dusted each glass, then lifted the prints using a piece of tape.

"There are newer methods, but I'm old school, and this works." Once he finished, he repacked the case and grabbed his computer bag. "I'll be back later," he said and headed out the door.

Tori stashed the glasses in the new dishwasher. "Let's talk in my office."

When she closed the door, David said, "This must be serious." He settled into a chair.

"It is." She told him about Myra's visit and the scene with Logan. "David, she was totally convinced the house was going to be torn down."

"You don't believe Myra is behind this, do you?"

"If I hadn't seen her talking to Logan, I wouldn't have thought so."

Troubled, he said, "There is that. And there doesn't seem to be a rational reason."

"Oh, I think there is." She handed him the drawing.

His eyes widened with astonishment as he studied it. "All this because of some guy buried years ago in the tunnel?"

"It would seem so. It's the only possibility that connects everything."

"How the devil could the murder of a man over eighty years ago affect anyone today?"

"I don't know."

"Then the attack on Ethel wasn't a random burglary. The intruder meant to shut her up."

Her tone grim, Tori said, "It's what's been haunting me. I don't even know if Ethel knows something. But she was almost killed because I made an entry on my tablet to visit her. It almost happened a second time." She told him about the latest attempt at the hospital.

"Thank god for Parker's heads-up thinking." A thoughtful look crossed his face. "Tori, there could be another reason. X may know something we don't. Ethel could be the key to all of this. Once the body was discovered, it may not have made a difference. X was going after her. Your note only precipitated the attack."

Tori let his comment settle in her mind. David wasn't saying it to appease her. She realized he could be right. "It means X knows my family, the history. Either Myra or

Judd fits that description. Parker described X as desperate, irrational. Not only because of how X reacted but the speed. Marshal said the city didn't receive the complaint until after the tunnel collapsed. The discovery of the body was front-page news. My permit was revoked the next day."

David's fingers tapped his knee as he studied the drawing. "When you look at the timeline, Parker is right. X acted fast and was willing to kill. But Myra? It still doesn't compute. What concerns me is when and where will X strike again?"

His words, echoing Parker's, set off a surge of chills. The first time she met Ethel, the woman said the house had secrets. Secrets that killed her grandmother. Were the secrets about to claim another victim?

Chapter 23

Shaking off her sense of trepidation, Tori said, "I still believe X is Judd. Marshal refused to tell us. He said he didn't want to make a bad situation worse. But it might account for that nasty scene on the driveway. I doubt there's anything Judd does that Myra wouldn't know. Inexplicably though, Logan seemed to be in control, not Myra."

David said, "It took a lot of stroke to have Marshal spinning in the wind. Judd's been a mover and shaker in this town as far back as I can remember. Old money and power. And Judd does know the history of your family. But I would have to point out, so does Myra."

He looked down at the paper he still held. "She's a Wainwright with social status and money that dates back to Frankie's era. Over the years, I've heard her make a few snide comments about how her grandfather made his money from the railroad, whereas Elly's father was a gangster and murderer. She always wanted to be one up on Elly."

With a wry smile, he added, "Your grandmother

tolerated her, but they were never close friends. What's more, Myra knew it, and it never set well. Myra likes to think of herself as Granbury's queen bee. The only problem is that was Elly. Still, I agree with you. All this seems to be more like Judd than Myra."

His comments reminded her about another incident. "After I announced my plans to turn the house into a B&B at Myra's party from hell, I was confronted by Judd *and* Myra. They showed up the next day and vehemently protested my plans. Judd warned me about the house's condition and what would happen if someone were killed or injured. He even threatened me. Told me I could end up dead like Elly if I stayed here. He hinted I didn't know what I was doing. What Marshal said echoed Judd's comments. According to his credible source, Elly had allowed the house to deteriorate, and my ignorance and naivety exacerbated the problem. Sure sounds like words from Judd Swanson's mouth."

"I remember," David said. "At the time, Judd led the charge about the condition of the house."

"That's not all. Dan confronted Marshal with the fact he had a condemnation order in his briefcase, ready to hand to me. Marshal didn't deny it. Then Myra shows up convinced the house will be torn down."

"If Judd is X, it makes sense." His brow crinkled with a worried look. "Tori, you should shut down the construction until we figure out what is going on."

For cripes sake, here she went again. "No, I'm not stopping any of the work."

David glowered at her. "X hasn't stopped you with any of his other attempts. Have you thought that you could be the next target?"

"Yes, I have, and it doesn't change a dang thing. How long do I live in fear in my home?" Frustrated, she pushed back her hair. "I've already had this conversation with Parker. I'm not doing it again."

His voice rose. "At times, you can really be bull-headed. If Parker is concerned, then you should listen to what we're telling you. This house isn't worth it."

"This is my life. This madman, whoever he is, isn't going to ruin it. I'll tell you the same as I told Parker, I will be careful. End of conversation."

David stood. "God, you can be annoying. Just remember this. You've got people who care about you. So don't get on your high horse when we want to be sure you don't end up dead. I never want to experience what I felt when you dragged yourself out of the tunnel a few months back."

Realizing David was afraid, Tori's anger faded. She walked around the desk. "David, I promise you, I won't take any chances." She gave him a tentative smile. "Okay?"

He grabbed her, crushing her in his arms. "I'm damn well going to hold you to that promise."

She eased back, looking up at him. A tender look replaced the fear in his eyes.

"What are your plans for the day?" His fingers pushed aside a lock of hair that had fallen across her face.

Emotions rolled inside her. She needed space. As she stepped away, Tori motioned toward the computer. "More research. I've got to find out the mystery man's identity. He's the key. There must be a record of him somewhere. Even in Frankie's era, a man doesn't vanish into thin air without it causing comment."

"I hate to be the one to throw a monkey wrench into this, but have you considered the mystery man may not have lived in Granbury or even in Hood County?"

Tori stared at him with a look of horror that turned into a glower.

David threw up his hands. "Don't kill the messenger. I'm only saying, what if?"

"Cripes, why didn't I think of it?"

"Probably because you've been too focused on the here and now."

She groaned. "How many newspapers in this area were there?"

David glanced at his watch. "More than one. I'd better get a move on. Walk with me to the door."

As they meandered their way to the front of the house, he threw his arm around Tori's shoulders. With a light squeeze, he peered down at her. An anxious expression crossed his face. "You're sure you don't plan to go anywhere today?"

"Yes, I'm sure. I'm staying right here."

"Good. If you do, let me know. Someone needs to keep track of you. I'll check in later." He flicked his finger across her cheek before striding outside.

A warm glow lifted her spirits until she settled in her chair and thought about expanding her search to other newspapers. With a sigh, she picked up where she had left off. Wading through the articles was tedious and time-consuming. When Ben stopped in the doorway, several hours had passed, and she was ready for a break.

"This was just delivered." He walked in and handed her a large envelope.

"Thanks, Ben."

After she slit it open, five credit cards spilled onto the desk. Delighted, Tori picked them up. These would make it easier for everyone and simplify the inn's accounting system. She set them aside, turning back to the computer.

Sometime later, a movement in the hallway caught her attention. Someone had walked past her door. But by the time she glanced up, they were gone.

Thinking it was probably Ben, she turned her attention back to the computer. Then it dawned on her, why would his footsteps have been muffled? Tori shoved back her chair. When she stopped in the doorway, Ben strode toward her. As he passed, he gave her a quick glance and kept going. Curious, she followed.

In the hallway, near the kitchen, Ben, in a no-nonsense tone, said, "Jack, what are you doing here?"

Tori looked around Ben's shoulder to see Crimshaw standing by the door to the utility room.

With a sheepish look, he said, "I've heard a lot about the house and took a few minutes to look at it."

"From now on, stay where you are assigned. We're

not here to sightsee. If you want a break, go outside. And, next time, use the front door."

Seeing her, Crimshaw said, "Sorry, Miss Winters. I didn't mean to cause a problem. But what you're doing with this house is amazing." He grinned. "It won't happen again. I'll be back in just a few minutes, Ben." Then he turned and walked out.

"He asked for a break to go to his truck." Ben scrubbed his face. "I expected he'd go out the front door. Instead, he headed to the back of the house. Barton alerted me. I'll let Colt know what happened."

Tori nodded. Though she couldn't see any reason for alarm, it didn't take much to spook her in her current state of edginess. On the way back, her phone chimed. Closing the door, she answered.

After greeting her, Dan said, "Good news! I received the permits and letter from Marshal. Everything is in order. There shouldn't be any more trouble with the city. I'll send them to you. The press release was sent out, and an article will be in tomorrow's Hood County News. It should be picked up by the other wire services."

"It's one problem solved. I need to run something else by you if you have a few minutes."

"Absolutely. What?"

Tori explained her new theory.

When she finished, he said, "I must say it makes sense. I haven't had a chance to talk to Parker. What is he doing?"

"Checking the fingerprints of the three men. I'm still

digging, trying to discover the identity of the mystery man."

"If there is any way I can help, call. And, please, Tori, keep me posted."

"I will. Thanks, Dan." She disconnected.

A tap sounded on the door. Tori said, "Come in."

"What's with the closed door?" Mia asked, walking in, and plopping in a chair.

"Oh, I was talking to Dan and wanted to make sure I wasn't overheard. What are you doing here? I thought you were taking the day off."

"Well, sort of."

"You've got the look."

"What look?" Mia said with an air of innocence.

"The one you get when you've been up to something."

"Maybe I have."

"Start talking."

"Hmm … I'll wait until the others get here. What's been happening?"

"A few things, but it'll have to wait."

Mia shot her a censuring look. "This isn't tit for tat." She stood, marched to the door, and shut it. "Now, *you* can talk."

Tori laughed. "Okay. Where do I start? Probably Myra. She stopped by."

Eagerness sparked in Mia's eyes. "Lordy be, yes, tell me all the juicy details."

"She showed up with the mayor's wife."

"Really! I haven't had a chance to meet her."

"You will, and you'll like her. I did."

Mia twirled her hand in the air. "Come on. What's the rest."

"Her reason for showing up was to offer her condolences and let Liz Talbot see the house before it was torn down."

"What?"

"Oh, yeah. The woman was totally convinced the city planned to demolish the house."

"Boy, I'd love to have seen her face when you burst her bubble."

"It was a doozy. But Liz Talbot was the real surprise. She fell in love with the house. And … are you ready for this? She's an antique lover and wants to meet you. She's going to help put out the word about the new inn."

"I bet that tidbit put Myra's nose out of joint."

"Oh, it did. After listening to Liz's enthusiastic comments, she couldn't make any more snide remarks. It wouldn't be socially correct to contradict the mayor's wife."

"Dang, I'm sorry I missed it."

"Hmm … all joking aside, the disturbing part was Myra's total conviction about the house." She wondered whether to mention Myra's hateful stare. Then decided it simply sounded too melodramatic. Instead, she explained about the scene in the driveway. "I've never asked, but do you know Logan or the other two men Colt hired?"

Mia shook her head. "No, I don't."

Movement on the camera monitor caught her attention. "Oh, my gosh, Cammie's on the way in. I've got to stop her from going into the kitchen."

Tori leaped to her feet, raced around the desk, flung open the door, and charged into the hallway.

Behind her, Mia exclaimed, "What the—"

The front door opened. Chattering and laughing, Heidi, Tina, and Cammie walked inside. They stopped to gaze in the living room, then the music room.

Tori said, "Got something for you, my office."

Clamoring their greetings, they filed in, and Tori closed the door.

"Uh, oh. Must be serious," Heidi said as she collapsed on the couch with Tina beside her. Cammie flopped in a chair next to Mia.

"I don't want anyone to overhear."

Before sitting down, she picked up the credit cards, handing each the one with their name.

For a few seconds, the women stared at them in amazement.

"Wow," Tina whispered. "This is so impressive."

Tori sat. "Okay, why are you here? I gave you the day off."

Mia looked at the others, who all nodded. In a stern tone, she said, "We need to talk about days off. There's something you don't quite get yet. This isn't a nine-to-five, five-days-a-week type of job. For us, it's an opportunity to share in something special. You've endowed us with your trust." She waved the credit card. "Here's a dang good example. You can't bottle it in a forty-hour week. It means we're involved, no matter the number of hours or days. We'll take time off when we feel comfortable doing it." She grinned. "I wanted to make sure we're all on the same page here."

Tori chuckled. Leave it to Mia to cut to the chase. The woman had never backed off an issue since Tori first met her. "I got it. Changes to the work parameters around here duly noted."

Cammie piped up. "Love the tablet, by the way. It really is handy."

Heidi and Tina chimed in with similar comments.

"I want to show you something." Tori stood and walked to the door. As the women followed her into the hallway, she grabbed Cammie's hand. "Close your eyes."

Puzzled, Cammie stared at her.

"Cammie, please, … close … your … eyes."

With a shrug, she did.

Tori motioned for the others to go ahead of her.

A look of understanding crossed their faces as they quickly moved into the kitchen.

Guiding Cammie, Tori stopped in the doorway.

"Okay. You can look."

Cammie opened her eyes and gasped. "Oh!" Her gaze wandered around the kitchen before walking to the counter. "Wow!" Her hand slid along the edge of the sink, then over the stove. She whirled to look at Tori. "It's wonderful! Absolutely wonderful!"

With a chuckle, Tori said, "Well, if you like this, you

will be ecstatic once the kitchen undergoes its next transformation. Colt said we need new countertops. So, pick out a pattern you think will look good."

With a swipe of her hand, Cammie wiped at the tears beading down her cheeks. "Sometimes I feel like I've fallen into another dimension."

With a dry tone, Mia said, "Don't we all."

Ben stepped into the room. "Hey, Mia. Didn't know you were here."

"Snuck right by you." She chuckled. "Some watchdog you are."

Looking sheepish, he said, "Well, it's been a little hectic around here today. Cammie, what do you think?"

"I absolutely love it," she said as she spun around.

A grin split Ben's face at her over-the-top enthusiasm. "Tori, I wanted to let you know we're done for the day. Colt's still out back, but he's heading out as soon as all the men are gone. Anything you need?"

"Thanks, Ben, but I'm good."

He looked at Mia. "If you're ready to go, I'll walk out with you."

"Yes. I am." Mia turned to see four sets of eyes fixed on her with an avid interest. Her eyes flashed a warning.

Tori grinned. "I'll see you tomorrow." Muttering, her voice low so Ben wouldn't hear, she added, "We'll want to hear all the juicy details."

Mia sniffed, ignored the comment, and walked out.

They waited until the front door closed before erupting into laughter.

Tina said, "This might be interesting. Ben's got her attention, and she's a tough nut to crack."

Heidi stood. "Of the four of us, I always figured she'd be the last one standing when it came to men."

Tori followed the three women as they walked out, making sure the front door was locked. Tired, she wandered toward the kitchen, stopping to get her tablet from the office. Eyeing the empty coffee pot, she decided it was too much trouble to make another one. Instead, Tori grabbed a bottle of water and a sandwich from the fridge.

Seated at the kitchen table, she glanced out the window. The two guards stood next to Carl's truck. As she ate, with an occasional gulp of water, she kept an eye on them. At least she didn't have to worry at night.

Nevertheless, her nerves twitched with a sense of urgency. Parker's words hummed in her mind—desperate, irrational. Her thoughts reverted to the key to it all, the mystery man. She still had one more way to find his identity. After cleaning up, she headed to her bedroom.

The boxes she'd found in the secret room were stacked in a corner. Most contained what she called diaries, but there were a few old newspapers and pictures. After a quick bath and wearing her oversized nightshirt, Tori sat on the floor, sifting through each box, checking dates.

At the bottom of one, she came across two notebooks from 1943. Scrambling to her feet, she climbed into bed, pushing the pillows into a pile. Leaning against them, she opened the oldest. The first entry was dated the second of

January. Elly would have been nine. Childish writing scrawled across the page. Snuggled against the pillows, she read aloud.

"*This was Momma's present. When I asked what I should write she said anything. How I feel what I did or want to do. Christmas was not fun. Daddy was mad. He is always mad at Christmas. There was a big party. Momma looked so pretty. I watched from the stairs. Momma sat in the living room with the ladies and the men went into the library. Momma said they like to gamble. I do not know what else to write. Elly.*"

With a sinking feeling, Tori realized the journals might not help. As much as she would enjoy learning more about a grandmother she never knew, what would a child know?

Flipping pages, she quickly scanned each one. About three months later, one caught her eye, and she stopped to read. "*A piano. I am so happy. I have a piano. Daddy gave it to me today. It is in the sitting room. Daddy said the room is now the music room. He is going to hire a teacher to come to the house. Elly.*"

It wasn't until near the end of the second journal she struck pay dirt.

Chapter 24

The date in the journal was December 15, 1943. "*Momma is scared. Something bad happened last night. Momma was in her bedroom. Sometimes when the men are here Daddy tells her to go to bed. She thought I was asleep. I walked real quiet so she wouldn't hear me. It is fun to sit at the top of the stairs and listen. Daddy never closes the door. Last night was scary. Daddy shouted at Uncle Denny using bad words. Uncle Denny is not my uncle but he likes me to call him that. I saw him when he came out of the library and fell. He had blood on his face. I ran to my bedroom. I heard Daddys voice when he came up the stairs. He was real mad at Uncle Denny. After he went past my door I opened it. Daddy was shoving Uncle Denny. Another man was with them. They went down the stairs to the tunnel. I hid under the covers. I fell asleep. This morning I asked momma what happened to Uncle Denny. She got an awful look on her face. She told me to never never tell Daddy I saw him or ask about Uncle Denny. She made me promise. I guess it is okay to write it. Elly*"

Tori flipped through the rest of the journal, but Elly never mentioned the incident again. Still, she had a date and first name. Denny probably stood for Dennis. She didn't want to wait until morning to check the newspaper archives and jumped out of bed. As she strode to her office, she didn't bother to turn on the lights.

Seated in front of the computer, she logged into the newspaper account, then started her search on the day after Elly's journal entry. Two days later, she found an article with the headline—*Missing Banker*. Avidly she read it. *"Longtime resident and local banker Dennis Kingston has been reported as missing. Local authorities have initiated an investigation. Mrs. Kingston was unavailable for comment."*

Unable to contain her excitement, she glanced at the time on the computer. Though late, Parker might still be up. Instead of calling, she texted—*Are you still up?*

His response was immediate. Her phone rang.

"I'm with one of my men on another surveillance. Something happen?"

"I know who the mystery man is, Dennis Kingston. A banker who disappeared in 1943."

"How'd you find out?"

She explained what she had found in Elly's journal, adding, "With a date, I found the newspaper article."

"Did you find any other comments in the journals?"

"So far, just the one. Obviously, Kingston was a friend of the family since Elly referred to him as Uncle Denny. It doesn't look like there is any doubt that Frankie killed him."

In the distance, sirens echoed.

"Something is happening outside. I can hear sirens."

Tori scrambled around the desk to look out. Since the windows faced the driveway, all she saw was a red glow. "There may be a fire. Hold on."

Clutching the phone, she rushed to the front door and opened it. Smoke and soot swirled in the air. Across the street and near the end of the block, a house was engulfed in flames. Fire trucks and police cars filled the street.

"A house is on fire across the street."

"I don't like it. You stay put. Don't leave the house. I'll be there in a few minutes."

The phone went dead.

Attired in a nightshirt that hung to her knees and barefooted, she couldn't do much anyway. Tori rushed inside, racing to her bedroom.

She stripped off the nightshirt, pulled on a t-shirt and slipped into jeans. Seated on the bed, Tori hurriedly laced up her boots. Once Parker arrived, she might be able to help.

When she stood, her gaze swept the camera monitor on the dresser. She stepped closer. Something was different. Wrong. It took a moment, then it hit. Even though the fire lit up the sky, there wasn't a light near Carl's truck and no guards.

Tori tapped the keyboard, zooming the camera facing the backyard. Two figures darted toward the tunnel, dropping into the hole. For an instant, a light flickered, illuminating the entrance, then disappeared.

She grabbed the phone she'd tossed on the bed. Trying to control the panic, her hand shook as she typed—*men in tunnel.* Tori hit send and shoved the phone into her back pocket.

Why would someone be in the tunnel? They couldn't get into the house since the door was kept locked. Or could they? Tori had to make sure. She couldn't wait for Parker.

On the way to the front of the house, she grabbed a flashlight from the utility room. As she ran, the phone vibrated against her butt, the ringing muffled. She couldn't stop. Taking the stairs two steps at a time, at the top, she smacked the light switch with her hand and kept going.

At the end of the hallway, she slid open the door leading to the tunnel. The beam of the flashlight bobbed across the steps as she ran down. At the bottom was a small room. When she stepped onto the floor, the door to the tunnel rattled. Fear, sharp and deep, bit into her. Tori backed up, ready to bolt up the stairs if they tried to break in.

A muffled, gravelly voice on the other side said, "It's locked. We'll have to leave it here."

"We could break it down. It looks flimsy," a second voice said.

"No time. Those guards won't be gone long. Besides, this tunnel gives me the creeps."

"Are you sure it will work here?"

"Her bedroom is on this side of the house. In fact, we may be under it. When this baby goes off, there won't be anything left." A malicious laugh echoed. "She won't cause any more problems."

The terror clawed its way into her brain. They were

going to blow up the house. Before she could move, the man said, "Okay, the timer's set. Let's get the hell out of here. We've only got a few minutes."

The sound of running footsteps faded. How much time did she have? Could she even get up the stairs and out of the house before the bomb went off? Her only chance was the tunnel.

She dropped the flashlight on the small table next to the door. With a heave, she lifted the heavy wood bar out of the brackets, letting it crash to the floor. She grabbed the flashlight, then threw the door open. The beam flashed across the dirt floor.

Horrified, she stared at a digital timer, wires, and sticks of dynamite held together with a black strap. Without thinking, Tori reached down and grabbed the end of the strap. With the bomb dangling from her hand and the flashlight in the other, she ran. Terror drove her as she plunged ahead. Her only thought, *get out of the tunnel*, echoed over and over.

The light barely cut through the sea of darkness. Unable to look down, Tori's ankles twisted on the uneven ground as she fought to keep her balance. All she could do was pray she didn't slip and fall.

The bomb bounced against her leg. A terror-laden thought electrified her. Could she accidentally set it off? Trying to stiff-arm it, she didn't slow down. Fear crushed her chest until her lungs heaved as she gasped for air. Her heartbeat pounded against her eardrums.

Ahead she could see the faint outline of the bend in

the tunnel. Almost there. As she neared it, a beam of light struck her eyes. Nearly blinded, she stumbled. *Oh, god,* she thought. Were the killers waiting?

A voice echoed. "Tori—"

She screamed, "Bomb! I've got a bomb."

Parker's light raked her body as he shoved a gun into his waistband. He jerked the device from her hand, turned and raced to the entrance.

Tori was on his heels. When he reached the top, he ran, shouting, "Bomb. Get her behind the truck."

Hands grabbed her, dragging her, then pushed her to the ground. A body fell on top of her. An explosion ripped the air. Dirt, rocks, and pieces of trees rained down. In her mind, she screamed—*Parker!*

As he rolled off her, Carl cried, "Miss Tori, are you hurt?"

Dazed, she pushed herself up. Her ears rang from the blast, and her mouth and nose were filled with dirt. She yelled, "Parker! Parker!" He didn't answer.

With Carl holding her arm, Tori staggered to her feet. Frantic, she screamed his name again and again. She pushed at Carl's arm. "Where is he? Can you see him? Find him!"

When she heard Parker shout, "I'm okay," the surge of relief took her to her knees. Carl reached to grab her, but Tori shook him off. "Check on Parker. Make sure he's not hurt."

Once she was sure her legs would hold her, she stood. In front of the truck, a beam of light lit up the ground.

Amazingly, Parker still had his flashlight as he and Carl walked toward her. Still unsteady, she hobbled to meet them.

Covered with dirt, blood snaked a trail down the side of Parker's face.

"You're hurt!" Tori exclaimed. Behind her, shouts echoed as help raced toward them.

"No. Just a scratch. I hit the ground pretty hard." He waved his flashlight over her.

A fireman shouted as he drew nearer. "What happened? Anyone hurt?"

Parker said, "A bomb. We all seem to be okay."

"What! Good lord." The fireman turned and hollered, "It was a bomb. Make sure there isn't any danger of a fire." More firefighters swarmed the area as two police officers joined the melee.

After retrieving her flashlight from where it had rolled under the truck, and on legs still shaky, Tori walked around to the other side. It had taken the brunt of the flying debris. Tori groaned with dismay.

Carl, who had hovered near her, rushed to reassure her. "Don't worry, Miss Tori. I've got insurance."

His truck was probably totaled. He had nearly been killed because of her. Yet, Carl was trying to reassure her, telling her not to worry. He had insurance.

Hysteria almost overwhelmed her. Tori gulped, fighting back the tears. Despite his confidence, Tori wondered if it covered damage from a bomb. Whether it did or didn't, there'd be a new truck in his future.

An officer trotted toward them, one she didn't recognize. This was surprising, considering how many times since she first stepped inside the house, the police had been there.

"Who owns the property?"

"I do. I'm Tori Winters."

"What happened?"

Parker spoke up, "We might be more comfortable in the house."

"Cripes. I don't have a key. I need to go through the tunnel."

"I'll do it." Parker turned to the police officer. "I'll meet you at the back door." Then he turned to Steve, who had run up with the officers. "Stay here."

The officer said, "How are you—"

But Parker had already taken off.

Sandwiched between a fireman, who insisted on checking her for injuries, and Carl, with the police officer following, they herded her toward the house. Still, they had to wait a few minutes before the kitchen light came on, and Parker opened the back door.

In the kitchen, she sank onto a chair, dirt and all. The fireman gave her a quick scrutiny.

"I'm fine. I really am. Just shaken up. I don't need medical treatment. I'm a nurse. I know."

Tori looked at Carl, leaning against the kitchen island, then Parker, talking to a police officer. They had all come so close to dying. She gulped, refusing to give in to another surge of hysteria at the thought of the moment when she picked up the bomb. It was Parker's calm insistence he was okay, as he waved off the attentions of the fireman, that steadied her.

After the officer finished talking to Carl, he headed toward the back door. Tori's voice stopped him. "Carl, thank you." The words seemed so inadequate.

He gave her a quick nod and smile, then walked out.

The officer came over, taking a seat across from her. The small notepad and pen ready, he said, "Tell me what happened."

While she talked, Parker started the coffee pot brewing. Once the machine beeped, he poured a cup, sliding it in front of her. Wrapping her hand around the cup, she flashed him a grateful look and took a sip. The hot liquid soothed away the grit she could still feel in her throat and mouth. Picking up where she left off, she finished the details, ending with Carl shoving her to the ground.

"You said you heard two voices. Did you recognize either one of them?"

Tori thought before answering. "I can't say for certain." She caught the look Parker shot her.

"Do you have any idea why someone would plant a bomb in your tunnel?"

"No, I don't."

He looked at Parker. "Did you see anyone when you got to the tunnel?"

With a shake of his head, he said, "No. They must have gone out the back of the property."

"I'd like to look at where you found the bomb."

"I'll show him," Parker said. "It's easier to go through the tunnel."

Tori said, "It was up against the wall outside the door."

After the two men left, her arms propped on the table, Tori dropped her head onto her hands. She still had the shakes. Nerves twitched. A residual of the adrenaline dump pulsated inside her. Her anger built, replacing the debilitating fear. Whatever it took, Tori swore to herself she would find X. Now that she knew the mystery man's identity, it was only a matter of time to find out why a crime so long ago had come close to killing the three of them.

She stood, refilled her cup, and stared out the window. Light from flashlights bounced around the new pit. As she watched, they started to move toward the house. Carl's truck was replaced with another one, and its headlights lit up the area. Tori figured Parker had sent Carl home.

Parker and the officer climbed out of the tunnel. After a few minutes, the officer walked toward the driveway, and Parker headed to the back door.

Tori poured a cup, handing it to him when he came in. Like her, he was still covered with dirt, though he had tried to brush off the worst.

"How is the head?"

With a sigh, he said, "It's okay. God, this was close. I talked to the fire department's captain. He believes the house fire was arson. It was meant to pull the guards away long enough to let someone plant the bomb."

He took a gulp. "I feel like I've swallowed a ton of dirt." He sat, setting the cup on the table. "Do you have an idea who it was?"

"I'm not sure. One of the voices sounded familiar, but I'd hate to accuse anyone, which is why I didn't tell the officer. But it sounded like Logan. He has a gravelly tone to his voice."

"I figured as much. I got the results of the fingerprint check, and Logan has a lengthy rap sheet, assaults, robberies, drugs. All are several years old, nothing recent. Crimshaw is the same, an assault, but it's also an old charge. There's nothing new. Martell is clean."

"Why didn't Colt learn about them when he did the background?"

"Depends on what type of background check Colt ran. Some only provide convictions, not charges. Neither man was ever convicted. They must have had one heck of an attorney."

He pulled out his phone and tapped the screen. When the call was answered, Parker said, "Yeah, I know what time it is. I need a man on Tommy Logan as soon as you can find him. Don't let him out of your sight. A bomb was planted in the tunnel at the Leichter place tonight. We got it out in time, but there's a new hole on the property. I sent Carl home and need a replacement as soon as you can get one here." He listened, then said, "No, he wasn't hurt."

He pocketed the phone. "I need to lock the door to the tunnel. I'll be right back."

Tori protested, "I can do it."

"No. It won't take me a minute, then I'm out of here. I'll be back in the morning. We need to talk more about what you discovered, but we both need to get some sleep." He finished off his cup.

While she waited, Tori washed the cups and pot, re-setting the coffee machine.

When Parker returned, he said, "A new guard should arrive within the hour."

"Both you and Carl—"

He cut her off as a knowing look settled over his face. "Nothing needs to be said. I'll see you in the morning."

Tori locked the door behind him. Turning off the lights, she made her way to her bedroom. Still amped, she wasn't sure if she could go to sleep. First, she had to get rid of the dirt. Her hair was thick with it. She groaned at the thought of sticking her head under the faucet. Why didn't Elly ever install a dang shower?

After filling the tub twice, she crawled out and tow-eled off. Tori pulled on the nightshirt she'd hurriedly stripped off earlier. With a last glance at the camera mon-itor, she settled into bed.

Her mind spun with thoughts despite her resolve to not think about that horrifying run through the tunnel and the sound of the blast. If she'd stumbled, lost a few pre-cious seconds … no, she wouldn't let herself go there. It didn't happen.

But even as she tried to calm her chaotic thoughts, a

new one rose. She had her answer to the earlier question. What would X do next? Well, she'd found out. Parker and David were right. She'd become the target. X missed this time. What about the next time?

Chapter 25

Every muscle in her body ached as she crawled out of bed. With a groan, she stumbled into the bathroom. It wasn't a promising start to the day.

Even worse, when she made her way outside with coffee and sandwiches, she got her first good look at the destruction. Dismayed, she stared at the rocks, broken trees and piles of dirt encircling the hole.

All the emotions, the terror and anger she had experienced, rushed back. With a shudder, she turned to say hello to the two guards gathered by the truck.

She brushed aside Steve's apology about leaving his post. "You did the right thing. The family could have been trapped. They had to be your first concern."

Not up to making small talk, Tori didn't linger. Instead, she hustled back to the house. As she stepped into her office, the phone's ring sent her scurrying toward the desk. It was Dan. He'd heard about the explosion on his car radio. After easing his concerns, she told him what had happened.

Next up was a call from Jonah, who had also heard it

on the news. As she disconnected, a sense of trepidation built. Disaster loomed.

The front door slammed as a loud voice shouted, "Tori! Where are you?"

What she feared had just arrived. Resigned, she hollered, "Office, Mia."

Mia marched in, followed by Heidi, Tina, and Cammie. Gimlet-eyed, they lined up in front of her desk. Mia's fisted hands rested on her hips. Her jaw tight, she said, "Explain! A dang bomb goes off, and we've got to hear about it on the news."

"I didn't want to wake you in the middle of the night. There was nothing you could do." With a sigh, she mumbled, "I didn't plan on it hitting the news this fast."

Mia snorted. "May I remind you we are a team? No, scratch that. We are family!" She angrily gestured with her hand. "It's not on a timetable. Whether we get awakened in the middle of the night doesn't matter! Whether there isn't anything we can do doesn't matter! What does matter is we support each other!"

Feeling she'd been suitably chastised, Tori said, "You're right. I should have called. Am I forgiven?"

"As long as it doesn't happen again," Mia said.

All four visibly relaxed. Mia plopped into a chair with Heidi next to her. Tina and Cammie took the couch.

Her face still tight with worry, Mia said, "Tell us what happened. And don't you dare leave out any details."

Nevertheless, Tori gave them an abbreviated version. Their faces twisted with a look of horror when she reached the part about grabbing the bomb and running out.

Mia whispered, "You could have been killed."

That the bomb was meant to kill her was one of the details Tori didn't mention. Hoping to divert their questions, she said, "I did find out the name of the mystery man." She told them what she'd found and how.

"So, we have a name, Dennis Kingston, and he lived in Granbury. I've never heard of him. And the mystery deepens. Who was the third man? I wonder?" Mia mused.

Tori asked, "Wonder what?"

"I need to make a phone call, then I'll let you know."

A knock sounded on the back door.

Tina jumped up. "I'll get it."

When she returned, Colt was close on her heels.

"A news van has pulled up in front. I didn't want to use the front door." While he talked, his gaze closely scrutinized Tori. "What happened? All I got was the lurid news on my truck radio."

With a wry tone, Mia said, "She's got a lot to explain today. We'll get out of the way. I've got groceries in my car."

Once they had left, Colt settled into the chair. Before she could start, the doorbell chimed. Cammie's voice echoed from the front of the house.

Footsteps pounded as David charged into the room. "Why didn't you call me?" he demanded to know.

Tori groaned. "Not you too. I might as well put everyone on an automatic caller. Plug in the message and list of numbers."

Frustrated, he glared at her.

"Have a seat. I'll tell both of you. And to answer your question, there was nothing you could do. It was late, and everyone was okay, so I didn't call."

He started to open his mouth.

Tori's hand shot up. "Don't want to hear it."

Muttering, he said, "You should have called," and subsided into a chair.

Mia, walking past the door, had overheard. She poked her head inside. "Don't feel bad, David. She didn't call any of us either. Someone tried to blow up the tunnel, but she didn't want to bother us."

Tori groaned again. "Don't you have something to do, Mia?"

"Yes! Annoy you. I've made it my mission for the day." With a wicked grin, she stalked off.

Colt started to laugh but turned it into a cough when Tori glared at him.

"Okay, enough said on the subject. Here's what happened." As she talked, she could see the anger build on the two men's faces.

When she finished, David shouted, "What happened to 'I won't take any chances.' My god, woman! What were you thinking to go charging into the tunnel."

Frustrated, she shouted back. "At the time, it seemed my only option." Her hands fluttered in the air. "If I'd tried to get out … I don't even want to think about what might have happened. We might not be sitting here with you yelling at me."

"Okay. I get your point, but still." He stopped when

she scowled at him. He cleared his throat. "What's being done about Logan?"

"What can we do without proof?" Tori said.

Ben's voice and the low rumble of other voices echoed along the hallway. The construction crew had arrived.

Her eyes flashed a warning, and she held up a finger before saying, "Colt, what do we do about the crater?"

Recognizing the reason for the change in the conversation, he played along. "I'll get rid of the broken limbs and tree trunks. Then bring in fill dirt and pack it down. By the time I'm finished, you won't even know there was a hole."

David stood. "Colt. I need to look at the tunnel. Make sure the explosion didn't cause a problem."

Aghast, Tori stared at him. "Oh, my gosh, it never occurred to me. Will this start up all the nonsense with the city again?"

David looked at her. "To be honest, I don't know. If it does, I want to be prepared. Colt, let's look at it."

Tori darted from behind her desk and followed.

Outside, Ben walked around the corner of the house, headed toward the crater where Parker and several construction workers stood.

"Ben," Colt shouted.

As he loped toward them, Ben's gaze swept the group of men. "I wanted to be sure Logan wasn't out here before I said anything. He's a no-show."

Parker had trotted up in time to hear Ben's comment. "I've got a man trying to locate him, but no luck so far."

Loud voices erupted. Parker whipped around. A news crew had snuck around the other side of the house, and a guard was trying to head them off. Parker took off at a run. Not wanting to give the reporter a chance, Tori sprinted to the back door. Still, the man tried. Evading the guard, he started toward her, shouting, "Miss Winters." Tori ignored him, rushing into the house.

Inside the kitchen, Mia was fixing another batch of iced tea. Heidi was seated at the table, typing on her tablet while she kept an eye on the melee outside. Cammie was busy rearranging the contents of the new refrigerator.

Heidi laughed. "I wondered if you would outrun him."

Tori leaned against the kitchen island. "What a mess. Now, David's worried again about the condition of the tunnel. Where's Tina?"

Mia said, "Getting pictures of the library. She plans to take several throughout the day to see which light works best." She laid aside the spoon and reached into a sack on the counter. "Your morning read."

Tori unfolded the newspaper and groaned. The reporter at *The Metro* had struck again. This time the headline was even more lurid. *Another Incident Strikes the Leichter Mansion. A Forewarning?* As she read, her anger grew. "She suggests the city needs to reexamine its position about the liability of the property. Oh, lord, this is going to stir it all up again." She straightened. "Wait a minute. There's something wrong. She said there was damage to the house and tunnel. There isn't. But if Parker and

I hadn't gotten the bomb out of the tunnel, there would have been."

With a cupful of sugar poised over the top of the pitcher, Mia glared over her shoulder. "You never said anything about damaging the house. Just where in the tunnel did you find the bomb?"

Well, dang, she'd done it now. Keeping her eyes on the newspaper as if still reading it, she mumbled, "A ways into it."

Mia dumped, then dropped the cup on the counter. "Tori!"

Heidi and Cammie froze. Their gaze was fixated on Tori.

Mia stepped forward, standing almost nose-to-nose. Or at least as much as she could, considering she was taller and had to scowl down. "Exactly ... where ... in the tunnel?"

Tori gulped. No getting around it. If she didn't tell her, Mia would worm it out of Parker. "Right outside the door."

Exclamations resounded, all the louder coming from three women.

Visibly shaken, her face pale, Mia stepped back to stir the tea. "You didn't tell us that. You would have been killed if you had been in your bedroom."

"It's what they intended on doing," Tori said. Might as well get it all out there. "Our main suspect, Tommy Logan, didn't show up for work."

"What's being done to stop all of this?" Mia banged

the metal spoon against the inside of the porcelain pitcher as she vigorously stirred.

Heidi observed, "You keep it up, and you'll break the dang thing."

"Cripes." Mia tossed the spoon in the sink.

Tori stepped over, sliding her arm around Mia's shoulders. "We're doing everything we can."

Mia's head dropped as a tear rolled down her face. Then with a sniff, she straightened, giving Tori a fierce look. "Don't you *ever* take a chance like that again."

With a wry smile, she said, "Scout's honor. I won't." She could only hope it was the truth.

Mia wiped her eyes with her sleeve before picking up the spoon.

Tori returned to the news article. "How did the reporter get the story so fast? Did someone give her an advance warning? If all had gone as planned, what she wrote would be true."

A phone chimed. It was Mia's. After a short conversation, she disconnected. "That was Fergie Ware. She's a historian and an expert on the history of Granbury. She lives at the senior citizen center. I left her a message earlier. She said she'd be home all day."

"Let's get going. I need to send an email. I'll meet you outside." Tori grabbed her bag from the bedroom and headed to her office. She typed an email to Sid, asking if he'd come across any mention of Dennis Kingston in his research before shutting down the computer.

Tori picked up the copy of the Kingston news article

she'd printed and her tablet, stuffing them in her bag. On her way out, she removed a poker chip from the safe in the library. They left in Mia's car since the construction equipment blocked the entrance to the garage.

During the short ride, Tori said, "Tell me about Fergie."

"She's a hoot, a real pistol. For years she managed the city library. Fergie ran the place with a hand of steel. She didn't put up with any nonsense from kids. Get too loud or cause a ruckus, and the parents would get a call. If that didn't fix the problem, she'd kick you out."

Mia turned onto the road leading to the center. "She retired five, six years ago. Since then, she has been compiling the history of Granbury. Says one of these days, she's going to write a book."

"How old is she?"

"Hmm … early seventies. She's one of those individuals who doesn't look her age."

Mia pulled into a parking spot. "Her apartment is on the second floor."

Trotting up the stairs, Mia led the way. She tapped on a door. When it opened, a tall, gangly woman dressed in sweatpants and an oversized t-shirt greeted them.

"Mia, dang, if you aren't a sight for sore eyes. Come in, come in."

She stepped back as Mia, followed by Tori, entered.

At Fergie's gasp, Tori smiled. Her resemblance to her grandmother had caused more than one comment.

"My goodness. You look just like Miss Elly. But then,

I'm sure you've been told that many times." In a strident voice, she said, "Have a seat."

Tori suppressed a smile. She had no problem imagining how the woman issued orders in the library.

Fergie motioned to the couch in the small living room. After they were seated, she dropped into a chair.

Mia was right. If the woman was in her seventies, it didn't show. Despite the short hair, more white than grey, her angular face with prominent cheekbones had few lines. Her light blue eyes sparkled with interest as she continued to study Tori.

"How's Ethel?"

Tori answered, "Better, but still in a coma."

"They ever figure out what the burglar was after?"

"No, the police haven't."

"Humph! Terrible, just terrible, when even in your own home, you're not safe. Would either of you like something to drink? All I got is fruit juice or water."

Both Tori and Mia declined the offer.

"Mia says you're looking into the history of the house and that skeleton you found. I don't watch much news, but it's caused a lot of chatter around here."

"Yes, I am. I have discovered his name, Dennis Kingston. He disappeared in 1943. He was murdered and buried in the tunnel Frankie built."

Looking down as she pulled the article she printed from her tote bag, Tori didn't see the flash of fear in Fergie's eyes that was quickly suppressed.

She handed it to Fergie while explaining about the

pocket watch and initials. Tori didn't mention Elly's journals, not wanting to broadcast their existence.

Fergie shook her head in amazement as her gaze scanned it. "I heard about the pocket watch but not the initials. All this time, he's been buried in that tunnel."

Mia, who had closely watched Fergie, spoke up. "You know who he was then?"

"Oh, yes. I know." A troubled look crossed her face. A slight tremble rattled the paper.

"What can you tell us?" Mia asked.

"Hmm … not much. I research a lot of old news articles. I remember this one, but I don't think I will be much help." She handed it back to Tori.

Disappointed, Tori slowly shoved it into her bag.

Mia said, "Fergie, what's wrong?"

Hearing the suspicious tone in Mia's voice, Tori's head snapped up. Mia was watching Fergie with an intuitive look.

"Why … nothing. What makes you think anything is wrong?" As if uneasy, Fergie shifted in the chair.

Mia's brow wrinkled. "There's something you're not telling us."

"It's best to leave this in the past." Fergie's hands twisted in her lap. "It all happened long ago. There's no reason to delve into it."

While Tori hated to pressure the woman about what was obviously a distressful subject, she didn't have a choice. "I'm afraid that's not true. Last night someone tried to kill me by planting a bomb in the tunnel. The same someone is why Ethel almost died and is still in a coma in the hospital. We believe these attacks are connected to Dennis Kingston."

Fergie huffed. Her face paled.

Leaning forward, Mia reached for Fergie's hand. "I don't know why you are afraid, but if you know anything that can help Tori, we've got to know before someone dies."

Fergie's hand clutched Mia's as she sucked in a deep breath. "Maybe it's time it all came out," she muttered. Fergie straightened, pulling her hand back. Her voice grew stronger. "There are some facts, but mostly rumors that have never been confirmed. Kingston was part-owner of a bank in Granbury, and a prominent member in the community."

"Did he have any connection to my great-grandfather?" Tori asked.

"This is where the rumors come into play. No one knew for sure, but for years it was touted that Kingston and his partner were Frankie's financial frontmen. Supposedly, Frankie used their bank to hide the profits from his casinos and other criminal activities."

Mia asked, "Who was Kingston's partner?"

"Archibald Hemphill."

Mia gasped. "Any relation to the Hemphill brothers?"

"Grandfather."

Tori asked, "Who are the Hemphills?"

Mia said, "They own City Bank & Trust. Norton runs the bank. His brother, Wayne, is a retired judge. Wayne's son, Graham, is a U.S. senator. There's been some talk about a run for the White House. The Hemphills are wealthy and powerful."

Fergie shot her a dry look. "And their bank is the same one their grandaddy owned. Only the name is different."

"So, that's where they got their money. From Frankie's gambling syndicate," Mia said. "That's one I've never heard."

"It was one of those rumors that, over the years, died out. After Kingston disappeared, his wife packed up the kids and headed back east, where her family lived. At the time, no one knew why, but the speculation was that Hemphill had taken everything, money, house, cars, even her furs and jewelry. She was left penniless."

Puzzled, Tori leaned forward. "How could that happen if Kingston and Hemphill were partners?"

"In those days, women had few rights. She had no family here to protect her."

Mia asked, "Did you ever come across any documents or articles about Kingston?"

She hesitated, staring at Mia with a fearful expression.

"Whatever it is, we'll deal with it, Fergie," Mia told her. "You're not alone. Tori has a lot of resources."

Fergie sucked in a deep breath, steadying herself. "Do you remember Clara Hopkins?"

Mia thought. "Vaguely. Didn't she work with you at the library?"

"Yes, she did. Clara and I had been best friends since we were kids. Like me, she was a history nut. The library had received several boxes of books from Marley Bennett's estate. Marley had started as a reporter and worked his way up to editor of the old *Granbury Chronicle*. In one, she found a notebook. After Kingston disappeared, Marley started digging into his disappearance and the rumors about the connections of Kingston and Hemphill to Frankie's gambling activities. He kept notes on what he discovered. I've often wondered if Clara would still be alive if she hadn't found Marley's notebook."

Chapter 26

*I*ntrigued, Tori leaned forward. "Why? What happened?"

"Clara couldn't resist a good mystery, and Dennis Kingston was one. Using what she learned from Marley's notes, she added to it with her own research. Once she had proof that Kingston and Hemphill were part of Frankie's criminal activities, she started corresponding with Kingston's widow. Betty Kingston sent her several documents proving Hemphill illegally took possession of the bank and her husband's estate. In essence, Hemphill stole everything Kingston owned, leaving his widow penniless. Clara figured Kingston had been murdered. Frankie and Hemphill were her primary suspects."

Fergie stopped as she looked at Mia, then Tori. An anguished tone crept into her voice. "Clara didn't plan to write a book. I'm the one who came up with the idea. We decided to keep the book a secret until we found a publisher. The thought that what we were doing was dangerous never occurred to us. It was the history of another era, prohibition, gambling, and gun running. For the most part, the people involved were dead. It might be a minor embarrassment for a relative, but it was still old history."

Tori asked, "What happened to Clara?"

Fergie looked at Mia. "You asked if I was afraid. I have been for years. Before Clara could publish the book, she was struck and killed by a car as she crossed a street. The driver was never found."

Mia reached out and gently squeezed Fergie's hand.

Fergie took a deep breath. "But that's not all. A few days after her death, someone broke into her house. The manuscript, notes, and research documents were gone. They were the only items stolen. At about the same time, the library was vandalized. The police believed it was kids, but I never thought so. The damage was only in my office, where Clara also had a desk. I think whoever broke in was searching for any additional documents Clara had. A couple of weeks later, a letter arrived from Betty Kingston's son saying his mother had died of an accidental overdose."

The stunning revelations set Tori back in her seat. Chills raced over her as she and Mia exchanged glances.

"Do you think Clara and Mrs. Kingston were murdered?" Tori asked.

"Yes. I do. Clara interviewed Sam Taylor, who died a few days after she was killed. He had cancer. Everyone assumed it was the cause of death. But I had to wonder after Clara's and Mrs. Kingston's deaths and the other incidents. Was someone cleaning up the loose ends?"

"Why did you think you were in danger?" Tori asked.

Fergie rose, leaving the room. When she returned, she carried two large envelopes and handed them to Tori. "In one envelope is Clara's manuscript. The other contains the Kingston documents, Marley's journal, and two cassette tapes of interviews."

Tori laid them on her lap. "I thought you said everything was stolen."

"Clara's copy was. I was editing the book and needed all the documents and tapes to check the accuracy of her statements. Whoever killed her didn't know I had them. I'm certain it's what saved my life. But I wasn't taking any chances. I hid them in an old footlocker with a false bottom. Even if someone had searched the place, they wouldn't find them."

"Was anything ever said about a poker chip with three lightning bolts?" Tori reached into her pocket, pulled out the poker chip with the lightning bolts on both sides and handed it to Fergie.

Her face frozen with shock, Fergie stared at the chip she held in the palm of her hand. She whispered, "Clara, here's your proof."

Tori asked, "What proof?"

"A missing piece of evidence for her book. Clara knew the chip existed but couldn't prove it. How did you get it?"

"Two were found with Kingston's remains."

Her hand trembling, Fergie handed back the chip. "Let me have the envelope labeled manuscript." After Tori handed it to her, she opened the clasp and slid out the contents. She held up the first page. Typed in the center was the title—*The Lightning Bolt Conspiracy by Clara Hopkins.*

Astounded, both Mia and Tori gasped.

"What did the chip have to do with Kingston?" Tori asked.

"I mentioned she had discovered Frankie, Hemphill, and Kingston were partners. It came from an interview with Sam Taylor. Marley had mentioned Taylor in his journal. When Clara first contacted Taylor, he refused to talk to her. But she kept trying, and he finally agreed."

She leaned back, her voice slipping into a recital tone. "According to Taylor, Hemphill and Kingston didn't want their involvement known. The proceeds from Frankie's illegal syndicate went through their bank, and they didn't want to draw the Fed's attention. Hemphill and Kingston were also involved in a secret, invitation-only poker club for politicians, government officials, judges. Influential men who couldn't risk being seen in a casino."

Fergie glanced at the paper she still held. "Frankie needed a special chip for the private games. Instead of the initials for the three men, Frankie used three lightning bolts. The special chip was given to a participant. If a player didn't have the chip with bolts on each side, he didn't get through the door. Another way to protect the men and keep a federal agent from sneaking in."

"What was Sam Taylor's role in all of this?" Tori asked.

"Taylor worked for the railroad. The line ran behind Frankie's house. Taylor handled the shipments of alcohol and guns. It was offloaded and stored in the tunnel. Taylor also played an active role in the operation of the clandestine poker games. He arranged the transportation to and from the games for the players arriving in their private train cars. Since reporters weren't interested in who came and went in Granbury, they disembarked at the Granbury train depot. Taylor had cars waiting to take them to either Frankie's house or a Dallas location. It depended on how many players showed up."

"The railroad! How did he get away with using trains for criminal activity?"

With a wry look, Fergie said, "Back in those days, a lot of cops and politicians were on Frankie's payroll. Everyone looked the other way, that's how. Taylor's boss was Loomis Wainwright, who controlled the operation of the railroads for this section of Texas. Wainwright was in this up to his neck, getting a cut of every shipment. Sam told Clara that Hemphill and Wainwright's fortunes came from their association with Frankie."

Surprised, Tori said, "Myra Swanson's grandfather?"

"Yes. Do you know her?"

"We've met."

Tori's dry tone didn't escape Fergie's attention. "Not the most pleasant of Granbury's residents, is she?"

"No, she isn't. Did Taylor know what happened to Kingston?" Tori asked.

"If he did, he wouldn't admit it. All he told Clara was Kingston disappeared one day, and no one knew why. She didn't believe him."

"Did Clara try to interview my grandmother?"

"Yes, but Miss Elly said she wasn't interested. She told Clara her father's unsavory reputation was already well-known, and there wasn't anything she could add."

Tori thought for a moment. "Was there anyone who was interested in her research?"

Fergie pursed her lips as she thought. "No. Clara never made a big deal out of it. Just told people she was researching Granbury's history. Clara did contact Archibald's son, Arthur, asking for an interview. He refused. I don't recall …" Her voice trailed off.

"Wait a minute, there was someone. I remember she commented on how unsettled she'd felt about the encounter. One day, Myra's father came into the library. He pulled Clara aside, asking questions about her interest in Kingston and what she'd found out. Even though Wainwright was a big donor to the library, Clara never liked the man and didn't tell him much. We blew it off, thinking he was just being nosy. The Wainwrights always wanted to have a finger in any pie that affected Granbury."

"All these years, I believed Hemphill murdered Clara. I have to wonder now if Wainwright was responsible?"

As Tori listened, a new worry built. Did her visit put Fergie in danger?

"Fergie, don't let anyone know why we were here. If someone asks, tell them I wanted your help stocking the library with books for the new inn."

Mia said, "That's a good idea."

An apprehensive look crossed Fergie's face as she slid the papers back into the envelope. "You think I could be a target like Ethel?" She closed it and handed it back to Tori.

"I'm not sure. You were part of what happened all those years ago. Someone might believe you know something. To be on the safe side, you are about to acquire a bodyguard. Parker Hayes, a private investigator who works for me, will call you."

After saying goodbye, they headed to Mia's car. Tori tossed her purse and the envelopes on the backseat.

Buckling her seatbelt, Tori said, "This is unbelievable. After all these years, who is still covering their tracks? And why? What is so important that they can't risk the exposure even now?"

Mia backed out. "As long as I've known Myra, she's always touted her impeccable background. She wouldn't like her family's dirty laundry becoming public."

"David said something along the same lines. Myra liked to lord it over Elly because her father was a gangster. I wonder if she knows her grandfather was a criminal, just like Frankie. Who do you think was the third man, Hemphill or Wainwright?"

"Either one is a good bet. What do you plan to do?"

"I'm not sure."

As she pulled out of the parking lot, Mia cast a troubled look at Tori.

She saw it. "Don't worry. I'm not going to take any chances."

With a scornful tone, Mia said, "Oh, right. This from

the woman who grabbed a bomb and ran out of the tunnel with it. Your definition of taking chances certainly differs from mine."

"When we get back, let's have a meeting. I wonder if David is still there?"

"I imagine he is. I don't think he's going to stay away for long. He's really got a thing for you."

As her lips twitched upward, she pushed aside the worry eating at her. "If he does, he's never done anything about it."

"Maybe you're sending the wrong signals."

Startled, Tori shifted in the seat. "Now, why do you say that? What signals? I'm not sending any signals."

"That could be the problem. You must admit the house has been your focus since you hit town. You haven't left much room for a relationship."

She grumbled, "Maybe so, but it doesn't mean I'm going to throw myself at him."

"Didn't say you had to, just a little encouragement now and then."

"That reminds me, what's up with you and Ben? I told you I wanted to hear all the details."

Mia shot her a wry smile. "I don't know. Whatever it is, I'm enjoying it. Did you know he was in the Marine Corps? He went from college into the military, most of it in Afghanistan. He's never been married, and his parents still live in McKinney, north of Dallas. Ben and Colt grew up together. When Ben didn't re-up for another tour, Colt contacted him, and he's been the foreman ever since. In fact, he's more than a foreman, handling a lot of the office activity."

Tori erupted with laughter.

"What!"

"Oh, nothing, other than that was quite a litany. Sounds like a heck of a guy."

"I guess so," Mia said as if she realized she had gotten carried away.

Another uproarious laugh erupted. "Who are you trying to fool, yourself or me?"

"Humph," Mia snorted.

When Mia pulled to the curb in front of the house, Tori spotted the excavator. It was back in action, dumping large clumps of debris into a dump truck backed into the driveway.

Excited, Tori said, "This must mean there's nothing wrong with the tunnel." She jumped from the car and grabbed her bag and envelopes from the backseat. She raced toward the house. After dropping everything in her office, she rushed outside. David and Colt stood nearby, watching the demolition.

As she trotted across the yard, David waved and shouted, "You're back in action."

She grabbed his arm to twirl him around. With a laugh, he clasped her shoulders, hugging her to his side.

"Nothing's wrong with the tunnel then?" she said.

"No, though Colt and I were worried."

Realizing she was still in his arms, she eased away, wondering what signal she'd just sent. As she shoved the thought aside, she said, "I've got unbelievable news whenever the two of you can break away. Where's Parker?"

"He muttered something about his office and left."

"I'll call him."

She hustled back to the house. Inside, Mia stood at the sink, washing the coffee pot.

"Where is everybody?"

"Heidi left a note on the counter. Cammie and Tina have a house to clean. Heidi is off interviewing possible replacements for the cleaning crew. I'll be glad when we get them hired."

"I've got to call Parker." She headed to her office to retrieve the phone from her bag.

Behind her, Mia muttered, "I'd better make another pot."

Tori dropped onto her chair, waiting for Parker to answer. When he did, she said, "You're not going to believe what Mia and I learned today. Are you coming back here?"

"On the way. Will be there in about ten minutes."

She laid the phone on the desk and booted her computer. Anticipation surged when she saw an email from Sid, and she eagerly read his reply.

He had found a 1942 article in a Fort Worth newspaper. It dealt with the murder of one of Frankie's competitors, another casino owner. Even though Frankie had been charged with murder, the charges were dropped when the witness disappeared. The reporter had caught Frankie outside a Dallas hotel with two other men. They were identified as Archibald Hemphill and Dennis Kingston. Sid had attached the article.

Tori clicked on the attachment and enlarged the picture. The two men were referenced as business partners. Her great-grandfather had the same predator's look as he did in the painting over the mantle. Archibald had a cold, emotionless stare. Kingston, by contrast, appeared almost boyish looking. She hit print.

Colt and David wandered in, each carrying a bottle of water. They dropped into chairs.

"Parker just drove up," Colt said.

"So, what's up?" David asked. An easy grin crossed his face as he gazed at her with a look that was more than idle interest.

A warm feeling rushed over her. Averting her eyes, she emptied the contents of both envelopes on the desk. "It's about what we found out from Fergie."

Parker strolled in with the computer bag over one shoulder and a cup in the other. One he set on the floor, the other on a small table before settling onto the sofa.

Mia brought in a tray of cookies. After setting it on the corner of the desk, she plopped on the couch. Parker leaned forward, snagging two cookies.

"We visited Fergie Ware, the resident expert on Granbury history. Parker, would you call her. I want one of your men to keep an eye on her?"

He paused, the cookies in his fist, to shoot her a sharp glance. "Give me the address and number. Why?"

"Let's just say what we found was enlightening and

could put her at risk." She told them what Fergie had said and what was inside the envelopes.

Ever the legal mind, Parker asked, "What are the documents?"

Tori picked them up, looking at the first stapled set. She quickly glanced through it before passing it to Parker. "It's a copy of Kingston's will."

Parker glanced at it before passing it to David.

As it got handed around, Tori picked up the next one. "A signed affidavit from Betty Kingston," and handed it to Parker.

With the next one, she exclaimed, "My gosh, this is a ledger sheet for Kingston's bank account. It has over sixty-thousand dollars in the account. It's dated a month before Kingston was killed. That was probably a small fortune in 1943." The last was a deed to a piece of property, Kingston's home.

Once everyone had examined the documents, Parker went back to the will, studying it. "Everything was left to his wife, including his half-share in the bank. Unfortunately, he made his partner the executor. Certainly left the hen house open for the fox."

He laid the will aside and picked up the affidavit. "This is a damning indictment of Archibald Hemphill. After her husband disappeared, Hemphill took everything, her share in the bank, their house, bank account, cars, furs, and jewelry. He even threatened to kill her children if she didn't leave town. All he let her take were a few clothes."

He laid the paper on top of the will. "Here's an

interesting twist. Kingston had only disappeared. No one ever said he was dead. Yet, Hemphill laid claim to Kingston's estate. How did he know Kingston wouldn't reappear unless he already knew Kingston was dead. It makes for a good argument that Hemphill was the third man that night."

Tori held up a finger. "That's not all." She went on to explain about Sam Taylor and Loomis Wainwright.

After she finished, David said, "Good lord, that was Myra's grandfather. So, he got all his money from Frankie's gambling syndicate. Not quite the respectable image Myra has always claimed."

Tori said, "Yep. Makes me wonder if Wainwright was the third man in the hall."

David said, "How far would Myra go to cover this up? Makes her a good candidate for X."

"Is Myra's father still alive?" Parker popped the last piece of cookie in his mouth.

Mia said, "No, he died several years ago."

Parker swallowed. "What about Archibald's son?"

"Dead," Mia said.

"What happened to the bank?"

"The Hemphills still own it. Different name, same bank."

"Interesting. We can't get around the bank connection, which adds Norton or Wayne to the mix as a possibility for X. We sure don't have a lack of suspects."

He took a sip of coffee. "While all of this is good information and connects some of the dots, none of it is evidence. Here's the issue. Since we don't know for sure who pulled the trigger, at the very least, Archibald may be an accessory to murder, and he did steal Kingston's estate. That was over eighty years ago and would probably only cause an embarrassment to the family. I doubt they would enjoy it, but after all, the current family members aren't responsible for the acts of a man eighty years ago."

Tori said, "What about Wainwright?"

"He's a viable candidate for the third man in the hallway. But the same argument can be made for him. An embarrassment, nothing more. And, we've got nothing to tie either Archibald's son or Myra's father to Clara's death. Again, with both of them dead, it would be a source of embarrassment, but is it enough to kill Ethel or Tori? I don't think so. We're still missing a piece of the puzzle, a motive for someone to kill."

Tori said, "Maybe there's something in the manuscript. I'll read it tonight."

Though they rehashed the details, they finally had to give up. David and Colt left, heading to their offices. Before he left, Parker called his office to assign a guard to Fergie.

Tori helped Mia clean up the kitchen and then strolled to her office. Sliding onto her chair, she tapped her keyboard and googled Judge Wayne Hemphill. She was surprised to see so few details. Most dealt with his career as a judge. He had no social media presence.

Her eyes narrowed as she stared at the image on her screen. Unsmiling, he stared into the camera. His face, locked in rigid lines, conveyed a ruthless appearance. Despite his stern look, she had trouble casting him, a judge, in the role of X.

She finally found a picture of Norton on the bank's website. He had the same harsh look as his brother. In fact, the only difference was he was dressed in a suit and his brother a black robe. She clicked back to the judge.

Mia walked in. "Whatever you're thinking can't be pleasant."

"It isn't. I'm looking at pictures of the Hemphill brothers."

Mia stepped around the desk to look at the screen. "I never liked the judge. He was rude and arrogant in the little contact I had with him."

"When did you meet him?"

"He visited an event at the school where my mom's a teacher. This was back when Graham was running for re-election. I was helping her set up the exhibits for her class project. Hemphill's visit was sheer publicity. When the cameras were filming, and the reporters watched, he was all smiles and glad-handing. It was another story when they weren't there. I'm not sure he even liked kids. If you're looking for clout, he's got it in spades. Judge Hemphill is as much of a presence in Granbury as was Miss Elly, maybe more. Of the two, though, I could see Norton as the mastermind before Wayne. But then, I've never liked either one of them."

She moved toward the door. "I'll see you tomorrow. I made sandwiches."

After Mia walked out, Tori locked the front door, then strolled to the kitchen. While soup heated in the micro-wave, she grabbed a sandwich from the new refrigerator. The neat order in the fridge brought a smile to her face. Seated at the table, only a light brush of sunlight on the horizon was visible. The two guards stood near the truck.

While Tori interspersed spoonfuls of soup with bites of the sandwich, her thoughts raced, replaying the astounding details Fergie had disclosed. An odd thought occurred to her. Frankie was shot down on a Dallas street four years later. Why didn't Hemphill do the same thing to her great-grandmother? Take everything.

After cleaning up the kitchen, she poured a glass of wine. She thought about the manuscript and its contents. Anticipation built. What else would she discover? With quick steps, she strode to her office.

Settled in her chair, she took a sip of wine before pick-ing up Marley Bennett's journal. Her gaze scanned the pages with the small, neat writing. Reading it, along with listening to the cassette tapes, could wait. She opened a drawer and dropped them inside. Then she turned her at-tention to the legal documents. Earlier, she had barely glanced at them. Now, she took her time to study each one. After perusing the ledger sheet and deed, they went into the drawer. Kingston's will was straightforward, as Parker had described. He made it easy for his partner to rip off his family. It was dropped on top of the others.

What she found truly disturbing was Betty Kingston's graphic portrayal of the events after her husband disappeared. Did she ever know the truth about what happened to him? She laid it on top of the will.

She took another sip of wine. Then with the manuscript in her lap, Tori propped her feet on the corner of the desk. The close-set typed sheets were occasionally marked, a line drawn through a word, or a comma added. Tori had to smile at Fergie's use of a red pen.

In the preface, Clara succinctly outlined the reasons for the book. She included a list of documents to support her conclusions. Tori briefly scanned them, only to go back for a closer look. One was missing, the partnership contract between Kingston and Hemphill.

So, where was it? Tori reached for the envelopes lying near the keyboard. Both were empty. Then she picked up the manuscript, flipping pages. When she spotted a change in the typing, she stopped. Concealed within the manuscript was the contract.

As she read it, her astonishment grew. A clause under a section titled *Dissolution* stated the partnership could only be dissolved by written notice of either partner. In the event of a death, the deceased partner's share reverted to the partner's estate. And Kingston's will left everything to his wife. Belatedly, she realized it was the original contract, not a copy. Since Kingston had been murdered, he couldn't have dissolved the partnership. Was it possible the contract was still valid?

Her feet hit the ground as she dropped the manuscript and contract in the drawer. Without thinking, she closed it. Tori knew nothing about the statute of limitations for contracts, but she might find something on the internet.

Out of the corner of her eye, she caught a light blinking on the camera monitor. Her head turned to look. The screen went black. She didn't know much about the new system, but Parker had told her it was top-of-the-line and reliable. Why would it go out? Suddenly, being alone in the house sent a ripple of apprehension down her back, raising the hairs on her neck.

A faint sound wafted in the air. Tori reached for the phone lying next to the computer.

"I wouldn't do that if I were you."

Her eyes flashed toward the doorway. She froze.

Chapter 27

onchalantly, he leaned against the doorjamb. Gone was the friendly, cheerful expression. Instead, he stared at her contemptuously while a gun dangled in his hand.

Tori's voice wheezed with fear. "How … how did you get in?"

Jack Crimshaw straightened, stepping into the room. "The back door. It's simple when you know how."

Crimshaw, not Logan. All this time, they had the wrong man. Her eyes flicked to the camera monitor. It was still black. What happened to the guards?

As if he guessed her thoughts, a chilling smile crossed his face. "Don't get your hopes up of another timely rescue. I've taken care of your watchdogs and the camera system."

An anguished cry erupted. "What did you do?"

"I didn't kill them. It would raise too many questions. This time, I drugged them. It was easy. I'm sure they thought the thermos of coffee I left was from you."

"You planted the bomb. Who was with you?"

He shrugged. "How did you get it out of the tunnel?" He lifted the gun, pointing it at her.

Paralyzed with fear, unable to look away, she mumbled, "The camera. When I saw two people enter the tunnel, I headed down the stairs. I was on the other side of the door. I heard what you said."

"I didn't have time to knock out the system. Well, it's not important now. This time I'll finish the job."

Icy frissons rippled along her nerves at his matter-of-fact tone. "Why?"

"The boss doesn't like loose ends. And you're one."

Loose ends? Fergie had mentioned loose ends. Tori struggled to keep her emotions under control while her thoughts, muddled by the agonizing terror, raced. She gulped. "What do you mean?"

A voice sounded in the hallway. "Jack, is everything set outside?"

With Crimshaw in the way, she couldn't see the second man's face.

"Almost," Crimshaw answered.

The man stepped into view. He stared at her with a cold expression, just as he had in the picture she'd found. The only difference, he wasn't wearing a black robe.

Wayne Hemphill glanced at Crimshaw. "Then finish it and get back in here. My business won't take long. I don't plan on hanging around."

Crimshaw nodded and walked out.

Hemphill's gaze swept the room as if he was an interested guest. "Well, my dear. We meet after all, though I would have preferred to forgo the pleasure. You have caused me no end of problems." He pursed his lips as his gaze scanned the bookcase. "I don't like problems. Especially ones that force me to get personally involved." He moved toward the table.

With a bravado she didn't feel, she forced a scornful tone into her voice. "Just what did I do to cause all these problems that have *so* inconvenienced you?"

He shot her a dispassionate look. "You decided to turn this house into an inn."

"So what? Why would you care?"

Hemphill gazed at the blueprints. "I didn't until your tunnel collapsed and that skeleton was found."

What could she do? She didn't have any weapons, or did she? Afraid to move her head, Tori eased her hand off the desk, groping to open the center drawer. Her fingers slid inside and grabbed the letter opener. It dropped onto her lap.

Hemphill looked up, and she froze, petrified he'd seen her hand move. When he glanced down to tap the blueprints, Tori gently closed the drawer before letting her hand rest on the edge of the desk.

"Quite impressive. Judd certainly misrepresented the condition of the house. But he's always had a tendency to embellish, even as a child."

"So, Judd was the one who lodged the complaint."

As he turned toward her, a disdainful expression flashed across his face. "Marshal would never have reacted to anything Judd said."

"You!"

"Of course."

"What did you hope to gain? You had to know such an idiotic plan wouldn't work. It sure didn't take Marshal long to realize he'd been had. Probably as soon as he walked in the front door. I don't imagine you won any friends there."

Her chest tightened when anger sparked in his eyes. It might not be wise to taunt him, but Tori didn't have many options. As long as he talked, she had a chance.

"Judd really dislikes you, and I can see why." With an easy motion, he slid a gun from beneath his jacket. "It didn't matter if it worked or not. Judd's obsession with this house was a convenient means to an end. It kept you occupied while I assessed the potential damage."

A gun against a paltry letter opener. As Tori tried to control the hysteria bubbling inside her, she asked, "Was Myra also involved in your little scheme?"

He grunted. "She doesn't like you either. Which was useful. I fed her information, knowing she'd run to the newspaper with it."

The scene in the driveway with Myra began to make sense. Then Logan was involved. Where was he? Outside with Crimshaw?

"Now, let's have a cozy chat before I bring down the curtain on this drama of ours." Hemphill sat, crossing his legs. Relaxed, he rested the hand holding the gun on the arm of the chair. It kept the barrel pointed at her while his other hand fastidiously twitched his pant legs into place.

"Why? It's obvious you plan to kill me."

With a mocking twist of his lips, he said, "A small matter that requires my attention. I can't leave it to Jack to handle. It's too important."

What was he talking about? What was important? The chime of her phone broke into her thoughts. Mesmerized, she stared at the screen. Hope flared. It was Parker.

Hemphill waved the gun. "Who is it?"

"Parker Hayes."

"Ah, the private investigator."

Tori hurriedly added, "If I don't answer, he'll show up to find out why." Somehow, she had to signal Parker.

"Answer it. Put it on speakerphone. Make a wrong move, and you're dead. By the time anyone gets here, I'll be long gone."

As she reached for it, it stopped ringing. Her heart sank.

"Call him back."

She tapped the screen. When Parker answered, she quickly said, "Parker, I'm in bed and couldn't get to the phone in time. Can this wait until we meet tomorrow?"

Hemphill's eyes never left her face.

With a conciliatory tone, Parker said, "I didn't mean to disturb you. I was calling to make sure tomorrow was still convenient."

"Yes, it is, though you won't need to buy a new coffee pot. Mia's going to pick one up."

"Thanks for letting me know. Saves me a trip to the store. I'm really sorry I was so clumsy."

"I'll see you in the morning." She disconnected.

Hemphill leaned forward to glance at the phone. "Just making sure you disconnected the call."

Though the idea had crossed her mind, with a gun aimed at her chest, she figured it would be unwise. Since Parker had played along, she clung to the small kernel of hope that help was on the way. But would it be in time?

"You won't get away with killing me."

"Yes. I will."

His absolute conviction set off another ripple of fear. "You shoot me, and there will be an investigation beyond just the police. But then your schemes don't seem to be too successful. The city reinstated my permit, and you certainly botched blowing up the tunnel. Besides, how many armed men does it take to kill one woman?"

His lips thinned. "No one is going to shoot you. I don't want the police to find a bullet. I have a better way. Burn your house. Such a terrible tragedy. Your death will be blamed on the arsonist the police believe is on the loose in Granbury. I'll have Jack torch another house to keep the cops running in circles."

The sour taste of bile filled her mouth. She swallowed, pushing it back. She wasn't sure which was more frightening, the gun pointed at her or the emotionless demeanor of the man holding it. A gritty resolve settled in her. She'd risk the bullet before letting them burn down the house with her in it.

Hemphill glanced at his watch. "Kingston. What do you know about him?"

Tori was running out of time. How could she keep him talking? Since he seemed to enjoy lording his superiority over her, she'd play to his ego.

"You knew who he was?"

"Of course. You'd be surprised at how much I know."

"Ah … the listening device."

He gave her a blank stare.

"That didn't work out so well either. I found it. It was sticking out from under my desk. Something else your man botched. Maybe you should consider hiring better help."

His jaw tightened. "Judd said you had a smart mouth. I'm going to enjoy making sure it's permanently shut. How did you discover his identity?"

His avid look of watchfulness raised the hackles on her neck. Was he looking for another loose end?

"The initials on the watch."

Dumbfounded, Hemphill said, "How could you have connected up the initials?"

"So much for you knowing everything. I found a 1943 newspaper article reporting the disappearance of a local banker, Dennis Kingston. Then another one popped up. This one had a picture of Archibald Hemphill, Dennis Kingston, and Frankie. It was quite informative. It referenced the two men as Frankie's partners in business. What was Archibald doing? Laundering money for Frankie?"

"Articles. That's all you've got?"

"What did you expect?"

His jaw tightened with displeasure. "What was in the

envelopes you had when you left Ware's apartment?"

"How did you know I was there?"

"I had someone following you. I knew you were trying to discover the man's identity."

"Why are you afraid of a couple of envelopes?"

"Don't confuse fear with practicality." Hemphill's lips twisted in a smile, though the humor never reached his eyes. "I've never had a reason to question what Fergie knew. Now, she's a problem, a loose end. The best way to handle a problem is to eliminate the source. I'll take great pleasure in knowing I'm rid of the two of you."

Chills crawled down her back. How many people had he killed? Where was Parker? Keeping him talking became a mantra over and over in her mind.

"Is that why Ethel was attacked? Another loose end?"

"Her mother was the housekeeper when Kingston was killed. Once the body was found, I couldn't take a chance on any memories it might trigger."

"Something else you bungled."

The hand holding the gun twitched.

She rushed to add, "I still don't understand. What possible harm could a skeleton cause you?"

Hemphill hitched his leg as if getting restless. "There's no reason not to tell you since you won't be able to repeat it. There is another loose end, a contract that disappeared. I couldn't risk what you might find if you started digging into Kingston's death. If it surfaced, the contract could cause undue interest in my business ventures."

Tori didn't bother to hide her revulsion. If she could

make him lose control, he might make a mistake. Give her a chance to escape. Or she could end up getting shot. A thought that didn't inspire confidence.

"Why does that not surprise me? Archibald was nothing but a gangster, a common criminal. Obviously, so are his descendants."

His eyes gleamed with hatred. "Someone like you would never understand what it means to have power and authority. I told Marshal you were an ignorant nobody. After meeting you, inexplicably, he told me I was wrong."

"Maybe he was more discerning than you could ever be," Tori taunted. "You certainly lost whatever credibility you had with him."

"Why, you stupid woman. What Marshal thinks is totally irrelevant. With one phone call, I can have him fired!"

"Who shot Kingston? Or don't you know?" Her gaze darted to the gun.

Hemphill chortled. "Of course I know. For years, my grandfather laughed about putting one over on Frankie. Conned him into believing Kingston planned to rat on the entire operation to the FBI. Frankie was livid. No one crossed him and lived to tell. My grandfather counted on his reaction."

Though she knew, she wondered if he would admit to it. "Why?"

"Money, of course. He acquired Kingston's estate."

"Is that what outright theft is called nowadays? Acquired?" With a deriding sniff, she said, "Archibald was good at letting someone else do his dirty work. And, wow, look at you. You've followed in the family's footsteps. Your power and authority are nothing but a front for your criminal activities. The upstanding judge, a respected citizen, is just like his grandaddy, another common criminal. I'd bet if the truth were known, so was your father."

His face twisted with rage. Hemphill pulled out his phone and tapped the screen. "How much longer?" He listened, then said, "Get in here!" He pocketed the phone and stood. With the gun aimed straight at her, he stepped closer to the desk. His eyes went blank as if there was no life behind them.

Fear churned her insides, locking her chest. She was out of time. Tori shifted in the chair and felt the letter opener slide across her legs. It sparked an idea, an act of desperation.

"Give me the contents of the envelopes."

Tori slowly opened the drawer. She lifted the stack of papers and laid them on the desk, pushing them to the edge. On top was the contract.

"Ah, that's better. Let's see what we've got here." He shoved the gun into his waistband as he stepped to the side of the desk. Bent over, he picked up the document, glancing at the next page under it. "*The Lightning Bolt Conspiracy*." He snorted. "Dad said it was a ridiculous title." Then he turned his attention to the contract.

Tori eased her hand into her lap, clutching the letter opener.

A look of satisfaction crossed his face. "It's the

original. This will be easier than I thought. Get rid of you and Ware, and any talk will die down. Whatever someone else knows would only be conjecture, no proof. What else is here?" He extended his hand to drop the contract on the desk.

Tori struck, driving the sharp point into the back of his hand.

A shriek of pain erupted.

She shot out of her chair, darted around him, and raced into the hallway. Tori was almost to the front door when his arm snaked around her neck, jerking her back.

The doorbell rang. The gun jabbed her ribs. With his lips next to her ear, Hemphill whispered, "Get rid of whoever is at the door. If you don't, I'll shoot both of you."

He let go, and she staggered forward. The doorbell rang again.

"Who is it?"

"It's David."

Fear spiked into sheer terror. Two armed men outside and one inside. David was defenseless. Tori couldn't risk trying to signal him. She had to make him leave.

Hemphill stepped alongside her, digging the barrel into her side.

Tori opened the door just enough to look around the edge.

His face wrinkled with worry, David asked, "Are you okay? Took you a long time to get to the door."

"I fell asleep at my desk."

"The poker game was canceled—"

She interrupted him. "David, I'm exhausted and not up to more company tonight. I'll see you tomorrow."

He slowly nodded, seeming to accept her explanation. "Okay. I'll be here for the meeting with Parker." Whistling, he walked away.

She closed the door, leaning her forehead against it. Behind her, she heard Crimshaw's voice.

"We're ready."

Tori turned.

Crimshaw walked into the foyer and stopped alongside his boss. His hands rested on his hips, only inches from the gun at his waist. Wide-eyed, he stared at the blood dripping from Hemphill's hand, hanging useless at his side. "What happened?"

"She stabbed me with a letter opener. I need a doctor. Where's Tommy?"

"In the car, waiting for you. As soon as you're gone, I'll set the timers. Within minutes this place will go up in flames. What about Tucker? Do you want me to kill him?"

"Let him go. He'll be able to say that he saw her just before the fire started."

Hemphill's eyes blazed with hate as he looked at Tori. "Get her back to the office and take care of her."

Tori stared at the pool of blood spreading across the floor. Unexpectedly, fury engulfed her, coalescing with fear and terror. The whirling vortex pushed her emotional state into a chaotic tangle.

Irrationally, she roared, "You've ruined my new floor!" Before either man could react, she charged, going airborne as she took a flying leap. All hundred and ten pounds slammed into Hemphill. He slipped in the blood and fell, taking Tori with him.

She pounded his face with her fists as he screamed, "Get her off me."

Crimshaw reached down and grabbed a hunk of hair. With it wrapped around his hand, he hauled her upright. His fist connected with her cheekbone. Though dazed by the blow, Tori twisted, kicking and screaming.

Hemphill struggled to his feet, holding the gun in his good hand. With Crimshaw in the middle, Hemphill couldn't shoot. He shouted, "Jack, get out of the way."

Focused on Tori, the men didn't see Parker race into the foyer. He tackled Hemphill. The gun fell and slid across the floor.

Crimshaw, trying to hang onto Tori, slipped. He let go, his arms flailing in the air as he tried to keep his balance. He dropped to his knees. Tori lifted her foot, driving her boot into his face. Blood spewed from his nose. Then she dove for the gun.

Cursing her, Crimshaw stumbled to his feet.

The front door flew open, and David charged in. He grabbed Crimshaw, driving his fist into the man's stomach. Bent over, the man stumbled back. David followed up with a blow to his face. Crimshaw crumpled to the floor.

Rubbing his fist, David looked at Parker. Despite Hemphill's screams about his injured hand, Parker was handcuffing the man.

"Got another pair?" David asked.

Parker glanced at Crimshaw. "He's not going any-where. That's a punishing right cross you've got. Where's the gun?"

David looked toward Tori.

Disheveled, her shirt torn, hair hanging around her bruised face and eyes that flashed with ferocity, Tori stood wide-legged. Her body was stiff, and her arms stretched straight out. She held the gun tightly clasped in her hands. It was pointed at Crimshaw.

David walked toward her, careful to not step in front of the barrel. "It's over. Let me have it." He reached for the gun, gently eased it out of her hands, then stuck it in his waistband. Belatedly, he noticed the blood on her shirt. "You're hurt!"

"No, it's not my blood. It's his." She nodded toward Hemphill. "I stabbed him with a letter opener." She cried, "David, he was going to kill me and burn the house down. Oh, god, Parker. Your men!"

"They're okay."

The relief was the final straw. Tori collapsed against David as shudders rocked her body.

He held her tight, stroking her back as he murmured, "You did good."

Caught up in her nightmarish emotions, Tori never felt the light touch of his lips to her hair.

Chapter 28

Several hours later, the cops had come and gone, taking Hemphill, Crimshaw, and Logan with them. After regaining consciousness, the guards were checked by the medics and released. Parker made arrangements to get them home.

A medic had examined the bruise on Tori's cheek. She wasn't happy to hear her eye would have some interesting colors by morning. Getting cleaned up and a change of clothes made her feel somewhat better. Not about to make her earlier mistake, she called Mia, who contacted the rest of her team. David called Colt, who in turn called Ben.

With all the police activity, there hadn't been a chance for everyone to hear what had happened. Gathered in the kitchen, Mia and the team set out sandwiches and boxes of cookies as they settled around the table.

In between bites of a sandwich, Tori told them, starting with the appearance of Crimshaw in the office and up to the point where David arrived. "I almost made it to the front door, but Hemphill grabbed me. Then the doorbell rang."

On the edge of their seats, no one commented as they intently listened to the horrifying details.

After a glance at Parker, who nodded for him to go ahead, David said, "After I left here, I went to my office.

When I finished, I decided to swing by and see if Tori was still up and if she'd learned anything new from the manuscript. Just before I reached the corner to turn onto the street in front of the house, Parker pulled alongside me, signaling for me to pull over. He said his men had missed a scheduled check-in call. When he tried calling, they didn't answer. Then he called Tori."

Parker spoke up. "As soon as I heard Tori's voice, I knew something was wrong. Then she threw in that bit about being in bed, a meeting we'd never discussed, then the coffee pot." At the interested looks, he said, "It was some heads-up thinking."

Tori said, "Since Hemphill made me put the call on speakerphone, I didn't know how to signal you other than to make some ridiculous comments. Thank god you realized it and went along. It completely fooled Hemphill."

Mia asked, "What did you mean about a check-in?"

Parker said, "When my men are on a surveillance or security detail, they call in every hour. A precaution for their safety," then picked up where he'd left off.

"David and I parked on the side street where the vehicles were out of sight and moved in on foot. We spotted Logan next to a car further down the block. I circled around, coming up behind him. Once I had him under control, we decided I'd go in the back door, and David would distract them at the front door."

Colt said, "Just what did you do to Logan?"

A satisfied look crossed Parker's face. "Knocked him out with the butt of my gun. The problem was the camera system. I figured Tori was in her office, and whoever was with her would see us on the monitor. That's why David went to the front door."

David said, "The plan was to get Tori and her captor out of the office so Parker could get to the back door without being seen on the monitor. With Logan out of the picture, we thought there was only one other person."

Tori said, "Of course, I was already in the foyer when David rang the doorbell." She took a sip of coffee. "Hemphill said if I didn't get rid of David, he'd kill both of us. I knew Parker had a gun, but David didn't."

David grinned. "Not true. Parker gave me his backup gun."

"What happened then," Heidi said.

"I played along with Tori's story about being tired and left. But I let her know that I wasn't buying it."

Tina said, "What did you do?"

Tori laughed. "I'll tell you. First, he mentioned his poker game. I knew there wasn't one. Then, he said he'd see me at the meeting with Parker. Of course, there was no meeting. I'd made it up for Hemphill's benefit. So, I knew he had talked to Parker." She shot a laughing glance at David. "Then he whistled, and I knew for sure."

Mia twirled her hand. "Don't keep us in suspense. What did he whistle?"

"The Lone Ranger theme."

Laughter erupted. "Oh, my gosh, how funny," Mia said.

Once the laughter died, Tori said, "Crimshaw and

Hemphill were in the foyer with me. I figured Logan had already been taken out. I just had to keep their attention on me." She touched her cheek. "I didn't plan on it being quite so painful."

Mia shot her an ironic look. "Dare I ask how you accomplished it?"

With a sheepish expression, she said, "I wasn't sure what to do. When I realized Hemphill was bleeding all over my new floor … well, I kinda lost it. I slam-dunked the judge."

For a moment, there was silence, then another roar of laughter echoed.

Wiping the tears, Mia said, "You actually slam-dunked the man? As in, knocking him down?"

With a smug look, she said, "Yeah."

David, with a note of pride in his voice, said, "She did. In case whoever was inside with Tori was watching, I had walked around the corner of the house. I heard Hemphill scream, 'get her off me.' I couldn't imagine what had happened. I figured I'd have to kick the door in, but Tori left it unlocked. When I got inside, Parker had tackled Hemphill, and Tori had kicked Crimshaw in the face. Her boot made quite an impact."

Tori snagged a cookie. She looked at David with a roguish grin. "When David got through with Crimshaw, he wasn't going anywhere."

Parker's lips twitched with a wry smile. "David, have you considered we were somewhat redundant. Thanks to Tori, Hemphill's hand may never be the same. She broke

Crimshaw's nose and possibly his jaw. She was a one-man wrecking crew." His eyes twinkled. "Or should I say—one-woman wrecking crew?"

Though Tori blushed, she said, "The only reason I could is because I knew I wasn't alone." She shot a glance at Mia.

Her eyes misting with tears, Mia huffed. "I won't forget what Myra and Judd did anytime soon. They sure had their nasty claws in this. At least we know why Myra was talking to Logan and who was the source for that news reporter."

"Not much I can do about it," Tori said. A thoughtful look crossed her face. "At least not right now."

Colt said, "And all of this was because of a contract."

"Yep. As Hemphill put it, it was another loose end, just like Fergie and me. He said it could cause undue interest in his business dealings."

Mia spoke up. "I don't remember any contract."

"I found it hidden in the manuscript. It states the only way the partnership could be dissolved was by written notification. If a partner died, the share reverted to the partner's estate. According to the will, Betty Kingston should have inherited it. But, of course, Kingston just disappeared, and Archibald took control of the bank. Since Kingston was murdered, I'd say it's a good bet the contract is still valid. I'll call Dan tomorrow. Some descendants might have a case to recover what was stolen."

Parker said, "That may be why Frankie hid the body, to make it easier for Archibald to take over. He didn't have to worry about the will. I'll call my FBI buddy. If there is something to be found in Hemphill's activities, he'll find it."

Mia said, "I wonder if we will ever know who killed Clara."

"I doubt it," Parker said.

Something pinged in Tori's mind, a comment. Suddenly, she straightened. "It may not be proof, but I know who killed her."

More than one voice said, "Who?"

She explained Hemphill's comment about the title of Clara's book. "The only way his father could have known was if he saw the manuscript stolen from Clara. And he knew she was researching Kingston. Clara had called Arthur Hemphill asking for an interview."

Her fingers drummed the table. "Hmm … I wonder if Arthur was responsible for Wainwright's visit to the library. Some sort of reconnaissance to find out what Clara knew. The Hemphills had a pattern of using others to do their dirty work."

Parker said, "An astute observation. At least, it's answered to our satisfaction."

Mia stood. "It's time we left. Let's get this cleaned up. Then we're out of here."

Parker was the first to leave. Tori walked up and hugged him. "Parker, thank you."

His cheeks turned red. "Hey, nothing needs to be said."

"That tough attitude doesn't fool me at all. I'll see you tomorrow."

David was the last to go. Standing by the open front door, he said, "Are you sure you're okay?"

She smiled. "Yes. It's such a relief to know it's over. I don't believe I'll have any trouble sleeping tonight."

He flicked a finger down her cheek.

She reached up and lightly kissed his lips.

His eyes lit up as his arms wrapped around her. This time the kiss lasted longer. When he stepped back, he said, "This will be continued. But not tonight."

As she closed the door, a warm feeling enveloped her. After a relaxing bath, she shrugged on her favorite nightshirt, one her mother had given her. Snuggled under the covers, her thoughts as she drifted off to sleep weren't about guns or fires. It was all about how she felt in David's arms and a promise of tomorrow.

Epilogue

Three weeks later

Tori sat by Ethel's bed, holding her hand. Two days after Hemphill had been arrested, Ethel regained consciousness. Still, she had a long recovery as the coma had severely weakened her. Tori didn't want to question her until she was stronger.

But today, her face had color, and her eyes were alert and bright with interest. Tori had just finished an abbreviated story about what happened after Ethel had been attacked.

"Oh, my, you've had a lot of trouble. Who would ever have thought Uncle Denny, as your grandmother used to call him, would cause so many problems? He was such a nice man." Her voice trailed off, and her eyes took on a distant look.

"You knew him then?"

"Oh, yes. I'd see him sometimes when I was allowed in the house. Of course, Miss Elly often spoke of him. She was quite fond of him. What happened to him, and his family was so very tragic."

"What do you know about it?" Tori had already told

her about the entry in Elly's journal.

"Miss Elly told me what she saw that night, though she made me swear not to say anything. Then Mr. Kingston disappeared. My mother never spoke of it, but I heard people at church talking about him. It wasn't long after that Mrs. Kingston left town. There was talk that the bank repossessed the house, and she was left with nothing."

"Did Elly know he was buried in the tunnel?"

"No, she didn't. In later years, we talked about it a time or two. She knew Kingston was probably dead, but she didn't have any proof. It never occurred to her that he was buried in the tunnel. She always believed they'd gone out the other end to keep anyone from seeing them."

"Did you know who the third man was?"

"No. Miss Elly didn't either. The hallway was dark, and she didn't get a good look at him. Miss Elly thought it might be Mr. Wainwright, but I told her I thought it was Mr. Hemphill."

"Why?"

"Every week Mr. Leichter had those gambling parties. Mr. Hemphill was always there." She shifted in the bed. "He was a hard man. After he had full control of the bank, he recalled loans. A lot of people lost their homes. He made a lot of money when he sold the properties." She sniffed. "I was taught that if you can't say something good about someone, then don't say anything. But Archibald Hemphill is the exception. He was an evil man."

Tori patted her hand. "He may not have received the

punishment he deserved in his lifetime, but his grandsons have."

"I hate that it caused you so many problems, though," Ethel said.

"Look at it this way. In every dark cloud, there's a silver lining." Tori smiled to herself. *About time for a good metaphor.* "We were able to put Dennis Kingston to rest."

"Well, there is that." Ethel smiled.

"I do have one other question. Do you know why Hemphill didn't go after Frankie's estate?"

"Jonah Greer's grandfather. He was the family attorney. I remember when he came to the house to tell Mrs. Leichter her husband had been killed. After that, he was always there, talking to Mrs. Leichter, helping her. My mother said, many times, she didn't know what might have happened if it hadn't been for Mr. Greer. You see, he was the executor of Frankie's will."

Seems she had more to thank Jonah for than Tori realized. One day soon, she'd take him to lunch and tell him what she'd learned.

"I've got good news for you. The doctor says you can go home tomorrow," Tori said. Rising, she bent over and hugged the woman's frail shoulders.

In a soft voice, Ethel whispered, "Thank you for everything you did. Gloria told me. How can I ever repay you?"

Tori pulled back. "Now, don't you go worrying about anything. You getting well is all I want."

"You are so like Miss Elly," she said. Tears glistened in her eyes. "I do miss her."

"Once you get settled, I'll come by and have a long chat."

In the elevator, she thought about everything that had happened. The other interesting development was the FBI's investigation of Hemphill's bank. Seems he used his position as a judge for more than legal cases. He still had ties to the underbelly of society, laundering money and making deals for individuals charged with crimes. Two of his recruits were Jack Crimshaw and Tommy Logan, his enforcers. The district attorney assured Dan that by the time the Feds got through with the Hemphill brothers, they wouldn't see the light of day for a long time.

After Dan found several relatives of Dennis Kingston, he forwarded a copy of the documents regarding Kingston's estate. The last she heard, they planned to file suit to claim restitution from the Hemphill assets.

As for Clara Hopkin's book, she and Fergie decided to work together to publish it. A prospect that Tori had en-thusiastically endorsed. Dan was already in contact with Clara's relatives.

When she stepped out of the elevator, her ride waited in front of the entrance. David had dropped her off to run an errand. As she walked up, he leaned over, opening the passenger door. "Hey, beautiful. Going my way?"

"Absolutely." Tori's joyous laughter rang out.

Inside, someone stood near a window, staring at Tori as she slid into the car. The watcher's face slowly twisted; the features disfigured with hatred.

The Story Behind the Fiction

The Chip Detective

The original inspiration for the Tori Winters Mystery Series was an article by Edward Hertel, the Chip Detective. His article dealt with the discovery of poker chips during the renovation of the Top O' Hill Terrace Museum. During the 1940s, Benny Binion, head of the Dallas gambling syndicate, had extended his illegal gambling activities into Arlington, Texas. He acquired the Top O' Hill Terrace, a popular restaurant and tea garden. Binion set up his casino in the basement, with secret rooms to hide the gambling equipment in the event of a raid. A tunnel allowed the clientele to escape and pose as innocent customers in the tea garden.

During my research for the series, I contacted Ed. After learning of my interest and upcoming book, he asked if I would like a chip like the one found during the renovation. I immediately said yes. When the package arrived, I was astounded that it wasn't what I expected. Instead of a couple of chips, there were nineteen, with different patterns and initials. All were original and had been used in Binion's casinos.

One of the chips had three lightning bolts. The chip immediately grabbed my attention. Due to my interest in the chip, Ed referred me to an article he wrote, *Benny*

Binion and the Dallas Gambling Wars. The article was first published in *Casino Collectible News, Winter/2017*. With Mr. Hertel's permission, I subsequently republished the article on the Mystery Review Crew website under my column, *On the Hunt*.

The article is a fascinating read about the history of Binion's gambling syndicate and the poker chip with three lightning bolts. Ed Hertel, the Chip Detective, used the manufacturer's archived records to backtrack to the casino that ordered the chips. Sam Murray, one of Binion's cohorts, ordered the lightning bolt poker chip from Mason & Co. in 1939.

Additional information can be found on Edward Hertel's website: http://www.chipster.net/

Casino Collectibles News. http://www.ccgtcc-ccn.com/vol30_4.pdf

https://mysteryreviewcrew.com/category/author-posts/anitadickason/

https://www.topohillterrace.com/

Granbury, Texas

The quaint town has proven to be the perfect setting for my Tori Winters Mystery Series. The many events and a dynamic downtown continue to provide a backdrop to add realism to my plot: Granbury Ghosts & Legends Tour, Arts & Letters Bookstore, Barons Creek Vineyards, D'Vine Wine Granbury, the historic Granbury Opera House, and more.

My fictional newspaper archives do exist. *Granbury News* ran from 1891 to 1945, when it transitioned to the *Hood County News-Tablet.* In 1971, the name changed to *Hood County News.*

For more information about this unique Texas town, please visit:

https://www.visitgranbury.com/

https://www.granburytours.com/

https://www.artsandlettersbooks.com/

https://www.baronscreekvineyards.com/granbury

https://dvinewinegranbury.com/

https://granburytheatrecompany.org/

About The Author

Anita Dickason is a twenty-two-year veteran of the Dallas Police Department. Anita served as a patrol officer, undercover narcotics detective, advanced accident investigator, and Dallas SWAT tactical officer and first female sniper.

Her law enforcement experience and knowledge provide an endless source of inspiration for her characters and plots.

Additional information can be found at:
anitadickason.com

https://www.facebook.com/AnitaDickasonAuthor
https://twitter.com/anita_dickason
https://www.pinterest.com/anitadickason
https://www.linkedin.com/in/anita-dickason-7b6b6650

An Author's World YouTube
https://www.youtube.com/@anauthorsworld

The Book Cinema Channel
https://www.youtube.com/@bookcinema